Reviews

"In some ways, the novel is a brutal cautionary tale, showing how one mistake can spiral into a life-changing series of events. In another, however, it is a moving coming-of-age narrative about a girl who discovers herself amid extreme circumstances...A nuanced yet plainly told novel."
Kirkus Reviews

"I found this to be a well-written novel about the trials, adventures and tribulations of a runaway girl in the 70's. A real page-turner, and at times likely to bring an open-minded reader to tears. Brought to life by a historically accurate backdrop, the story is a bridge from a life of bad decisions and misunderstandings of an uninformed youth to another life of hope and happiness."
Amazon Reader

Peg's Story
Detours

A NOVEL

Sheri McGuinn

Durare
Publishing

Bullhead City, AZ

This book is a work of fiction. Real locales and events have been used fictitiously. Each character is a composite of multiple moments with multiple people, blended with a hefty dose of the author's imagination. None should be considered representative of any real event or real person, living or dead.

www.sherimcguinn.com

smcguinn@sherimcguinn.com

sherimcguinn.substack.com

Copyright 2020

ISBN 978-1-942069-02-7 Paperback

ISBN 978-1-942069-03-4 EPUB

ISBN 978-1-942069-06-5 Kindle

Library of Congress Control Number 202914857

Cover Design by Sheri McGuinn

Original Photo by Michael Bry manipulated by Sheri McGuinn

HUMAN
AUTHORED™
Authors Guild
8813674

Table of Contents

Chapter 1: Detours

When I started high school in 1971, my plans for the future were not clear, but they included an exciting career that would take me all over the world, far from the boring small town of my parents. Instead, a series of detours became my life.

Telephones were all land lines and long distance calls were expensive. No one had a personal computer, the World Wide Web didn't exist, and it was still considered scandalous for TV to show a married couple sharing a bed – in pajamas, of course. Nice girls guarded their innocence; only bad girls were careless with theirs. Pregnant girls were forced to leave school in shame. Abortion was illegal. There was little coordination among police of different states and missing children couldn't be put into the FBI's database.

That Christmas I missed the first sign my world was about to be shattered. By June I would run away; by August I would be running again, from far worse, convinced I could never go home.

It was easy for me to disappear for ten years.

Chapter 2: First Kiss

Journal: Christmas 1971

Most of this house is older than I am - clean, but old - worn carpeting, patched wallpaper, ancient kitchen appliances. Mom doesn't care. She lives in her garden.

When Dad fixes anything, Mom repairs his repairs while he's at work. Before I was born, she hung baby animal wallpaper in my room. I got stuck with those little critters until I was ten. Then Mom finally let me paint my room pink and we bought café curtains with tiny purple flowers. She thought we should get the pink ones, but once she saw them on my windows, she decided the color mix looked good. It's kind of little-girlish for me now I'm in high school, but at least it's not baby animals.

The ninth grade English teacher had decided we should keep journals for writing practice and as a source of material later in our lives. She said description and critical analysis of our environment and world events would make it a journal instead of a diary.

I'd decided to write first thing each day.

My initial entry followed her dictates, until I noticed the college catalogs I'd borrowed from the guidance office to show Mom. My parents both went straight to work after high school and married that summer. They wanted me to go to college to find a doctor or lawyer to marry. Mom of course thought that should be done with the least possible expense. She always worried about money. Seeing the catalogs set me off on a diary-style rant.

I have to convince Mom to let me go away to college. Northwestern is the best for journalism, but American University would help me get into a Foreign Service job, something where I'd get to travel and live in amazing places. She keeps saying how nice it is I can live at home while I go to Fredonia State. If she makes me do that, my life will be as boring as hers!

I wouldn't want Mom reading that; I hid the journal in the bottom of my desk. I hadn't been downstairs yet, even though it was Christmas morning. With no extended family and no siblings, holidays were never a big deal. However, I knew my parents would be waiting for me.

Our silver tree glittered on a small table in the corner of the TV room. A real one would be too much bother. I plopped onto the couch next to my dad, who was still in his terrycloth bathrobe, with a beer in hand, of course. My new Fredonia State sweatshirt was big enough to cover my feet when I curled them under me. My best friend Jan had given it to me the day before. She knew what I liked.

Mom came in from the kitchen, wiping her hands on the apron she wore over her slacks. She sat next to me on our small couch. I felt like peanut butter between two slices of bread. My parents weren't fat, but they weren't skinny, either.

Dad urged me to open a present. I picked the biggest one first. Laughing, I peeled layer after layer of boxes and filler until I found Mom's annual underwear and socks gift.

"Thanks, Mom."

She pointed to a medium-sized box. "Open that one next."

Spiral notebooks, a package of Bic pens, a drawing pad, drawing pencils, and an eraser filled the box with each item, even the eraser, wrapped separately. I pretended to be surprised, but it was one of Mom's standard tricks to make our Christmas seem bigger.

"I used the materials list for that course you're going to take," she said. "They weren't sure what an art eraser was at Murphy's, but I figured an eraser's an eraser."

Dad looked at me, puzzled. "I thought you wanted to be a writer."

"I like drawing, too, and this way Jan and I can have a class together."

"Jan?" he asked.

"Janet, Dad."

"Oh, she's going by Jan now?"

I smiled, shook my head, and teased him, "You do know they moved, right? They don't live next door anymore."

He pretended to be serious. "They moved because she changed her name?"

Even Mom smiled.

Three presents remained under the tree, one for each of us. I picked up the packages I'd wrapped for my parents. They never bought stuff for each other anymore.

"You first." I handed Mom her gift.

I'd made a fancy bow, winding the wide ribbon loosely around four fingers, notching it at the center, and tying another piece around the notch to snug it all together. Then each loop had to be separated and twisted. The bow was small, but the package wasn't very big, so it looked okay.

Mom touched it and smiled. "This looks like my begonias."

I didn't know a begonia from a daisy - Jan and I grew up staying clear of the garden so we wouldn't ruin anything. Mom carefully peeled the tape back on one end of her gift and slid the paper off as we spoke. She opened the box and pulled out the apron I'd folded tightly to fit into the tiny space.

"We made them in Home Ec. I didn't want you to guess what I was giving you."

"I had no idea," she said as she shook it open. "Why, it's lovely."

I'd picked one with roses for her. I knew which flowers were roses, and she had them climbing the fence and growing in bushes, different colors all over the yard.

"Thank you," she said, then put it aside. "Who's next?"

"You open mine," I told Dad.

I'd made him a tie. It hadn't turned out quite right, but he smiled as if it were pure silk from an expensive store.

"Thank you, Honey. I needed one for work." He draped it around his neck, picked up his beer, and posed like an ad. It looked silly against his terry bathrobe.

It was time to open the last present, the one for me from Dad, a little box, a flat rectangle. The paper was heavy with gold in the design and the bow was perfect, so he probably had had it gift wrapped at the store. I saved the paper and bow for Mom, then lifted the lid.

"Dad!" I gasped. "It's beautiful!"

As I held up the necklace for my mother to see, Dad swallowed some of his beer the wrong way and choked.

"Are you okay?" I asked.

"Fine, I'm fine," he sputtered, still coughing a bit.

"Let me see that," Mom commanded. She looked at the fine gold chain and the clear crystal it held. She glared at Dad. "This is too expensive for a fourteen-year-old girl."

My heart fell. It was about money again. Dad looked miserable, too. I went over and gave him a hug. "That's okay, it's the thought that counts. It's okay if you take it back. I love you."

I collected my other gifts and left the room without looking at my mother. Upstairs, I sat down with my journal. The teacher had said he wouldn't read or collect them. We were on our honor to report how many pages we wrote each day, so it was safe to let my emotions out on the paper, all the things I wanted to scream at my parents.

My mother's garden and money are the only things she cares about. She didn't get me any real presents, she just wrapped up stuff she had to buy for me anyway. I don't know why she bothered having a kid. Dad actually got me something nice and she's making him take it back. I hate her. At least Jan got me the Fredonia sweatshirt. Her mom let her visit with Steve when they were up there doing Christmas shopping and they went to the Student Store. One from Northwestern would have been better, but it's still a college sweatshirt.

My mother was of course too cheap to drive twenty-five whole miles and buy me REAL art supplies instead of the kiddie stuff she got from Murphy's. Maybe I can return the junk she bought and get Dad to take me to the art store in Fredonia.

I was a teenager and so unhappy with my life. It never occurred to me that my parents might have their own problems or that my life could be much worse – and soon would be. But this was supposed to be a journal, not a diary, so I tried to get back to description, with spotty success.

Jan's almost two years older than me. We grew up next door to each other and were best friends all the way through her first year in high school, when I was in seventh grade. But that summer her parents bought a place outside of town and we didn't see much of each other the whole next year. High school classes are in a separate wing. And when she started dating Steve Hartfield, a senior and captain of the football team, she didn't have any time for me at all. So last year was pretty miserable.

This year, Steve's at Fredonia State, about twenty-five miles from us, and his Dad took a job in New England or something, and freshmen can't have cars, so Steve doesn't come here at all. Jan says they're still going steady, but I don't know how.

Anyway, I thought it would be different between Jan and me this year. What I hadn't realized is she got close with a bunch of girls last year who all date jocks. I'm not allowed to date until I'm sixteen.

But since Thanksgiving, Jan's been talking to me more and she suggested I take the art class so we could spend more time together - an elective like that's the only place a freshman and a junior can be in the same class. She misses me, too.

At the beginning of the year I'd joined MYF, the Methodist Youth Fellowship, to spend more time with her. My family didn't go to church, but the pastor didn't mind. MYF was co-ed but it wasn't dating, so my parents approved. Jan hardly ever came, but I knew everyone else from school. Gradually I'd been becoming less dependent on her. Still, I was excited she wanted to be close again.

A few days after Christmas, MYF had a sledding party on the hill above Jan's house, and then we went inside for hot chocolate. She brought out her Twister game and whoever was spinning the dial would cheat to make the positions more interesting. Eric and I were on the mat when his buddy Phil took the dial. Eric was really cute. All the girls liked him and he'd already gone steady and broken up a few times.

I kind of had a crush on him, but my competitive instinct took over in any game, so I thought nothing of reaching between his legs when Phil called "right hand green". My legs were crossed and on green and red, so I was twisted up under him.

"Left hand red," Phil called quickly.

This let me untwist, ending belly up, arms and legs spread wide – right under Eric.

Phil yelled, "Kiss her!"

Eric gave me a wet smack right on the lips and I collapsed on the mat. I squirmed out from under him, wiping my mouth and making a face.

"What's the matter, is that your first kiss?" Eric laughed.

I stood up, gave him a haughty look and said, "I thought you were trying to drown me."

Everyone laughed at Eric and the game continued with a new challenger for him. At the end of that party, Eric invited everyone to his house for New Year's Eve.

"No Twister, though," I joked. And everyone laughed.

I described the afternoon's activities in my best journalistic style, then finished with the important stuff.

December 28, 1971

That really was my first kiss. When everyone else had left, I told Jan and said it hadn't done a thing for me, that I thought it was gross, that his mouth was partway open and slobbery with spit. She laughed and said kissing doesn't count until you French.

She realized I didn't understand what she was talking about, so she explained that you actually kiss with your mouths open and do stuff with your tongues. She laughed at the look on my face and said I'll like it when it happens.

I wish I wasn't so stupid about sex. I don't know anything. But if I ask Jan to explain more, she'll think I'm weird and she won't want to hang out with me at all. She might even laugh about it with those girls at school. And I can't ask my mother. When I got my first period, she shoved a box of pads at me and started fumbling around trying to figure out how to begin and I told her some of the other girls in my class had already started, so I knew about that stuff. She was relieved and that ended the conversation.

That was sixth grade. I was already wearing a trainer bra, but by the end of seventh grade I was bigger than my mother and boys snickered about my "balloons." Of course I never talked to my mother about the teasing.

I worried there might be kissing games at the New Year's Eve party. I didn't want to be grossed out, but I didn't want people to think of me as a baby, either. Then Eric called.

"Sorry, I can't have the party. I've got chicken pox."

"What?" I yelped. "How did you get that?"

"From my little cousin."

My voice dripped with sarcasm as I thanked him for kissing me. "If I miss my new art class with chicken pox, I'll have to kill you."

Fortunately for Eric, I stayed healthy. But New Year's Eve was the pits. Dad always had beer but Mom wouldn't allow anything else in the house; she didn't drink. So for New Year's Eve she made a bowl of punch with grape juice and ginger ale to make it fizzy. We could have pretended it was champagne, but she added sherbet. We were fixing food when Dad came into the kitchen wearing a jacket and tie.

"Cool," I said. "I'll get dressed up, too. It'll be more like a party."

I dashed up to my room and changed into a dressy blouse, but by the time I got back to the kitchen, he was gone. "Where's Dad?"

"He's going out to celebrate *properly*," Mom huffed, her head inside the refrigerator.

"Most people have something besides beer or juice, Mom."

"I suppose."

She kept her back to me, so I went to the living room and turned on the TV to find Dick Clark. Eventually she came in with cheese and crackers and we played Rummy while we listened to the TV. At midnight we watched as the big glittering ball slowly fell in New York City with all the people in the street counting down and screaming and kissing each other. At least *they* were having a good time, and I was sure Dad was, too.

He hadn't come home when I went to bed. When I got up at noon and he was gone, I assumed he'd left to watch football games with friends. I spent the afternoon curled up on the couch reading. Mom had already taken down the tree and had a jigsaw puzzle on that table. She worked on it the whole day, which told me she was really mad.

She didn't even make dinner. I fixed sandwiches from leftovers. She said she wasn't hungry. But when she finished the puzzle, I managed to coax her into eating one. We played Rummy until Dad came home, a little after midnight.

"Did you have a good time?" Mom asked sourly, staring at her cards.

"Yeah, at Tony's." He went straight upstairs.

Tony lived by himself and he was a drunk. I thought I knew why Mom was mad.

Chapter 3: Virginal Crushes

Once we got back to school, my lofty goals for my journal fell by the wayside. I worried about how much I was writing about boys, but justified it.

January 12, 1972

Relationships are at the core of our existence, aren't they? Most successful men are married to smart, supportive women. So, as a woman, I need to find a smart, supportive man to be successful in my career.

While Eric was out with the chicken pox, my fickle attention turned to Andrew, a junior. I was sure kissing Andrew would be *much* more exciting than Eric's slobbery peck, even if I didn't want to French. However, as the new captain of the basketball team, Andrew did not notice honor students like me. So I contrived to sit near him at lunch. Jan thought he was a jerk, but sat with me to help draw his attention.

That was a really big deal. Normally, Jan ate lunch with her junior and senior girlfriends. They all used eye shadow and mascara and had long, glossy straight hair. I didn't own any makeup and my hair frizzed on humid days.

Jan was at my table in art class, too. I truly believed we were best friends again, until she passed her driver's test the third week in January and took me for a ride.

"I can visit Steve now!" she crowed.

I felt our renewed closeness starting to dissolve.

January 20, 1972

This Saturday Jan has permission to drive to Fredonia for Steve's basketball game, but she wants to go every weekend. She says her parents will believe we're doing whatever she tells them as long as I'm with her. Part of me wants to tell her to take a hike. I know she was planning this all along. She didn't really care about being friends again. But maybe I'm being oversensitive. She'd do this for me, probably. I'll see what it's like and decide.

That Saturday we drove up to Fredonia State to see Steve play. He sat on the bench most of the game. His roommate watched with us and explained that none of the freshmen played much.

The roommate's name was Brian, and he was studying to be a science teacher. He was eighteen, a college freshman, and absolutely adorable. I lost interest in Andrew and stopped worrying about lying to our parents. I knew Jan was using me, but being partners in crime drew us closer. I went along for the ride and had fun hanging out with Brian.

Jan took care of the details. She decided on our story each weekend, and she always bought gas in Fredonia before we headed home. She had the attendant put in exactly three and a quarter gallons every time, enough to replace most of what we'd used, but not so much her father would notice she was buying gas. He wouldn't expect her to use much around town.

Brian and I would hang out at the Student Union while Jan and Steve stayed back at the dorm. I got to know a few other people on campus that way and was thrilled to be passing as a college student. Then Brian gave me a rose the weekend ahead of Valentine's. I thought he might be the supportive mate I'd need.

We hadn't kissed.

We hadn't held hands, either, aside from a brief moment when he led me through a crowd. But the night he gave me that rose, even though I knew he picked it off a bush on campus, my journal entry rambled on about how many children we should have. I even mused about names. I was so ignorant.

The day after Valentine's, Susan Robinson complained about her parents while we dressed for gym. "My dad brought her flowers, took her into the city for dinner and a show, and then ..." Susan rolled her eyes and shuddered. "The bed actually banged against the wall! That's what woke me up. I could hear my mom trying to shush my dad, then there was this panting and ... Anyway, it was really hard to look at them this morning."

"Do they want more kids?" I blurted out.

"No. My mom's on the pill," she said.

That night my journal entry was very serious.

February 15, 1972

Susan threw it off so casually, "My mom's on the pill," like wouldn't everyone's mother be on the pill? I'm sure mine isn't. My parents never touch. I can't imagine them ever having sex. When I was little, I saw two dogs locked together and Jan told me that was to make puppies. I know it's not exactly the same with people, but still, it has to be even grosser than French kissing, and it definitely requires touching.

Boys talk like sex is all they think about, but why would a woman want something shoved inside her? To have children, I guess, but then the pill makes no sense. Unless married women are expected to let their husbands do that even if they don't want more children. But Jan makes it sound like women actually want sex too?

Maybe there's something wrong with me.

The next couple weekends, Brian and I played a lot of pool at the Student Union and he was always nice, but he never tried to hold my hand or anything. I worried that he might have given me that Valentine rose out of pity, because he knew no one else would ever give me one.

March 8, 1972

If nobody ever wants me, I'll never have a family. But he is taking me to a concert this weekend. I'm not sure it's a date, because he said he got two tickets for helping with the posters. It's not like he bought one for me. It's some band from England - Yes. I never heard of them, but it'll be cool. I've never been to a concert except ones at school. Those don't count.

Yes was fantastic. The music lifted me on a wave and kept me up there until the last note faded away. The entire time, I was mesmerized by Rick Wakeman and his light golden hair down to his knees, flowing among the keyboards that surrounded him.

The best and worst parts of the evening came after.

We stopped in the Grove and kissed. Brian was the one to stop and remind me that Jan would be waiting. We ran, but she was sitting in her car, angry at me for being late. I got in quickly and she drove off, too fast. She said she and Steve had broken up.

"No!" I wailed. "I'm in love with Brian!"

"Since when?"

"Tonight. We were late because we were kissing in the Grove."

She snorted. "You finally Frenched."

"Yes. And you're right, it's not gross when you're in love."

"Love, schmuv, it's all hormones. You only think you're in love because it was your first time Frenching."

I wanted to make it better. "You love Steve, and he loves you."

"Steve just wants to get in my pants." Jan still sounded angry, but a tear slid down her cheek. "He wants to go all the way. College girls do."

"But you're not on the pill, are you? Does he want you to have a baby?"

"No. He had rubbers." She hit the steering wheel. "I've been doing everything else, but I want to save going all the way for when we get married. Why can't he understand that?"

I stayed quiet the rest of the drive home, my emotions bouncing between joy and despair.

March 10, 1972

*On the way back to the dorm, we stopped in the Grove and Brian kissed me!!! It was French, and it **wasn't** gross! Not the least bit of slobber! We walked a little way, then he pulled me into a hug and kissed me again and I kissed him and we kissed for ages.*

I am definitely normal!

But Jan's mad at Steve. So now I'm in love but I don't know if I'll ever see Brian again. I can't even call him or write because I don't know how they get mail, and it's just a payphone in the hall there. And it's long distance, so if I had the number I couldn't call from home.

Jan kept babbling about Steve's rubbers and saying she's done everything except go all the way. I wish I knew what she was talking about. Maybe they teach that stuff in Health class, but the guidance counselor put me into Earth Science. She said it'll look better for college. And my mother will probably wait until my wedding day to explain whatever little she knows about sex, if then. What if I have to ask my husband!

If you've grown up with internet access, you need to understand, books were my main hope for learning about sex, and if the library had them, they kept them hidden away somewhere for adult eyes only – at least I didn't find them. I did look, but I was too embarrassed to ask the librarian for help.

All I thought about was Brian and how we were meant to be together forever. The second week, with Easter vacation looming, I looked through Jan's notebook while she was cleaning her brush in art class and found the number for Steve's dormitory. During lunch I called it from the payphone booth they'd put into the main entry, so students wouldn't bother the office staff when they wanted to call home for a ride. The boy who answered got Steve instead of Brian.

"Brian's in class. I'll tell him you called. But please, Peg, tell Jan I'm sorry. I love her. I'll do whatever she says."

I ran to the cafeteria and told her right away. They made up over the phone, but he and Brian were both leaving for home, so we couldn't see them until after vacation. I never did get to talk to Brian, but I thought that was because he was in class.

Much to my surprise, my mother saved me from two weeks of moping around by lining me up with a job. We lived in Concord grape country and in spring the vines had to be tied onto the wire trellis. She dropped me off before seven each morning and picked me up at six, but I wasn't going to complain. They paid minimum wage. Babysitting didn't come close to that.

Easter Sunday was the only day I had enough energy to make a journal entry.

April 2, 1972

Tying grapes is hard and easy at the same time.

Over the winter, someone trimmed each vine so there are only two strong branches coming off the trunks. Two heavy wires run parallel to the ground from post to post, making a trellis for the vines. I wear an apron with thin copper wires in the pocket and bunches of twine tied to the sides, with a slip knot holding each bunch tight as it gets smaller. I use a piece of twine to tie the trunk loosely to the trellis wire near my knees, then drape one branch to the right, the other to the left, over the wire that's near the top of my head. The branches reach all the way down to the lower trellis wire, where I attach them with copper wire. That has to be pretty tight so the wind doesn't rip them loose. The vine ends up draped over the trellis in an umbrella shape.

It's easy now I'm used to it, and I can zone out and think about Brian and imagine what life with him might be like. I bet he'll want a bunch of kids. I'd like six, close together so we're one big happy family. But we could go into the Peace Corps together first. I know I'm rushing it, but I'm in love with him. The way we kissed in the Grove, I know he must feel the same way.

Anyway, back to now. Mom's been treating me like an adult, which is really cool. My hands got sunburned the first day, so she gave me her gardening gloves, but I couldn't tie that way, so she had me take zinc oxide and keep putting it on my hands. That seems to work, and she said she was proud of me for not quitting.

There's another week before we go back to school and I've already earned over a hundred dollars!

They're not tying today because it's Easter. Dad was upset I didn't put out a basket or dye eggs. It's the first time, even though I can't remember believing in the Easter Bunny. He got me a big, fluffy stuffed rabbit, as if I'm still a little girl. Mom gave me some Easter candy. She said she figured I could use the energy boost halfway through the day, the way I'm working. She didn't mind not having to hide it. She knows I'm not a little kid.

I went to church with Jan and her parents and MYF had a party afterwards. Jan's been babysitting for the Little Tyrant. No one else will, but he's some kind of cousin to her. He took off on his bike and she had to chase him all the way across town! I am SO glad to be tying grapes. And it's been cool getting closer to Mom. I always thought she loved her garden more than me, but maybe she's just better with adults than kids.

The first week of school dragged by, then Saturday morning Jan picked me up to go see our boyfriends – that's how I thought about it. I didn't say it out loud though, or tell her why I wanted to stop at a jewelry store in Fredonia before we went on to the college.

While she was busy looking at rings, I bought Brian a gold ID bracelet, had my name engraved on it, and paid extra to have it gift wrapped. When she realized what I was doing, she warned me that maybe I should wait and give it to him later. I pretended to agree but knew I'd give it to Brian right away – after all, he'd given me my Valentine rose and taken me to the concert, and we'd kissed.

Brian and Steve were waiting in front of the dorm for us.

"Let's give them a chance to talk," said Brian.

He started walking down the street. I was disappointed that he didn't take my hand, but we hadn't spoken to each other since that night in the Grove. I felt better when I realized that's where we were headed. When we got there, he took my hand long enough to pull me onto a bench. He turned to face me and sat up so straight it pulled him away from me.

I fished his gift out of my pocket and held it out.

"What's that?" he asked.

"A late Valentine."

He looked like he might throw up. "I can't take it."

"Why not?"

"I got back with my girlfriend at home."

"Girlfriend?" I froze in shock.

"She's in high school but she'll be here next year. She's going to be a teacher, too."

"You never said you had a girlfriend," I whispered.

"We started going to the skating rink together in seventh grade. Neither of us ever had a date with anyone else. That's why we agreed we should see other people this year."

"What about ..." I waved my hand. We were near where we had been that night.

"You're the only other girl I've ever kissed, and it felt wrong."

"You didn't act like it bothered you."

"It didn't right then, but afterward I felt horrible. Guilty. I called her that night and told her about it and she said the same thing happened to her when she tried to go out with someone else. It was okay as long as it was just friends, but … Anyway, we decided not to see other people. She's wearing my ring again."

I couldn't say anything. My heart was in my throat, choking me.

He stared at his feet. "We only kissed the one time. It's not like we were dating."

Part of my brain actually recognized this as the truth, so I managed to save face by choking out, "Yeah, we weren't dating."

"I can't take your present." He looked up, his face pleading for understanding.

"Of course not. It wasn't that big a deal anyway." I shoved it back into my pocket and forced a smile. "It was mostly a thank you for the concert."

"So we can be friends?" he asked. "I know Jan needs you to cover for her when she comes up here. We can still hang out."

"Sure." I wanted to be mature and say the right things.

"No more kissing, though."

"Of course not," I said. I wondered why he couldn't hear my heart cracking open.

The more I smiled and pretended it was okay, the more it hurt.

I didn't want to wear a bracelet with my own name on it. I threw it out the window on the way home. Jan reminded me she'd said I shouldn't give it to him yet. She said I was being ridiculous.

When I tried to write about it in my journal, the intensity of the pain stopped me. I cried myself to sleep every night that week. I considered telling Jan I wouldn't go with her anymore, but what else would I do? Sit at home alone?

It was a relief when Brian had to work on a paper the next weekend. I didn't have to see him at all. Steve borrowed an ID from a girl who looked kind of like me, so I could get into the movie at the Student Union by myself. Jan said we'd leave about eleven – her parents thought we were at a school dance again – so I stayed at the Union after the flick. I hovered on the edge of a group of girls, trying to blend in, until they left.

It was time to head back to the dorm, anyway. I stopped at the machine to get a Coke. Three good-looking guys came up as I popped off the cap and took a sip.

"Hi," said the nearest one. He turned away from his buddies to focus on me.

I returned his greeting and smiled shyly, then started to walk away. He came along.

"We're having a kegger at the frat next Friday. We're inviting all the pretty girls on campus. You want to come?" he asked.

I blushed. "Maybe. Which frat?"

He gave me the name and directions, then returned to his buddies.

My journal entry that night glossed over my heartbreak.

April 21, 1972

I was so ridiculous, thinking I was in love with Brian. Kissing's not a big deal. Some of the kids in my class have gone steady with three or four people and we're only high school freshmen. They've probably done lots more than kiss.

That's what I wrote, but I still cried every night, believing no one would ever love me. By Wednesday morning I was desperate, afraid I'd break into tears if I saw Brian, but I tried to dismiss those feelings by forcing excitement about the frat party.

April 26, 1972

Sure, my heart feels like it's been torn apart. Physically, it really does feel like that, but I need to get over it. I should make sure I kiss someone at that party. They think I'm in COLLEGE!

Maybe I'll even do more than kiss!

I still didn't know what "more than kiss" might mean, but the attitude in that entry kept me from falling apart at school.

It's also the reason I blamed myself for everything that happened at the frat that night.

Chapter 4: End of the World

My world shattered on Wednesday afternoon.

Any day Jan's mom wasn't using her car, she let Jan drive to school instead of riding the bus. We were going to the Tastee Freeze that afternoon, but I needed money. Jan waited in the car while I ran into the house to get some out of my room, but as I came in the kitchen door, my ears were assaulted by angry yelling.

I'd never heard my parents argue. I'd never heard my mother raise her voice. Now she was in the living room and I could hear every word.

"I've been working for months! Why should I quit now? You wouldn't have found out if Tony hadn't come into The Diner!"

"You don't need to work," my father said gently, trying to calm her down. "Why would you want to sneak around like that?"

I had to go through the living room to get to the stairs. I peeked in at them, not sure what to do. They didn't notice me. Tears poured down my mother's blotchy red face.

I'd never seen her cry, either.

"Sneaking around?" The words ripped from my mother's throat. She began to shake. "You know about sneaking around. I'm working because you buy your girlfriend diamond necklaces instead of paying the bills! I'm working because you drink away half your paycheck! I'm working so we don't lose this house! Because I want Peg to be able to go to college!"

"If I was working at the grocery store you wouldn't be upset!" she screeched. "You're just afraid the girlfriend you dumped might tell me about you. But she didn't have to!"

I backed into the kitchen so they wouldn't see me. I wanted to stick my fingers in my ears, but I needed to understand if my parents were going to get a divorce. I listened with clenched fists as my mother berated my father for having a string of girlfriends. She'd known about it for years and was sick and tired of being pitied. Of course everyone knew. We lived in a small town.

He tried to tell Mom she shouldn't listen to gossip, but she got really quiet and recited names in a dead voice, starting with Louise, her boss at The Diner, who gave Mom the job out of pity after my father dumped her, too. So many names, so many I knew. The father I'd always trusted was a cheat and a liar.

Tears welled up in my eyes as the sense of loss poured through me, but at the same time the fledgling bond with my mother that started over Easter vacation began to grow and solidify. Then that, too, disintegrated. He broke down and cried and said he loved her and promised it would never happen again. He said he couldn't bear to lose her – and she forgave him. Instead of feeling relieved, I felt I'd been cut adrift, that nothing in my life had been real.

I wiped the tears off my face and made my way back to Jan's car on autopilot. I couldn't talk to her about it. What if she'd known all along? I was mortified by the possibility. I pretended to be wiping at a spot on my jeans while I told her I hadn't found my money. She drove to the Tastee Freeze anyway and bought me a burger I couldn't eat.

She jabbered about Steve the whole time and didn't notice.

I was relieved she had to go home after she ate. When I went through the living room to the stairs, my parents were sitting on the couch with my mother cuddled against my father, all lovey as if that's how they'd always been, while I'd never seen them touch like that. I rushed by, mumbling something about a lot of homework.

Desperate for an outlet, I pulled out my journal.

April 26, 1972

I felt so good this morning, but now? She forgave him!!!!!! I can't believe it. She even apologized for yelling at him! I snuck out, so they still don't realize I was there. I think they're both disgusting—him for being a liar and a cheat, and her for putting up with it. She apologized!!!

Money's not the only reason my mother wants me to live at home while I go to college. She's been afraid he'd leave her once I was gone!

I don't ever want to be that weak.

I will never need someone like that.

That day shaped the rest of my life.

I avoided Jan the next day at school. I didn't want her to ask me what was wrong. But we worked at the same table in art class and she said she had the car again and insisted on giving me a ride home so we could talk. I tried to think of a lie, but I wasn't any good at it. I waited stiffly for the questions to start.

I shouldn't have worried.

"I've decided to do it," Jan announced as she drove.

"Do what?"

"Go all the way."

"Really? Are you sure?" I turned to stare at her.

"Steve and I are going to get married when we're done with college. It *is* silly to wait that long. We've already been dating almost two years."

"What if you get pregnant?"

"We'll be careful." She dismissed that worry with a wave of her hand. "Remember that time we camped out at the creek when we were kids? I want to pretend we're staying over at each other's houses like that. You can crash on a couch in the dorm."

"Where's Brian going to sleep?"

"On a couch, probably."

That would be too close. "I'd rather sleep in the car."

"I guess that's okay if you lock the doors. You can use that old blanket my parents keep in the trunk."

When she dropped me off at home, I went straight to my journal.

April 27, 1972

Jan is so self-centered! She didn't even consider how I might feel sleeping on a couch by Brian. So I get to spend the night in her parent's car with the dusty old blanket they keep for emergencies. I'd tell her to go to hell, but I'm really looking forward to that kegger. I've never even sipped Dad's beer, but he's always chilled out. Maybe it'll work for me. Maybe it'll loosen me up enough to kiss someone I don't care about.

That's why I thought everything was my own fault, why I was too ashamed to talk it out with anyone, why I never looked closely at what happened that night. Why I assumed I was drunk.

My parents were quick to let me spend the next night at Jan's –
they'd have the whole house to themselves.

We left right after dinner. I insisted we stop at the jewelry store
in Fredonia to get my ears pierced. Jan and most of her friends had
pierced ears. I'd always been chicken and my mother didn't
approve of altering the body like that.

"Finally," said Jan.

"They'll make me look older," I said. "My hair is long enough to
hide them at home."

Having gold studs shot into my ears hurt, but not nearly as much
as I had anticipated. Jan agreed it would help me continue passing
as a college student. She and Steve headed up to his room as soon
as we got to the dorm. Brian offered to go with me to the party.

"That's okay," I said. "I'm meeting up with some people there. I
know frats aren't your thing."

Besides, I didn't want to be around him. I wanted to drink and
have fun. I wanted someone else to kiss me, someone I didn't care
about, so my heart wouldn't hurt afterwards.

They were checking college IDs at the door.

"Sorry," I was told. "The cops have been busting frats for letting
in local high school kids. You'll have to go back and get your ID."

I nodded and turned to walk away, wondering if I could get that
girl's ID again.

"It's okay, I know her." The guy who'd invited me grabbed my
elbow and pulled me into the house. "You came!" He walked me
down stairs past people to the party in the basement. "You want
beer or some punch?" He gestured to a large plastic garbage can
filled with liquid. "It's whatever anyone's thrown into it."

"I think I'll have a beer."

"Good choice." He grinned and led me to the keg. "You've got to
be careful to hold the cup at an angle or you'll get all foam," he
explained as he poured the draft and handed it to me.

"Thanks."

"Hey, Robbie," another guy called. "They need you upstairs."

"I'll be back," he promised.

I stood alone with my beer, in a room full of people I didn't
know. A stereo blasted out The Doobie Brothers and everyone

stood around drinking. No one was dancing. I took a sip of beer and almost spit it out. It was awful. How could anyone like it? I watched and saw people were swigging it down, not sipping, so I tried that. I gagged and it came right back up into the cup. I found a bathroom next to the stairs, dumped the beer, and rinsed my mouth.

Back in the party room, there was nothing but alcohol to drink.

"There you are." Robbie put an arm around my shoulders. "Whoa, ready for another already? Cool."

He poured me another beer. This time I kept my mouth closed as I pretended to drink. Even that left the foul taste on my lips.

"Want to dance?" he asked.

I had fun dancing. After a while, we went outside to cool off. Around the corner from the entrance, Robbie backed me against the house and kissed me. I was startled at first, my body tense, but he took his time. His lips felt like butterflies caressing my face and neck. This is what I'd wanted, to be kissed by someone I didn't really care about, and his teasing was effective – when he finally brought his mouth to mine, I was fully aroused and amazed at the sensation. Brian had been much more direct; nothing like this. I kissed Robbie back enthusiastically, knowing it was just physical, that my heart was not in danger.

When I realized his hand was *under* my shirt, not on the outside, I pulled away.

"I'm not ready for this," I told him, still not certain what 'this' might be.

He looked at me straight in the eyes and slowly slid his hand down my back, then along the outside of my thigh and back up the inseam to the crotch of my jeans. I gasped at the sensation.

"Are you sure?" he asked.

"We need to go back inside," I whispered hoarsely.

He laughed and gave me a closed-mouth smack on the lips as he slid that hand to my back and guided me into the house. He poured another beer from the keg.

"Here, this'll help." He smiled.

He moved on to another girl and one of the other guys asked me to dance. I put down the glass without touching a drop. I had fun for hours, dancing with all the guys. Dancing worked better than alcohol would have. I won a kissing contest with a cute guy who kissed more like Brian and kept his hands where they belonged.

Robbie danced with me again after that. He slid his hands down on my butt and pulled me tight. It didn't make me feel the way I had outside – it made me uncomfortable – but other people were dancing the same way and I didn't want them to think I was too young to be there, so I didn't say anything. After that, they played more slow dances, and every one of my partners pulled me close like that.

I didn't want to go sit in Jan's car all alone yet. I wasn't sleepy and it was chilly outside.

Finally, I found myself yawning and realized there were only two other girls left at the party. Most of the guys were gone, too. The other girls were really drunk. One was making out with her dance partner right in front of everyone, then they headed upstairs. I decided to leave.

Robbie caught me on my way out. "Wait while I get my jacket. You shouldn't walk across campus alone this late."

"Will the Union be open? I really need something to drink that's not beer."

He held up one finger, disappeared through a door I hadn't noticed, and returned with a glass of Coke. "Here you go. It was warm, so I put it on ice."

"Thanks."

"I'll be right back. Wait here."

I shouldn't have waited.

Chapter 5: The Stranger

I woke up on the bathroom floor, naked except for my new earrings. My throat hurt. My private parts hurt. My stomach was burning. Painfully, I stood. Someone had puked in the sink. I rinsed it down the best I could and cupped my hands to drink some water from the faucet. I looked at a stranger in the mirror, but she was me. My hair was a wild, stinking mess. Something sticky had dried chunks of it together like glue. Everything after the Coke was blurry. I hadn't even finished one beer. I obviously shouldn't drink.

What had I done?

My hair could wait. I wanted my clothes. There were none in the bathroom. I peeked out where the remains of the party were strewn about – empty cups everywhere, the keg still in the corner, my jeans on the floor by the stereo. Nobody was in sight, so I hobbled out and picked up my pants. My blouse was in another corner, one button on the floor near it, the others nowhere to be seen. My sandals were under a ragged couch. My underwear and bra were gone.

I made my way back to the bathroom as quickly as I could, but it hurt to walk. Once inside, I locked the door. I couldn't let anyone see me like this. I rinsed out a cup and used it to pour water over my hair, finger-combing it until most of the goo came out, then splashed water on the rest of me, not caring if that left a puddle on the floor. My blouse had to serve as a towel. At last I put on my jeans and the wet top, which I held closed with my left hand.

I headed up the stairs as footsteps came down from the second floor. Robbie got to the landing by the outside door and stood above me. My heart pounded its way up into my throat.

"Hey, leaving already?" He shifted so his body blocked the way out. "You were so busy with the other guys last night, I only got one turn. Come on up to my room."

When he grabbed my arm I found my voice. "Stop it!"

I pulled towards the exit. He lost his balance at first, but his grip didn't loosen until I stopped clutching my blouse to claw his face.

That made him let go, but as I started for the door again, he grabbed my hair and yanked me back.

A hippie with a ponytail saved me. He came down the stairs with a leather saddlebag over his shoulder. He towered above Robbie.

"Let her go." He said it quietly, almost peacefully, but there was no doubt in his tone, no uncertainty in his face or stance.

"Fine, she's all yours." Robbie pushed me toward the hippie and disappeared out the door.

I burst into tears and pulled my torn blouse together, grasping it with both hands.

"I'm not going to hurt you," the hippie said softly. "Do you want a T-shirt to put over that?"

I nodded.

He swung the saddlebag off his shoulder and pulled out a tie-dyed T-shirt similar to the one he wore.

"Here you go," he said as he handed it to me. "My name's Joe."

"I'm Peg," I whispered. I turned my back to him and pulled the shirt over my torn blouse.

"Are you okay?" he asked.

"Yeah," I lied. I turned around but avoided looking at him. "Robbie's going to be mad at you."

He shrugged. "I don't live here. I'm on my way to Canada on my motorcycle. It looked like rain last night, so I came by the campus looking for a place to crash."

"You were here last night?" A knot formed in my stomach.

"I found a couch up on the third floor and went to sleep early."

"You weren't ...?"

He shook his head. "We should probably get out of here. You want a ride?"

I nodded and asked, "Can you take me to my friend's car? It's on the other side of campus."

He led the way. His bike was parked down the street. He put the saddlebags on the back.

"You sit right here," he said, patting in front of the bags. "Do you need help getting on?"

I wasn't ready to be touched. "No, I think I can do it myself."

He steadied the bike while I sat sidesaddle, then gingerly pulled my leg over the seat. I winced as my weight shifted onto my crotch. He guided my feet onto pegs.

"Keep your feet on these until we're parked and I tell you it's okay. There's some slide when you take off or stop, that's why I wear boots with leather soles, so they don't catch. Those sandals would rip right off."

Pushing against the pegs took some pressure off of my crotch.

"There's not much room," he apologized as he got on in front of me. "You can hold onto the frame or put your arms around me, whichever is more comfortable."

I leaned back a bit and grabbed the frame.

"You'll have to give me directions," he said.

"Right at that stop sign, then follow the drive around to the dorms and you go left into visitor parking."

"Just tap my shoulder for the left."

Jan's car wasn't where she'd parked. I scanned the lot, in case she'd moved it or I'd remembered wrong, but it wasn't there.

"She left without me," I sobbed.

"Do you want a ride to the hospital?" He turned to look at me.

My eyes widened in fear and I shook my head. I couldn't let anyone know what I'd done.

"I can take you home," he offered.

"It's a half hour the wrong way, if you're going to Canada."

"I'm not on a schedule."

I shifted on the seat uncomfortably. The vibration from the trip across campus had made everything hurt even more. The seam of my jeans dug into me. I wasn't sure I could last a half hour. But I didn't know how else I would get home.

"Thanks," I said, and gave him directions.

"Okay, hold tight."

About halfway, he pulled onto a side road, drove up the hill, and stopped by a meadow overlooking Lake Erie.

"Figured you might need a break." He parked and got off the bike, being careful not to bump me.

We were right next to the road, in the open, with a house not too far away, and I did need the break. He stood with his arm out. I grabbed it for balance as I awkwardly brought my leg over and dismounted. He got the saddle bag and went ahead. I had to walk with my legs apart and my knees bent some to keep my jeans from rubbing against my sorest parts. It would have been embarrassing, but Joe wasn't looking at me. He was staring out over the lake.

"This view is copacetic," he said.

I looked at the lake. "It *is* pretty. I guess I kind of take it for granted."

He pulled a thin blanket out of one of the saddlebags and spread it on the ground. From the other bag he got a thermos and a jar of seeds, raisins, and nuts. He poured a light brown beverage into the thermos cup and offered it to me.

"Herbal tea," he said.

I tried it cautiously and found it soothed the burning in my stomach. "It's sweeter than the stuff my mother drinks."

"That's probably black tea. It's acidic and has caffeine in it."

He plopped down near one edge of the blanket, opened the jar and poured some of the mix into his hand. He stared off at the lake.

For the first time, I took a good look at him. His slightly flared jeans were faded blue denim. His shirt was a bright sunburst of colors. A small glass dragon dangled from a leather thong around his neck. The green in it matched his eyes.

Realizing I'd been caught gazing at him, I turned away and blurted out, "I didn't think hippies rode motorcycles." I realized how unfriendly that sounded and tried to fix it. "I mean, shouldn't you have a VW bug or something?"

"I'm not actually a hippie. I help my dad run the family restaurant."

Shyly I glanced at him. "I like your necklace."

"Thanks. I made it myself."

"Is it stained glass?"

"Yeah. I'm working on a big piece that I'll be able to hang in a window. There's a wizard using a crystal to cast a spell on a huge fire-breathing dragon. It's the most detailed work I've done so far. There are tiny flowers at the foot of the dragon, in multiple colors, and the flame coming out of his mouth is red, orange, and yellow."

"Why do you work with your dad when you're so excited about making stained glass?"

"He needs my help."

Cautiously, I sat down on the edge of the blanket as far away from him as possible. I gave him the empty thermos cup and he shook a little of the nut mixture into my hand.

I picked one piece at a time, a walnut, a raisin, then stopped.

"Do you mind if I put it back? My stomach's kind of upset." It was still burning and now it was knotted up as well.

"Sure." He held out the jar. "Did the tea help?"

I nodded. He poured some more tea and as I sipped it our gazes met and stuck. I was afraid he would suggest a hospital again. Maybe he read that in my face, because he didn't. Instead, he looked away as he talked.

"My brother had to go to Canada to avoid being drafted," he said. "So I got drafted into the restaurant."

"Oh. You're going to visit him?"

"Yeah."

We sat there in silence for a while. If my body hadn't been so sore, I might have been able to pretend nothing had happened. But I kept feeling the pull on my hair as Robbie started dragging me up the stairs.

"I'm glad you were there," I whispered.

"Do you want to talk about it?" he asked gently.

I shook my head, but tears began to flow and when he opened his arm, I moved closer and leaned into his shoulder. The crying turned into sobbing and I was comforted when he brought his other arm up and rocked me gently.

When I could talk again, I asked him to tell me about his family and their restaurant. He kept holding me and rocking me while he spoke softly, as if it were a child's bedtime story, all about his father's sisters, who spoke mainly Greek, and how his father refused to talk to his brother since he'd run from the draft.

"Jorge was the one who lived for the restaurant. He's got his own place up in Canada. My mother sent him the money to start it. Dad pretends not to know or care, but he'll be listening to everything I say when I get back."

Finally, he took me home. Well, around the corner from my house. I couldn't let my parents see a hippie on a motorcycle bring me back from my overnight at Jan's. It was bad enough to be wearing Joe's tie-dye. I offered to return it, but was relieved when he said to keep it. It would have been worse for them to see my torn blouse.

They wouldn't have though. I heard them when I started up the stairs to my room. They were in their bedroom, making up some more. Gross. I took a long, hot shower, then called Jan.

"God, Peg, where have you been? When you weren't in the car I panicked. I didn't remember which frat you'd said, and they all have parties every weekend."

"I fell asleep there. On a couch. You were gone when I got to where you parked."

"I told you my dad needed the car this morning. I waited as long as I could," she insisted. "How'd you get home?"

"Got a ride."

"It's like three o'clock."

"We stopped for a picnic."

"Who we?"

"Me and the guy who gave me a ride."

"Shoot. My dad's coming in," she whispered. "I'll talk him into letting me borrow the car again and pick you up."

While I was waiting, I opened my journal. For a long time, I sat there. Finally I wrote about the night before – not much, but enough to bring it back with startling clarity when I read the entry so many years later – and enough to realize how little beer I had.

It was easier to write about Joe, every little detail. He was a lifesaver with his gentle calm support, but I wonder now what would have happened if he'd made me go to the hospital. It might have been better; it could have been worse.

There's no way to be sure.

I slapped my journal shut when Jan barged into my room with my overnight bag. I put the notebook away in my desk drawer before we left, then went back to writing as soon as I got home.

April 29, 1972

My parents apparently heard me in the shower, so they were in the kitchen playing Rummy when Jan came for me. I'm sure they headed for their bedroom the minute we left. No wonder I'm a slut. My mother's glowing all the time. Gross.

Jan acted as if I'd forgotten my overnight bag at her house. She brought it up to my room and then we went to the Tastee Freeze. That gave me a good excuse to skip dinner. My stomach's still burning like crazy. I didn't know beer did that, or maybe sex does? I'm never having either again, so I won't ever know. At least the milkshake at the Tastee Freeze made it feel a little better.

On the way there, I remembered the whole reason for our visit to the campus was so Jan could lose her virginity. I didn't really want to hear about it, but she'd expect me to demand all the details, so I asked "How was it?"

She chickened out again. She said he was really sweet about it, though, and once the pressure was off she relaxed and they made out for hours, then fell asleep in each other's arms - naked. She whispered "naked" because it was so important. She said "I just couldn't... you know ..." as if going all the way was a big deal even when they've been together forever and figure they're getting married and even get naked with each other.

I almost puked.

Jan asked about the guy who got me home and I told her about Joe and his family and his motorcycle, which totally amazed her. Me, the girl who just finally got her ears pierced, riding a motorcycle. So I told her how cool it was but that it left me kind of sore, like when you ride a bike too long. There's no way I can tell Jan or anyone else the real reason I'm sore. Jan can't even go all the way with a boy she's been dating for two years. I'm a drunken slut who did who-knows-what with who-knows-how-many guys I don't even know. Actually, I'm beginning to have flashes of memory, some of the things I did and let them do to me.

I did like it, at least some of it.

I'm such a slut. Who will ever want me?

I was perilously ignorant. I had never heard of a date-rape drug and so had no clue they could work by increasing the libido and lowering inhibitions, by creating false desire. I spent most of my life blaming myself for everything that happened that night.

It changed the way I felt and thought about myself.

It put me on a dark and dangerous road.

Chapter 6: Lies

The next weekend, Jan's family went to visit her grandmother. The weekend after that, I pretended to have really bad cramps. Jan was not happy.

"I can't go to State without you. You're the only reason my parents don't give me the third degree about where I've been with the car. They know you're such an angel."

I knew I was no angel, but I couldn't talk about it, and I couldn't go back to that campus. In art class the next week, Jan accidentally spilled some paint, ruining my project. I used that as an excuse to stop speaking to her. I didn't say anything to anyone, unless they asked a direct question, and then I gave the shortest answer possible.

My parents didn't notice. They were wrapped up in themselves. I didn't even bother keeping my ears covered, and my mother didn't say a thing about my having pierced them.

I became obsessed with my father's philandering.

May 17, 1972

My math teacher has a picture of his wife and kids on his desk. I looked at it this week, to see if any of the kids look like me. None of them do. But I probably have at least one half-sibling out there somewhere. I don't really want to know, but I'm fascinated by the idea, too. I even have imaginary conversations, where I drop the bomb, "Oh, did I mention we share the same father? Yes, he really got around, There are several of you bastard children." Except that makes it sound like a gothic romance, and I don't find it at all romantic.

I hate being here with my parents. They're constantly touching each other, all lovey-dovey. It's sickening. They've hardly noticed my existence since they had that argument.

I've got to get out of here. I wonder what Harrisburg is like? I wonder how long Joe's staying in Canada?

Near the end of May, I realized my period was three weeks overdue. Abortion was still illegal. If it had crossed my mind, I wouldn't have known how to get one.

May 29, 1972

Pregnant.

What am I supposed to do about that? Maybe I'm not. I've skipped a month before. But I can't stand it here anyway, and I don't want anyone to start wondering. I feel fatter already. Maybe it's just bloating because I'm late. God, I hope I'm not pregnant. But if I am, I'm pretty sure people will be able to tell by the end of school. Another month? Yeah, it'll be obvious by then. I think.

There is no way I will ever give this town another scandal.

I have to leave. But if I go away, give it up, then come home, everyone will count months and know why. So there won't be any coming back. That probably means I won't ever finish high school, so there's no reason to worry about leaving before finals. I'll go to Harrisburg. Joe's really nice, and he won't look down on me for being pregnant. He'll understand. Maybe he'll help me again.

I focused on Joe because everything else seemed cold, dark, and frightening. But I couldn't get to him by myself. Hitchhiking was a foreign concept. Catching a bus would be daring enough. But if I started anywhere near home, my destination would become public knowledge.

If I could convince Jan to take me to Erie, I could leave anonymously. I had to make up with her. At school, she now snubbed me. She had plenty of friends from her own grade; she didn't need me. I called her at home.

"Jan, please don't hang up. I need to talk to you." No click. She was still there. I rushed into her silence. "I'm sorry for being such a jerk about the paint."

"You should be. I haven't been able to see Steve at all."

"I'm sorry. I need your help." I wound the phone cord around my hand three times.

"Why would I help you?"

"You're the only one who can." I shook off the cord and clenched my fist with crossed fingers.

"Can what?" She was suspicious.

"I'll explain, but not on the phone."

Curiosity won. "I'll pick you up in twenty minutes."

We drove down to the lake and sat on the rocks.

"All right, what do you want?" Jan demanded.

I wanted to tell her the truth, but she might tell someone about me, tell them what I'd done. So I told a lie I wanted to believe.

"It's Joe," I stalled.

"Who's Joe?"

"The guy who gave me a ride home, remember?"

"Oh, yeah. What about him?"

I couldn't say anything about being pregnant, under any circumstance. "He's taking off for California, and I'm going with him."

"Are you nuts?" she exclaimed.

"We've been talking on the phone every night, after my parents are in bed."

"*That's* why you look like you haven't been sleeping. How old is this guy?"

"Nineteen." That sounded old enough to be responsible, but not too old.

Jan was impressed. "He actually wants you to go with him?"

"Yeah. We love each other." I wished this was true.

"He came out and said he loves you?"

"Yes, he did, and I love him." My desire made it sound believable.

"It took forever for Steve to say that. I mean, I knew he did, but to actually come out and say it..." Jan tossed a flat stone toward the waves, but we weren't close enough to make it skip. "Okay, if you're sure, I'll help. But what about your parents?"

"They're like having a second honeymoon or something. It's really gross. They won't even notice I'm gone." I didn't have to fake the feelings about my parents.

"My mom's bridge club is talking about how they're holding hands and kissing in public."

I had to ask. "You know what everyone talked about before, don't you?"

There was an uncomfortable silence before Jan answered. "Yeah. This is better than that, isn't it?"

"I guess. But I'm glad I've got Joe." The wistfulness in my voice was for the wish, but it made the lie convincing.

"When's he coming for you?" she asked.

"Friday. He wants me to meet him in Erie so no one sees us leaving together."

"That's smart. He could get into trouble, especially crossing state lines with you."

"Yeah, that's why we have to do it this way. Will you give me a ride to Erie?"

She couldn't resist being part of my romantic adventure, but she wanted a key role. "Sure. But if I don't like him, you're coming home with me."

June 1, 1972

I can't believe Jan hasn't asked if we've done it yet. She probably figures there's no way I would have.

I found an old duffel bag in the attic and cleaned it out good yesterday. It's packed and ready to go, with my life savings in it. After Mom left for work this morning, I told Dad that my friend Ellen, an imaginary new kid in town, wants me to go shopping in Buffalo with her family for the weekend. He picked me up after school so I could get money out of my savings account.

It was easier than I expected at the bank, because he ran into one of his drinking buddies and started talking. He signed a blank withdrawal slip and handed it to me. I filled it out for five dollars less than my account held and went to the teller by myself. She asked me about taking so much out, but I told her I'd be putting most of it back on Monday after shopping. I tucked the money in my pocket before Dad saw it.

When Mom got home, she of course wanted to call this new girl's parents, but I said I'd left the number at school. When she insisted on calling information for it, I made up a Polish-sounding last name. When the operator said there was no listing, I said I might not be saying it right and had no idea how to spell it. Mom kept saying no, but I reminded her how I'd worked for the money, and I really do need some shirts for summer.

She finally agreed, on condition I leave the phone number where I'll be on the table before I leave tomorrow.

I'm supposed to be home Sunday morning. So I'll have at least a couple days before they start looking for me, and they'll look the wrong direction. Of course, they're so wrapped up in themselves now, it may take a week or two for them to notice I'm gone.

On Friday I woke up early, looked at the pink walls and purple café curtains, and pulled out my journal.

June 2, 1972

I'm never sleeping in this room again.

My stomach's doing flips, but no way can I stay longer. I can barely snap my jeans.

When I told Jan I'm meeting Joe at the bus station, she asked about his motorcycle. I told her he sold it so we'd have money to get started. I'm getting really good at this lying thing. I always used to get caught when I tried to lie. Now it's kind of like writing stories.

If you wish hard enough for your lie to be true, you start believing it yourself, at least a little bit. In my more rational moments, I kept telling myself Joe probably thought of me as the slutty girl he helped out with a ride, if he thought of me at all. But in my heart, I hoped the lie would become my reality. I slipped my journal into the duffel bag, next to my clothes, thinking I'd write daily, hoping Joe would be a central character in the pages to come.

That was my last day in high school, forever.

Jan rode the bus home to get her parent's car, so I had time to change and get my things ready before she picked me up. I didn't leave a note for my parents. What would I say? Jan would give them my phony story eventually.

I scribbled a fake phone number on a paper for my mother and left it on the table. I waited impatiently by the door. As soon as I saw Jan, I hurried to her car before anyone could see me.

"*Where* did you get that outfit?" she demanded.

The Jesus sandals were from the new shoe store in town. The felt hat had been on my closet shelf ever since my father gave it to me on my twelfth birthday. The cotton flower-print skirt and peasant blouse had come from Murphy's last summer. I'd planned to wear them as a costume for Halloween, then decided the top looked stupid with my bra.

I wasn't wearing one. That's probably what rattled Jan the most. I always dressed to hide my figure. But my bras were painfully tight now. Besides, if I was running away to California with Joe, I might as well look like a hippie. And if my parents called the police when I didn't come home, they'd never describe me this way. I kept telling myself they probably wouldn't notice I was gone for a week or so.

"How's your boyfriend getting to Erie?" Jan asked as we drove out of town.

"A friend's giving him a ride that far. Can you find the bus station?"

She nodded. "You know my mom. She's got maps for any place we've ever been. I have the one for Erie, and the bus station's marked on it. What time do you have to be there?"

"I'm not sure."

"Well, when are you supposed to meet him?"

If I told her too early, she'd insist on waiting with me. "Eight," I said, "but he may be later. His ride has to make some stops on the way."

"Good. We can stop at the Red Barn for dinner, my treat. You didn't give me enough warning to get you a real going away present."

"You don't have to do that. Your parents will be expecting you."

"They play bridge on Fridays. They won't be home until midnight."

"Great." I pretended to be glad, but she wouldn't need to leave Erie until ten.

As we ate, Jan drew me into remembering all the good times we'd had as we grew up. It occurred to me that this was probably the last time I'd ever see her. I didn't have to pretend. I was missing her already. We walked out to the car with our arms around each other.

When we got to the bus station, she insisted on parking and coming in with me.

"I am not leaving you in this neighborhood alone."

"I'll be okay, and Joe will be here soon."

"He better be. You're not taking off across country with some guy I've never even seen!"

We sat on a bench and chatted some more about the good old days, but I kept watching the clock.

"You don't think he's changed his mind?" she asked.

"No, I'm sure he's coming. You don't have to wait, really."

"I'll wait, or you'll go home with me."

The bus station *was* dirty and some of the people looked pretty rough.

"You sound like my mother," I said, but I added a smile. I didn't want to make Jan leave by starting a fight, not when I'd never see her again.

"It's probably filthy, but I need to use the bathroom," she said. That was definitely what my mother would say. "Come with me?"

"No, I'd better stay out here where Joe can find me."

I scanned the crowd, wondering if I could pretend someone was Joe, but what would I say to them? Jan might go off about how I was underage or something.

"Hi."

The deep male voice startled me. Could he be talking to me?

"Going far?" He was wearing camouflage fatigues, but his dark hair was long and he had a guitar strapped across his back. And he was looking straight at me.

"Kinda." I stammered.

"Your friend seems a little uptight," he said.

"Yeah, she won't leave until my boyfriend shows."

"Oh," he seemed disappointed.

"Thing is, there's really no boyfriend, so I'm not sure what to do." I glanced at the restroom door. No sign of her yet.

"How old's this boyfriend supposed to be?"

"Nineteen."

"Think I could pass? If she saw me at all, it was only my back."

My prayers were being answered! "Maybe."

"What else should I know?"

"We met a few weeks ago, at a party up in Fredonia, that's in New York, at a frat house. We've been talking on the phone every night and we're running away to California together."

"You're headed to California?" He frowned.

"Actually, I'm going to buy a ticket for Harrisburg, but I don't want *her* to know that."

His smile flashed brightly. "That's home."

"Really?"

"Just bought my ticket," he said.

"I can't get mine until she leaves."

Jan came through the restroom door. "That's her," I squeaked.

He threw his arms around me and whispered by my ear, "Who am I?"

"Joe!" I cried, pretending he'd just arrived.

He pulled me closer and gave me a long, deep French kiss, then leaned back to look at me and exclaimed, "God, I've missed you!"

Stunned by the effect his kiss had on me, I stood there with a goofy grin on my face. I was vaguely aware of Jan, who was staring with her mouth hanging open.

I pulled it together. "This is my friend Jan. Jan, this is Joe."

"Thanks for getting her here." He gave Jan a warm smile and reached out to shake her hand. "It's really nice to meet you."

"Nice to meet you, too," she said haltingly. "You're nineteen?"

He did look older.

"Yeah, a couple weeks ago," he claimed.

"Well, I guess you won't have any trouble getting a job in California." Jan looked at me, concerned. Realizing she couldn't change my mind, she turned back to the stranger. "You'll take good care of Peg, won't you?"

He pulled my hip tightly against his. "You better believe it."

"I'll be fine." I was beginning to believe it myself.

Jan let out a big sigh. "I still think you're crazy not to finish school."

"I told you Joe has to leave now."

He nodded with an apologetic smile. "I figure Peg can study for the GED while I work and save some money, then we'll both go to college."

"What part of California are you going to?" Jan asked.

"The Bay Area." When she looked blank, he added, "San Francisco. I've got a friend out there who's setting us up with a place to stay and all."

"Oh, do you have an address?" Jan asked.

"Not yet," he answered.

The detail going into this lie made me nervous. I just wanted Jan to leave. I slipped away from the stranger and gave her a hug. "This is the best thing that's ever happened to me. Be happy."

She smiled. "Okay. I'm happy for you. Call me when you get a phone, though. Let me know where you are."

"I will."

I lied.

Chapter 7: Pyra is Born

The stranger insisted on walking Jan to her car. He carried my bag, as well as his guitar, and kept his arm around me until I'd waved her out of sight. Before I could slip out of his grasp, he pulled me into another kiss. He didn't stop until I melted into him.

Then he pulled back and smiled. "I'm Nick."

"I'm Peg," I gasped.

"So I heard. Are you still Peg?"

I was having trouble breathing. I knew it was dangerous, but every nerve in my body was tingling and hoping he'd kiss me some more. When my brain accused me of being a slut, it didn't matter anymore – Peg and her virginity were history.

"I think I'll be Pyra." I looked like a hippie; I might as well take a hippie name.

"Nice meeting you, Pyra."

He kissed me again, and I kissed him back. When he finally lifted his face from mine, our bodies were still pressed together and my heart was pounding.

"Let's get your ticket," he said.

Nick insisted on paying for it. "I've got plenty of cash, Pyra. Don't worry about it."

He'd never have offered to buy Peg's ticket, and she would have been too scared to let him if he did. I pushed those thoughts aside. It wasn't like I had to protect my virginity anymore, and he'd already helped me with Jan, and besides, he was a good kisser, and older.

I *liked* knowing he would take care of me.

"Thanks," Pyra said casually.

Pyra knew men would do things for her, right from the start. I was a new person.

Nick came back with my ticket.

"The bus doesn't leave until midnight." He had a deck of cards in his hand. "Do you play poker?"

I'd expected him to want to pass the time necking, but if he wanted to play cards, that was okay, too. Whatever he wanted was fine with me. Nick wrote out a list of what beats what. We played for pennies. I won the first three hands.

"You didn't mention you're a card shark," he pretended to complain.

I grinned and sat straighter, which pushed my breasts forward. "I'm a fast learner."

When he grinned back, I shifted my shoulders to make my naked nipples rub against the material of my blouse. I felt hot and tingly just like I had when he'd kissed me.

"How old are you?" he asked.

"Old enough." The reply popped out.

I was playing with fire and it was exciting. He reached over and brushed my right nipple, making it swell even more against the thin cotton of my blouse. I glanced around nervously, but no one seemed to be watching. He did the same to the left one while he stared deep into my eyes. I could hardly breathe.

He put the cards away, grabbed our gear, and nodded toward the back door. He didn't have to say a word. I followed.

It was dark. He found a spot between two buildings and put down our things. He shoved me against the wall and kissed me, hard, demanding. He worked on his belt with one hand and slid the other up under my shirt. He grabbed my swollen breast, then rubbed the nipple. He took it in his mouth and sucked on it, nipping it. I shoved my pelvis against him and he bit harder. I gasped.

He backed away and stared into my eyes. I was panting. I had this overwhelming desire to belong to him and he knew it. He watched my face as he reached under my skirt and pushed my panties down. I stepped out of them. He watched my eyes open wide as he shoved his thing into me all at once, banging me against the wall. It hurt and felt good at the same time. Then he lifted my legs around him and I grabbed him tightly, biting his neck as he pounded into me. The bricks of the wall scraped my back through my thin peasant shirt. It felt so good!

He smothered my moans with his mouth. When he began pulsing in his climax, my entire body shuddered violently. I clung to him, feeling we were one.

As our bodies parted, he asked, "Is that what you wanted?"

"Yes," I whispered. "Thank you."

"Pyra," he paused to nip my neck, "is the right name for you."

He straightened my clothing, then threw my panties into a garbage can. I smiled. We walked back into the bus station as if we'd just taken a stroll, but I could feel his juices sliding down my legs. Having no panties on left me wanting him inside me again. I looked at him, eyes wide, and he laughed.

"Later," he said.

I used the bathroom and wiped off my legs and crotch. I didn't care if I was a slut. Sex was fantastic, when you weren't drunk. No wonder my parents were at it all the time now. Well, there's no way I'd go back to being a little kid again.

I'd always been embarrassed by my big chest. Now, I strutted with shoulders back, deliberately shifting my breasts so they were more noticeable and my swollen nipples brushed against the fabric and stood out. Every male who glanced my way stopped and stared. If they knew I didn't have any panties on, if they knew what I'd just done with Nick ... I could be with any of them. But I was Nick's. It was in his eyes as I came back to him. He knew what I was doing, and he knew I was his. He patted the bench beside him.

"Sit and cool down, fire lady."

I obeyed.

"Why are you going to Harrisburg?" he asked as if nothing had happened. He pulled out the deck of cards we'd been playing with earlier.

I suddenly realized it was probably illegal for him to have sex with someone my age. Of course we had to be casual. I could do that. "I had to go somewhere, and it's as good as anyplace."

"Do you know anyone there?"

Joe was a fantasy. Nick was real. "No."

"Where were you planning to stay?" He shuffled the cards but looked at me.

"I hadn't thought that far ahead." Panic gripped me for a moment as I realize how poorly I'd prepared for anything beyond getting away.

"Then I guess you'll move in with us." He smiled.

He wanted me! "Us?"

"The Second Street Coalition."

"Who's that?"

He stopped shuffling and held the cards. "Our band. We live in Crazy Mike's house."

"Crazy Mike?"

"Yeah. He's the drummer. We have a gig weekend after next at the coffeehouse. Can you sing?"

"Sing?"

"Like Joni Mitchell? Gracie Slick would be great."

"I'm not sure." We only had AM radio, and the strongest station not playing country was CKLW, Motown out of Detroit, Michigan.

He put the cards aside, got out his guitar, and played songs I'd never heard, or had heard only a few times. Finally he played *Leaving on a Jet Plane*, a Peter, Paul, and Mary song I knew. I sang along.

"You sound just like Mary," he said. "Once you've heard the other songs, you'll be able to sing them."

I glowed. I'd been in chorus when I was in grade school, but hadn't done much singing since then. Now I was going to be part of a rock and roll band. He started teaching me some of the lyrics while we waited.

On the bus I slept with his arm around me.

The house was on the corner of Second Street and an alley. It squeezed against its neighbor in the morning light. A grimy picture window with curtains drawn and a narrow door over a cement stoop offered little encouragement to enter.

Inside, it was gloomy. A couple of guys were dozing on a couch with the TV flickering. Nick led me straight up the stairs. They tilted to the left and creaked as if they might give way at any moment. On the second floor, he took me into the bathroom. I stared out the window at a small patch of tar roof with a lawn chair on it while he peed. I was glad I'd gone at the bus station. It was gross enough listening to him. When he finished, Nick came over next to me.

"That's our sunbathing area, if you're into that. You just climb out this window."

Blank walls of the neighboring houses rose on one side and the back, inches away from the roof. The remaining side was open to the alley. My mother would hate this place.

Nick's room was the entire third level. Stereo equipment and TVs were stacked away from the windows that overlooked the street. On the floor under the windows, tangled bedding did nothing to cover the stains on the mattress. A wire milk crate served as a nightstand, with a small lamp and an alarm clock on it. A thin rug covered part of the floor. A wooden orange crate on its side held records and a slab of plywood across the top of it supported Nick's record player.

"Don't mess with my stereo," he warned. "I'm picky about how my records are handled."

Nick opened the closet door and made a separate space for my things.

"Here you go," he said.

"Thanks."

I unpacked my bag while Nick went downstairs to see what had happened while he was away. There weren't any empty wire hangers, but there was room for three piles on the shelf he'd emptied for me—pants, shirts, underwear.

I'd been with Nick every minute since Erie. Now I had a moment alone, I wrote in my journal.

June 3, 1972

We had sex in the alley behind the bus station! I thought we were just going to make out some, but then I realized I wanted it, and it's not like I'm a virgin anymore. There's no reason to stop. It made me feel really powerful and at the same time so ... submissive, I guess ... like willing to do anything. I guess that's what happened at the frat house, but I was too messed up to know what was going on. Now that I've had sex on purpose, I like it. Being close to Nick makes me ache for him. The sex makes me feel as if I belong to him. I want to do it again. If that makes me a slut, I don't care. I'm Nick's slut.

I hid the notebook inside my Fredonia sweatshirt, under my T-shirts, just before Nick came back.

"Let's take a bath," he said.

There was no shower. We squeezed into the old cast iron tub together. At first, I was shy about him seeing my entire body naked, but that was silly considering what we'd done in Erie. He washed me and had me wash him. He was playing with my breasts when someone knocked once, then rushed into the bathroom. I hugged my knees to my chest.

"Man, I gotta take a shit," said one of the guys from the couch.

"Let us get out of here first." Nick stood and stepped out of the tub.

He took a hand away from my knees and pulled me up. There was no way to cover myself. The stranger looked right at me as Nick introduced us.

"This is Pyra. Pyra, this is Crazy Mike."

"Nice to meet you." Crazy Mike sounded like he met naked girls every day. He grabbed our towels off the toilet seat and shoved them at us, then started unbuckling his pants.

Grossed out, I turned for the door, wrapping the towel around me as I left. Nick stayed behind a moment to talk to Crazy Mike about his trip. I peeked down the stairs. No one else was coming. I rushed up to Nick's room.

I dried off, then snugged the towel to cover me while I stared at the closet, trying to decide what to wear. Nick came up and wrapped his arms around me. His thing poked at my bottom through the towel and he rubbed it against me. He took away the towel, turned me around, and looked me over. Then he started touching me.

We made love the rest of the day.

I wanted to do everything for Nick that I'd done at the fraternity house. Since those memories came in vague flashes, I was simply willing to do anything he wanted. At first, aware of the other people in the house, I held back when I wanted to moan or cry out – because it felt so good or sometimes because it hurt some. But Nick urged me to let it out, to scream if I felt like it, and by the end of the afternoon I wasn't worrying about making noise. It felt good to let go completely, to belong to somebody completely, even if everyone in the house knew what we were doing.

We were wrapped together naked when he finally dozed off. I laid there wondering if everyone did all the things Nick had done with me. I couldn't imagine my mother letting my father take her like that, or doing the things Nick had me do to him.

I hoped he'd keep me when he found out I was pregnant.

Nick worked with me on songs that first week. He had me listen to Jefferson Airplane and Crosby, Stills, Nash, and Young and Joni Mitchell and a lot of other music I'd never really known. He wrote down lyrics and I sang along with the albums until I was pretty good, then we started rehearsing with the band and I learned to work with the microphone.

Nick kept me right there next to him even when we weren't working on music, even when he wasn't paying any attention to me. I wasn't wearing a bra or underwear anymore, and mostly I wore skirts to make it easy for him to take me anytime, anyplace. Waiting like that left me wet and ready. The next time I had a few moments alone to write in my journal, I described how I felt.

June 11, 1972

I love belonging to Nick. When he takes me in the kitchen, knowing the guys are in the next room, knowing they have to know what we're doing, makes it more exciting—because it tells them I'm Nick's and he wants me that much.

This must be how my mother feels about my father, why she kept quiet about his sleeping around for so long, and why they kept touching each other when they made up. Sex is so much more powerful than the silly little crushes I had when I was a virgin. I'd do anything for Nick.

I don't think I ever fooled myself into believing Nick loved me, but I certainly thought that's what I was feeling. I so needed to belong to someone, somewhere.

There was more to the belonging than Nick, too—by the next weekend, I was ready to sing with the band. We loaded the amps and speakers and instruments into the back of Crazy Mike's bread truck. It had to be convinced to start.

"You got to fix that before our next gig," said Jim, the bass player.

The coffeehouse was across the street from the river. They sold natural juices and snacks. There were only a few people there when we started setting up.

Jim looked around and shook his head. "Won't have much of a crowd this time. Everyone's gone home."

"Gone home?" I asked.

"Tons of people were here for the Berrigan brothers' trial, and when Angela Davis came to speak," he explained.

"Yeah," laughed Crazy Mike. "There were guys in trench coats and shiny shoes taking pictures of us the last time we played here. We're in a file somewhere."

"It's still light out," said Jim. "More people'll come later."

Even after dark, the audience was small, but they liked me. While the guys unloaded the truck, I slipped upstairs and wrote about it in my journal, and about what happened after.

June 17, 1972

Jan would die! I'm not the little mouse she knew, always shy and embarrassed by my big boobs. Not only did I sing at the coffeehouse, I let strangers sneak peeks inside my shirt so the guys could shoplift our dinner! While I kept all eyes on me, they walked out with steaks and stuff to celebrate.

I'm sure the cashier saw my nipple, and it turned me on. I was so hot, Nick and I made out on the way home and he pulled one out and sucked on it and nipped it, right in front of the guys. It was so exciting, having him show them I'm his, and I'm not even on 'ludes.

I'd do anything for Nick.

By then, I'd tried pot and pills. The only thing I liked was the Quaaludes. If I was on 'ludes, I always got off on sex, even when Nick deliberately made it hurt. I was on them more often than not.

Now I had the lyrics down, I only had to practice when the guys did, which wasn't often. They didn't have any more gigs set. Nick and I screwed every day, but not all day. We watched cartoons or played poker with the guys, and when there was a break in the rain, we took walks.

We got ice cream cones at the mom and pop grocery store two blocks away. The Susquehanna River was right down the street. We walked along the river and played music by the Sunken Gardens – beautiful flower beds close to the river's edge, down twenty or more feet from street level. Kind of like a deep, empty, three-sided swimming pool with a garden on the bottom and the river running along the fourth side. Mom would love it. On down the river was Walnut Street Bridge, which connected the shore with City Island, and farther on was Market Street Bridge.

There was another house full of girls across the street. At first I wanted to make friends with them, but Nick didn't like that.

"They're whoring themselves out for their drug money. Those marks on Mary's arms are from shooting up heroin."

I paid more attention after that. Those girls stood on the corner in hot pink fishnet stockings and tight, short skirts. They took rides from men or took them inside that house. Nick pointed out their pimp to me. He was the darkest man I'd ever seen in person, as dark as Sidney Poitier but clearly nothing like him.

I didn't connect those girls with the changes in me.

Chapter 8: The Hurricane

For the first time, I understood what old folks meant when they talked about it coming down in buckets. And it didn't stop. Hurricane Agnes had come north along the coast and turned inland. It ran into the front that had been dumping so much rain on us and stalled.

The news was all about flooding upriver and how high the Susquehanna was getting. The National Guard got called in to help with evacuations. Helicopters flew up and down the river searching for people caught in the flood waters.

Then I started bleeding. Nick said having sex might help the cramping. It didn't, and I didn't enjoy it much, but I couldn't say no. I did pretend to fall asleep when he was done, though. He went downstairs and I curled into a ball of agony, rocking and listening to the rain pounding against the windows. When the cramps eased enough, I padded quietly over to get my journal. Nick rarely left me alone long enough to write in it. No way did I want him to see it.

June 22, 1972

I'm bleeding a lot, with clots and terrible cramps. I don't usually get cramps. I'm scared it's a miscarriage, but I never told Nick I was pregnant, or probably was, so I don't know what to do now. Jan's mom had a miscarriage when I was in sixth grade, and they kept her in the hospital for a week.

I'm so scared.

I wanted to call home to tell them I'm okay—the flood's on national news—but Nick won't let me. He says they'd make me go back and he's right that I couldn't go back now. I'm not the little girl they'd remember, not even close. That girl wouldn't even like me.

Like Nick said, my parents think I'm in California, anyway, and they probably don't miss me. They didn't pay much attention to me when I was there. Now I'm not in their way. I belong here.

Late that afternoon, I was still hurting. The guys were playing poker and listening to music. For once the TV was off.

"I need Midol."

I wasn't going to say it out loud, but I should get more pads, too. I'd only packed a few, hoping my period would come. Since I wasn't a virgin anymore I thought I could probably use tampons, but not while I was cramping so bad.

Crazy Mike got me to take a few hits off his joint. It helped some, but not enough. Nick folded his cards.

"We should check things out, anyway," he said.

The two of us walked to the corner store in the rain. We were soaked in minutes, but it was warm, so it didn't bother us much. Some families were loading furniture into a truck. We were from the freak house, though, so they didn't talk to us.

The store was locked, barricaded shut.

"We need to check the river," Nick said.

"I can't walk that far. I hurt."

"Here. These'll help. They're phenobarbs."

Nick handed me four little pills and I swallowed them all. By the time we'd walked down to the river, the cramps didn't hurt so much. I began to feel like I was walking in a dream. The reality before me reinforced that sensation.

Where we first hit the riverfront park, the water was almost to the top of the bank. A few days earlier, it had been nearly thirty feet down to the water. We followed the sidewalk along the river. In places the water actually spilled over onto the park. When we came to the Sunken Gardens, they'd disappeared. Not only had the river filled that hollow in the bank, it pushed on across the road into a gas station. Beyond, we could see the sidewalk and road reappear from the water.

"It can't be that deep," said Nick.

We followed the sidewalk into the rushing water. When it came up over my knees, I looked where the gardens were deep under water and, as if through a fog, I realized the current might be cutting into that bank, moving the edge toward us. The ground could disappear beneath our feet. Then something heavy rammed into my legs and I stumbled, temporarily shocking me into a more wakeful state. Nick grabbed me and held on until we reached the other side of the breach. Without him, the river would have taken me.

It was getting dark when we got to Walnut Street Bridge, but we could still see that the water was almost touching the bottom of the roadway, and the supporting pillars were being rammed by debris. We walked out on the bridge. I stared down at the rushing water.

"It would be so easy to swirl away," I said dreamily.

"That's not a bad idea," said Nick. "It would be easy to disappear now, get listed as missing in the flood."

I swayed as another tree hit below us. Nick took my arm and walked me off the bridge. We went a couple more blocks down to Market Street. Ahead of us the land dipped and people were being evacuated from the hospital's second floor by boat.

"Shit, we better get out of here," said Nick.

We walked up to Second Street away from the flood and rushed to the house. Jim was perched on the couch in front of the TV. I'd never seen him look so alert.

"This is the Emergency Broadcast System," came from the tube.

"They announce that every few minutes, then go back to updates. It's on every channel," Jim told us. "We turned it on when Mary came over and told us that Jo-Jo's dead. She was stoned in the back seat of a car when they drove into a low intersection. The storm sewer exploded and flooded the place so fast that she didn't make it out of the car."

I'd only met Jo-Jo once. She'd seemed kind of empty. I wondered if she'd wanted to float away, too.

"They're evacuating people from the hospital by boat," Nick said.

"They were talking about gas tanks floating down the river and graveyards getting washed out, the whole state of Pennsylvania is a disaster area. We're right in the worst of it."

"Shit. Where's Mike?"

"He had the truck apart. He's out there trying to get it back together."

Nick took charge. "Pyra, you stay here and watch for any warnings. Jim, help me load the truck so we can leave as soon as Mike has it running."

I sat on the couch while they came in and out, and soon felt drowsy.

"Hey, you've got to stay awake," said Jim as he passed by the living room. "How can you sleep at a time like this?"

"Nick gave me some phenobarbs for my cramps."

"How many?"

"Four."

Jim looked shocked. "Here. Take the rest of my speed."

He held out three little white tablets and I took them. It got easier to stay awake. When they announced that a dam had broken, I ran out and told the guys.

"That's downriver from here," said Jim.

I returned to watching the TV, wide awake now.

We'd already seen for ourselves that every bridge across the Susquehanna had been closed. Then a chlorine gas leak made them close another bridge out of the city the other way.

"We'll have to go out up near the armory," said Nick when I told them.

The armory was the main evacuation center. The truck was almost ready. All of our music gear had been loaded.

"What about those stereos in your room?" I asked.

Nick scoffed. "We can't drive around with those. Go back inside and keep us posted."

I was obediently watching for more news when Jim came in to see what was happening.

"You feeling okay now?" he asked.

"Yeah. My cramps are gone."

"And you're not sleepy anymore?"

"No. Jim, why can't we drive around with the stereos?" I asked.

"They're hot. Didn't you know that?"

"They're stolen?"

"Yeah. Why'd you think he had so many?"

Another warning came on. Another dam had cracked. They weren't sure it would hold.

"Shit," said Jim. "If that one goes, we'll be under water in no time. Come on, let's go."

Mike was trying the truck. It turned over and quit, then turned over and caught. We piled in and took off. No one talked until we got across the last open bridge. We all let out the breaths we'd been holding in one communal sigh of relief.

"Armory?" asked Crazy Mike.

"Yeah, let's check it out, anyway," said Nick. He didn't sound happy about it, though.

I looked around the truck and realized they'd brought our music gear, but no clothes. That meant my journal was still safe at the house where no one would see it.

We pulled into the armory parking lot. The shelter was a warehouse lined with rows of cots. Nick insisted we sign in with phony names and called me Jo-Jo Jones. When the guy registering everyone looked at me funny, I said my parents had a sick sense of humor.

We gathered in one area together. Nick pulled out his guitar and started to play songs that sounded good acoustic. Most of them I'd learned by then and I sang along, until he started playing *Tin Soldiers and Nixon's Coming*. It didn't look like anyone was paying attention, but the National Guard were the ones running the Armory. They had to realize the song was about students shot down at Kent State by National Guardsmen.

"Nick man, that's really not cool," said Jim.

"It's not cool to be here with a bunch of killers," said Crazy Mike.

Nick packed up his guitar. "Let's get out of here."

I wasn't sure where else we'd go, but I was Nick's girl. I went with them.

I celebrated my fifteenth birthday in a Red Cross shelter in a church, but I told everyone it was my eighteenth and they believed me, thanks to my big boobs. I was still going by Jo-Jo Jones. We'd been there two weeks, and my period was still heavy and full of clots.

At least I didn't have to sit and worry the whole time. I helped keep the little kids entertained at the shelter. Also, as Jo-Jo and Mac, Nick and I had volunteered for the Red Cross to search for missing people who might still be trapped in their homes. We had to have special passes to go into the city because it was under martial law.

The only other people we saw were trucks of National Guardsmen. Most were driving around, but one was parked and they were taking stuff out of a house. We turned a corner instead of passing them.

"Looters," Nick spat out.

"Maybe they're helping someone who lives there," I offered.

"Don't be stupid."

I shut up. Nick had told me he'd demonstrated against the war and hated the military. I should have known better than to say anything.

We were still having sex every day, quickies in the truck. He was going to make me do it in the church bathroom, but we almost got caught. He finally asked me about the bleeding. He sounded angry.

"Do your periods always last this long?"

"No."

"Did you leave your pills at the house?"

"I don't have any pills."

"You're not on the pill?" He grabbed my chin and yanked my face close to his angry glare. It frightened me. "What are you, stupid?"

"I never ..."

"There's no way you were a virgin when I met you."

"No, but ..."

"As soon as things are back to normal around here, you need to go to the clinic and get on the pill. I guess I'll have to use rubbers until then, if I can find them. There still aren't many stores open, you know."

I didn't dare ask him how rubbers would help. I didn't want him to call me stupid again. I didn't know if it was a heavy period or if I'd been pregnant. I'd wait and ask them at the clinic, if I didn't bleed to death first.

Our house was in one of the last areas to get electricity back, so we had to stay in the shelter an extra week. At least I finally stopped bleeding. Nick had only taken me out to the truck once since I told him I wasn't on the pill. I found out what a rubber was and felt really stupid. He complained it wasn't as good with it on.

I was afraid he had stopped wanting me.

Chapter 9: Belonging to Nick

The house hadn't been flooded. The water had stopped two blocks away.

Nick grabbed my hand and pulled me up the stairs first thing, saying, "I'm going to screw you until tomorrow."

He did still want me! But when we walked into the room, the stereo equipment was gone and he yelled and punched the wall and hurt his hand and cursed out the National Guard for being looters. I wanted him to make love to me, not be angry.

"You can tell the police. Maybe they can get it back," I said, putting my arm around him, trying to make him feel better.

He pushed me away so hard I fell down. "You stupid little bitch."

I remembered what Jim had said. The stereos had been hot, stolen. Of course he couldn't tell the police they were gone. "I'm sorry. I wasn't thinking."

"Do you ever?"

He punished me with sex. He'd been rough before, but only when I was already so turned on that I was into it, usually when he'd given me Quaaludes. This time he didn't try to excite me. It was all about making me cry.

He left me alone when he was done. I checked that my journal was still in my sweatshirt pocket, under my shirts, and wrote one short sentence.

Nick hurt me, but it was my fault for being stupid.

Later that week, Nick and I got jobs with the Red Cross Disaster Services as Jo-Jo Jones and Mac Nicholas. Basic data processing, putting things people bought with their relief allotment into categories. One woman spent it all on underwear.

The gas still wasn't on at the house, so there was no way to cook. Nick let me keep part of every paycheck for food. The rest went to house expenses. We walked through the Farmer's Market on our way to work and every day I bought a donut. I'd eat part for breakfast and part for lunch, unless someone was driving to McDonald's. That's where we ate dinner every night. I'd get a burger, fries and a drink, but it got so I couldn't eat more than a bite or two. I'd drink the cola and give most of my food to the guys. My clothes started getting loose.

Nick gave me Quaaludes every night now. Without them I was tense, afraid it was going to hurt. With them, it all felt good. Then came the night a guy named Bob was over doing 'ludes with us and Nick shared me with him. Later, when I knew they had both left the house, I got my Fredonia sweatshirt and put it on, along with a pair of panties, and curled up to write in my journal.

July 21, 1972

Nick shared me with some guy. I don't know if it was the Quaaludes or if I'm a total slut, but I remembered doing two at a time at the fraternity and instead of getting freaked out, I started getting into it more.

So when the guy left, Nick slapped me around some and took me really rough, to punish me for being such a slut. But I liked that, too, because he's right. I deserved it.

I hope he forgives me.

Nick was an expert. He didn't touch me for two weeks, which left me frantic. I didn't know what would happen to me without him. I certainly couldn't go home, not anymore.

Then we played at a fundraiser out on City Island. It lasted all weekend with lots of local bands. The crowd really liked me. People camped out wherever they wanted. There were drums going in the crowd between bands. It was cool. Nick took me off in the bushes, in a good mood and gentle, even though having to use a rubber still annoyed him.

"If you don't get on the pill soon, I'm done with you," he said. "Abortions are expensive."

A week and a half later, I finally got into the clinic. The nurse talked to me first.

"You're eighteen?"

"Yes."

"When was your last period?"

"I had a normal period last week, Monday through Thursday, but the one before that was late and really heavy, with lots of clots."

"Any chance that you were pregnant?"

"That's what I'm worried about."

"Any chance you might be pregnant now?"

"My boyfriend's been using rubbers, but I want to get on the pill instead."

"Have you ever had an abortion? If you have, I'll record it as a miscarriage so you don't have to worry about that. But the doctor will check you for any damage done if you have had one."

"No. I wouldn't do that."

She left me to put on the gown. She came back with the doctor, but it was still so embarrassing. I stared at a spot high on the wall while he examined my breasts. There were hickies on them from Nick, but he didn't say anything about that. It was better when he covered me back up, but then I had to put my feet in the stirrups and scootch down to the edge with my legs spread wide.

"This might pinch a bit," he said. He stuck something cold and hard into me and spread me wide open. It did pinch, but I didn't make a sound. The nurse stood back and watched him.

I wished one of them would explain what he was doing.

Finally he pulled it out, but then he stuck his gloved fingers in me. "Um-hm," he muttered as he pushed from the outside against the fingers inside me. "Uterus seems normal." He stepped back.

"You can sit up now," the nurse finally spoke.

"I can't say for sure," the doctor said, "but I think your period was late because you were worried. I doubt very much that you were pregnant."

"So there's nothing broken?"

He smiled. "No, there's nothing broken."

"I can have kids someday?"

"I didn't find any reason you'll have a problem."

I hadn't realized how important that was to me.

"But if you're not planning on having them now, you need to use some contraception."

"I want the pill."

"You're sure? We have an IUD that's ideal for young women, the Dalcon Shield, or you can use a diaphragm in conjunction with condoms. That's very effective and not as risky as the pill or an IUD."

I just wanted to be on the pill so Nick wouldn't dump me. The doctor wrote the prescription and left the nurse to explain it.

"Here's a sample. There are complete directions inside. It's best if you wait until your next menstrual period to start, and another month before depending on the pill for protection."

"You mean we have to keep using rubbers?"

I almost threw up.

Nick wasn't happy about having to use rubbers, but he didn't want me to get pregnant, either. He had Bob over again to be with me. I didn't want anyone but Nick, but to make him happy I took the Quaaludes he gave me and followed his order to strip for them, taking off one piece of clothing at a time, trying to be sexy about it.

Once I was naked, Nick went downstairs without a word.

I let Bob do whatever he wanted to do. What did it matter? Nick didn't want me anymore. When Bob finally left, I curled up to go to sleep. No one would ever want me for anything but fucking; I was a worthless slut.

Nick yanked me off the mattress by my hair and shoved me against the wall. Maybe he did care.

"You like being a whore?" He was grinning at me.

I wasn't sure what he wanted to hear. I wanted to please him.

He grabbed my boobs and squeezed until I cried. "You're my whore. He paid me for you. Do you like being my whore?"

"Yes," I whimpered.

He pushed me face down onto the mattress and took me fast and hard. Then he beat me.

I was his.

We were still working at the Red Cross. Nick was careful not to leave marks where they would be seen at work, but sitting all day was a constant reminder of our new relationship. He'd come by and whisper in my ear, "Whose whore are you?"

"Yours," I'd reply obediently.

The job wasn't going to last much longer. My boss gave me a letter of recommendation, to help me get another job. I took it and hid it from Nick, in my journal inside the Fredonia sweatshirt. At night now, he'd bring strangers to me. They seemed to expect to use rubbers. There was still a sliver of hope that Nick would want me to be his alone again, once I'd been on the pill long enough. But I was beginning to wonder.

He found the letter from my boss and burned it in front of me.

"What did you think you were going to do with this? I make more on you in one night than we both make in a week at those shit jobs. We only took them to drum up business."

He flipped through the journal, making fun of the early entries. Then he got to the part about the party.

"You took on a whole fraternity? You little slut."

I tried to tell him I was drunk and didn't even remember it, that I'd been a stupid little virgin, but he slapped my face so hard my lip began to bleed.

"Now you're my whore. Don't you ever forget it." He grabbed my hair and pulled my head back, then spat in my face. "You can be my gang-bang specialist."

He worked me over, inside and out, not worrying about where the bruises would be. Nick went to work alone the next day and told them we were moving out of town. They gave him both of our final checks.

Then he made me move across the street with the other whores. He let me keep my journal. I still kept it hidden in my Fredonia sweatshirt, because I didn't want the other girls to find it and laugh at me, but I wrote a little the first morning after he made me move.

August 23, 1972

Nick moved me in with the other whores across the street. He shoved me into a room where they were all sitting around watching TV and I was crying and promising to do whatever he wanted if he'd please take me back and he said he had a new girl moving in and I was not to speak to her or he'd make me wish he'd killed me. I kept begging him not to give me away to a pimp, but he laughed at me and left.

The girls laughed at me, too. There were four of them.

"You are so stupid. Who do you think's in charge here?" When I didn't answer, the black girl who looked about my age continued, "Nick's the boss. Julian works for him. You been set up, girl. You were a target from the moment he laid eyes on you."

"No!" I refused to believe it. I remembered how I'd acted at the bus station. "I came on to him, not the other way around."

"Yeah? And where was your head at when you did? And did you *really* make the first move? Or did he come and offer you some kind of help?"

While I stood there shaking my head, she started to say more, but a thin girl with scraggly hair spoke over her. "Let her alone, Angie. She'll figure it out soon enough."

"Fine." Angie stalked out of the room and Mary, the one Nick said was a heroin addict, went with her.

I started to explain that it really wasn't the way Angie said, but the girl waved away my words.

"I'm Lisa, and that's Rainbow in the corner. She doesn't say much." Then she plopped down on the couch and stared at the TV, my signal to stop talking.

When Julian gave me Quaaludes before we started working that night, I took them gratefully, knowing sex was always easier with them. He gave me enough, I didn't care what anyone was doing with my body. I did whatever I was told to do in that dreamy Quaalude state.

But I dreamed my way back to the bus station and saw myself the way Nick did – a screwed up little girl bouncing her tits around, trying to get her normal friend to leave. I woke the next day knowing that girl was right. I'd been a target from the beginning. Careful to wait until Julian wasn't nearby, I asked the girls why they stayed.

"Don't even try to leave," said Mary. "You don't cross Nick unless you like hurting."

"Most of us do," whispered Rainbow.

"She speaks! The world must be coming to an end!" Angie shouted.

"We want to be hurt?" I asked.

"Punished," Rainbow murmured. "For whatever we did wrong that landed us here."

"We're all sluts," Mary said. "That's what got us here."

Angie snorted. "The 'ludes make you feel that way. But what the hell, if you gotta be a ho, might as well enjoy it."

I wondered if she was right. I hadn't been on Quaaludes or drinking at the bus station. But I wondered.

That night I swallowed obediently with the Quaaludes under my tongue. Fortunately, I kept the pills where I could take them later. It was awful. The first customer smelled like a dead woodchuck I'd come across when I was tying grapes. I started to cry and that excited him more. I took the pills and once they kicked in, I thought I liked it, all of it.

Angie was right.

Once my head cleared the next afternoon, I started to plan.

I didn't dare write anything in my journal about that or how I really felt, because Nick had probably let me keep it so he'd know if I was going to try anything stupid. So the first thing I did was write an entry just for Nick, telling him exactly what he'd want to hear.

August 25, 1972

What's wrong with being a prostitute? It's the world's oldest profession, and with Quaaludes, I like it. I like being a whore. The next time Nick's with me, I need to show him how much I love him for showing me who I really am.

Writing that made me realize part of me believed it. But I didn't like being a whore, or I'd have liked it without the drug.

I needed to get out before I completely lost myself.

First, I had to figure out how to keep my head clear. I couldn't work without the drug, but maybe I could take less. Julian gave me four each night. That night, I only swallowed three and still floated through everything. The next I tried two and was more alert, but still too relaxed. On one the night was miserable and I was still not clear enough to get up early and escape.

To get away, I would have to whore my way through one night without any help.

Chapter 10: Escape

It was hell working without the Quaaludes, especially since they kept me busy most of the night, but it was worth being able to get up early the next morning. Everyone else would sleep past noon. Still, I washed off in the kitchen to avoid waking anyone.

I put on bell-bottoms and my Fredonia State sweatshirt, the only modest top I could find. It would be too hot, but I didn't have a bra anymore and didn't want to look slutty. The only shoes I had now were my Jesus sandals, but my feet were used to them. I stuck my journal into the front pocket of the sweatshirt and headed downtown.

Joe had saved me once before, maybe he'd help me again.

It was easy to find the restaurant. It was the Greek one with stained glass ornaments hanging in the windows. But Joe wasn't there. An old lady, probably one of his aunts, told me that he and his bride were on their honeymoon.

No wonder he hadn't given me his phone number or address.

Crushed, alone and helpless, I started walking back to my life as a whore in defeat. But I thought about my boss at the Red Cross giving me that letter of recommendation and how Nick burned it and said I was worth more as a whore – worth more to *him*.

Nick didn't get to decide my future.

It was still early. I could get away. But I'd need some money and I'd earned it. I'd been paying attention. Julian kept each night's take in a metal box by his bed.

Back at the house everyone was still asleep. I stepped carefully to make as little noise as possible. I pawed through our dirty clothes, piled in a closet off the kitchen, taking the least whorish and bundling them into a long-sleeved shirt that was probably Julian's. I left that by the door and padded silently to his room.

I opened his door so slowly, so carefully, so quietly. Then I waited, listening to his soft snore. Mary was in bed with him. She wouldn't hear me, she always shot up at the end of the night. Maybe he did, too.

I crept across the floor on my belly to the box, then wiggled back the same way, holding it in front of me, with my fingers cushioning it from the floor. I didn't stand up until I was well away from the still-open bedroom door. I cautiously made my way down the stairs, grabbed my bundle of clothes, and slipped outside quietly.

I headed for the river with the box.

Inside I found a stack of twenties and lesser bills, and a few fifties – at least a thousand dollars. They never let me handle the money, so I didn't know how much was from me or whether they took in this much every night or what.

I didn't care. I stuffed it all into my pockets and threw the box far out into the river. The sun was still climbing. I turned my back to it and started walking. I couldn't go home, but I would never let myself be used like that again.

Soon I shoved up the sleeves of the sweatshirt. When I got to a highway entrance ramp headed west, I turned around and stuck out my thumb. As Peg, I never would have considered hitchhiking, but I'd left Peg far behind. Pyra, of course, would do anything, but I was determined to leave her behind as well. Fortunately, my first ride didn't ask for a name.

An old Corvair pulled over, blowing greasy smoke. There was one person in it, a clean-cut innocent-looking young guy. I slipped in without hesitation. I needed to be out of the city before they realized I'd taken off with the money.

"Thanks," I said.

"Where are you headed?"

As far as I can get, I thought. But that might scare him, so I said, "I'm not sure. I just got an itch to see some of the country."

"Oh, I thought you might be going to that festival they're talking about. Some rainbow thing out in Colorado."

"Rainbow thing?"

"Yeah. Hippie back in New York gave me this fat flier about it. It's all about connecting with nature and stuff."

"No, I hadn't heard about that. Sounds interesting, though. Is that where you're going?"

"Nah. I'm headed back to Carlisle. Sorry I'm not going farther. Can't miss work. I have a job that's keeping me in Dickinson."

"College?"

"Yeah, a rich kid school, but they give out scholarships. That covers tuition, but I have to work for my room and board. My folks can't help out much. I've got four little brothers."

"How far is it?"

"About twenty miles. I'm not using the Turnpike, don't want to pay the toll, but I'll leave you at the west on-ramp just outside Carlisle."

"Thanks. Maybe I'll check out that hippie thing. I know I want to see something besides Pennsylvania."

I wouldn't feel safe until I was far, far away from Nick and Julian. The driver talked some more about himself and how his parents were so excited when he got into Dickinson because neither of them had even gone to college, but he couldn't tell them how hard it was after public school and how everyone else seemed to be from prep schools.

When he stopped, he dug in the back seat and pulled out a fat yellow booklet and handed it to me. "Here, maybe you'll want to go meet up with them," he offered.

"You're sure you're not going?"

"No, I wouldn't even if I didn't have the job. It sounds interesting, but from the looks of this, there'll be drugs and other hippie stuff happening, and I can't afford to look like I'm into any of that. Don't want to lose my scholarship or miss getting into law school, you know?"

"Well, thanks," I said. I fanned through the pages. "I see what you mean. Well, thanks." I unlatched my door.

"Hey, wait a minute." He lifted a backpack out from behind my seat and unzipped it. He dumped some books out and emptied the small pockets as well. Then he held out the empty bag. "If you're traveling, this'll make it easier to carry your stuff."

I took it, amazed by his generosity. "Thank you. But don't you need it?" I sat there, not sure I should be accepting his gift.

He pointed to a tear in the seam, held together with a safety pin. "My books are too heavy. I need a new one, something tougher than this. Sorry I don't have any food."

"It's okay, I've got money to buy food."

"Don't keep it all in the pack. Too easy to lose it that way."

"I won't." I stuffed my clothes, my journal, and the booklet he'd given me into the pack, then got out of the car. I thanked him again and slung the bag over my shoulder.

"Well, be careful," he said.

"I will." I closed the door.

He waved goodbye, then did a U-turn and drove off.

It was going to be a sunny day. My pockets were bulging with the cash. First making sure no one was watching, I put most of the small bills in my pack so they wouldn't be so obvious. Fifties went into my back left pocket, the twenties folded so I could pull out just one got tucked into the back right, and enough smaller bills for a couple meals in my front pockets.

I put out my thumb again. I didn't think it was legal to hitchhike, so I took the first ride, even though my instincts warned me to let it pass.

When the guy started to open his fly, I had to decide if I was going to whore myself out for rides or not. Pyra would. Peg wouldn't. She'd freak out completely.

I sat staring straight ahead, as if I didn't notice what he was doing, then leaned my head against the window and closed my eyes. I yawned, not too wide, and said, "The sun's making me sleepy. Hope you don't mind if I nap a little."

"Uh, no, that's okay." He sounded confused.

"How far are you driving?" I asked without opening my eyes.

"Pittsburgh."

"Can you make sure to let me out where I'll be able to catch a ride west? If I fall asleep?"

"Uh, sure. Where're you headed?"

"Colorado, Denver."

"That's a long haul."

"Um-hm," I murmured, pretending to drop off.

I heard his zipper and the snap of his jeans being closed. He probably felt stupid, and lucky that I hadn't noticed.

I still didn't know who I was, but I knew who I wasn't.

I did doze off for a while, and stared out the window when I woke up. He didn't try anything else and didn't talk much, either. Then he pulled off the turnpike at the New Stanton toll booth.

"What are you doing?" I demanded. "This isn't Pittsburgh."

"You said you're going to Denver."

"Yeah." I thought that was what I'd said.

"This is Interstate 70." He pulled into a gas station. "It'll take you to Denver. You don't need to go into Pittsburgh."

"Oh, thanks." I wasn't sure whether to believe him, but still, he'd given me a ride.

I used the gas station bathroom, bought a snack, and took a free map labeled Pittsburgh Tri-State Area. Then I sat outside the store with my back against the wall to eat.

I opened the map and found where the turnpike met I-70. The perv had been telling the truth. Highways made a big triangle around Pittsburgh. It probably wasn't a good idea to hitchhike in a big city, anyway.

I-70 would take me across the bottom of the triangle to Washington, Pennsylvania. The side heading north from there was I-79, which went to Erie. I could be home by dark.

Back in the store I bummed a pen, then sat outside again, this time pulling out my journal. It was time to make an entry.

August 29, 1972

On my way West.

I will NEVER let myself be used like that again.

I'm not Pyra anymore.

I shut the notebook. There were still empty pages, but a fresh start deserved a new book. The store had a few for sale. I bought one, got situated outside again, and cracked it open.

My Journal #2: August 29, 1972

Well, I didn't fill the first journal, but that's all about what needs to be left behind. This journal is about where I'm going.

I'm on my own now. There's a road that could take me home if I turn north, but I can't do that to them. They'd expect me to be their innocent little girl. I couldn't even tell them what I did at the fraternity, and what I've done now is so much worse.

And they have each other. They don't need me in the way.

Besides, I need to figure out who I am. I was always a good student for my teachers, a good daughter for my parents, and then a good whore for Nick. From now on, I need to be whatever I am for me, not anyone else.

I closed the journal and packed up. I should use daylight to get as far away from Nick as possible. The sun made it easy to tell which way was west, so I walked over to the right ramp and stuck my thumb out. There weren't that many cars, and most of them buzzed past me without slowing down. It took almost an hour, but I finally got a ride.

It was a minister who preached at me about how dangerous it was for me to be taking rides from strangers, and how it was illegal.

"I know." I agreed, my eyes wide with pretended fear, then I gave him a story. "I had a ride to Washington, the one west of here, not D.C., but my friend's car broke down here. They told her they may have to order a part or something so she's stuck waiting, and my brother's already on his way to meet me in Washington to take me the rest of the way home, and I don't want him to get there and worry about where we are."

Back then, cell phones didn't exist, so this was a believable story. And then I went on about how grateful I was such a kind, good person stopped to give me a ride and he said he'd take me to Washington, even though it was farther than he'd been going.

"Then I will deliver you to your brother," he said.

"Oh, I couldn't ask you to do that."

I should have kept my mouth shut. He would have let me off sooner with no problems.

"I wouldn't sleep tonight if I didn't know you were safe and sound," he insisted. "Where exactly is he meeting you?"

I'd never been anywhere but Erie and Buffalo before I took that bus to Harrisburg, so I paused. He got suspicious.

"Are you telling me the truth about meeting your brother?" he asked.

"Of course," I said. "I'm just trying to remember the name of the gas station where I'm meeting him. He told us to take the first exit after I-79." There had to be a gas station where two interstates crossed.

"Well, we should be able to find him, then. You'll know his car?"

"He'll be in our folks' station wagon."

He quit pushing me for details and talked some about religion and his calling. Then he asked what church I attended. I figured he might stop the car and order me to get out if I admitted I'd only been to church a few times with Jan's family. He wasn't wearing one of those backwards collars like priests do, so I told him my parents were Catholic, hoping that would save me from having to know much.

"But I'm not sure it's right for me," I said. "Can you tell me more about your church?"

And that kept him busy until we got to the exit past I-79 and there was a gas station with a blue Ford Country Squire being filled up by the attendant. As we pulled in, we could see the only person in the car was a woman in the driver's seat.

"My mom came!" I exclaimed. "She'd be upset with me for hitching a ride. Please, just watch me."

I figured I'd ask the lady something, then go use the bathroom. As long as she didn't pull out before he left, that would work.

"No, I'll talk to her," he said. He parked next to the station.

The attendant had finished pumping gas and was walking around to get the lady's money. I used that as an excuse.

"She'll want to get going right away. I better use the restroom so I don't hold her up."

"Okay. I'll let her know where you are."

As soon as I got out of sight around the building, I took off running. I felt bad not apologizing, because he'd been trying to be nice, but I couldn't take a chance on his turning me over to the police. I ran for a backyard and hid in some bushes.

He came around behind the building and looked my direction, but I guess he decided not to go trespassing, because he shook his head and left. Still, I waited in those bushes a good half hour before

I dared to slip back to the gas station and use that restroom. It wasn't locked. Businesses didn't do that yet.

I wasn't sure what to do. He might have called the cops. To avoid trouble, I needed a plan, but my brain wasn't working. The last thing I'd eaten was some pizza the day before. A Dairy Queen was right down the street. There weren't any cop cars yet, but I walked fast, just in case they were on the way.

That cheeseburger was the best thing I'd tasted in weeks, because I was free. I'd planned on having a banana split, too, but decided on a small hot fudge sundae because the burger and fries filled me up. I guess my stomach had shrunk. My brain started working again.

It was nice to stop for a bit, but the sooner I was out of Pennsylvania, the better. Not only to get farther away from Nick, but out of range for Pennsylvania cops, too. If they were looking for me, it would be at this on-ramp. If I tried walking to the next one, I'd be in the open longer, and anyway, it might be twenty miles away in another town.

I could let them catch me and they'd probably get me home, but I couldn't go there. Not the way I was now. My raw nipples rubbing against the rough lining of my Fredonia sweatshirt and other sore places were a constant reminder of all the men who'd used me.

As I sucked the ice cream and fudge off my spoon, I checked out the other customers. I settled on three girls a little older than me because one of them was wearing an Ohio State T-shirt. She wanted the others to hurry, so she could get back and study for an exam.

Aside from that, they were giggling and talking about boys, the same as Jan and I used to do. They seemed so immature; it was hard to remember I was the young one. They were almost done with their ice creams when I walked over and said hi.

"Fredonia State." The one who seemed to be the leader read my sweatshirt. "Does someone you know go there?"

"I do," I lied. "But my boyfriend goes to Ohio State. Jim Anderson. He's an English major. Do you know him? He's a freshman."

My time at the student union in Fredonia was paying off. They accepted me at my word and my guess that they were older was right. The leader dug her keys out of her purse while sweatshirt girl answered.

"No. I'm an English major, but I'm a junior. He'll still be stuck in intro classes."

"I know it's a huge campus," I said. "He doesn't know I'm coming, either. We need to have a serious conversation. I plan on calling him once I'm there."

I let that dangle and could see they were curious, probably guessing I was knocked up or something equally dire.

"Good luck," said the driver. "Let's go, girls."

As they started to leave, I sighed. "The thing is, my friend from Fredonia was only driving this far. Then the plan was to hitchhike, but now I'm getting cold feet."

"Good grief!" exclaimed the one who hadn't said a word yet. "Are you crazy? That's dangerous! And it's illegal, I think. Mary, there's plenty of room in your car. Can't we give her a ride?"

The police car was waiting near the on-ramp, but they weren't looking for a carload of college girls. I dodged the girls' questions about my boyfriend and why I had to talk to him by getting them to talk about themselves. They were too polite to say anything, but the girl in the back seat with me kept her distance. I'd been sweating all day in that heavy shirt. So when we got off the highway in Columbus, I asked them to stop at a motel. After some discussion, during which they pointed out which ones were not for nice girls, they took me to one of which they approved.

After they'd driven away, I walked back to one of the not-nice places, where identification was not required with cash. The air in the room tasted like cigarettes, but it wasn't too bad after I opened the window. I'd spotted a Murphy's while they were driving. I walked back to it and bought a bra, underwear, jeans, and a couple T-shirts that weren't at all sexy.

Back at the motel, I soaked in a long hot shower. With new underwear and a new T-shirt I felt a lot better, even wearing the too-short cutoffs I planned to throw away. I wanted to soften the jeans up by washing them before I wore them. The motel clerk directed me to a nearby laundromat, and I washed everything else I had with me. Pyra and Nick seemed a little farther away.

Sitting there in the laundromat, I pulled out the booklet the first ride had given me. The cover declared it was *The Rainbow Oracle of Mandala City*. He was right, it sounded as if there would be a lot of drugs and I didn't need to deal with that. I pulled out my new journal. After writing details of the day, I finished with my thoughts.

August 29, 1972 Evening

So, I'm finishing my first day as the new me in a laundromat in Ohio. There's no plan. I'm not sure what I'll do tomorrow morning, or tonight even. But I am sure I will never take Quaaludes again. I don't think I'll ever want to have sex again, either. And I WON'T if I don't want to.

Actually, I think I'll head to California. Nick knows that's where I pretended to be going before, but it's a huge state. He won't even waste his time trying to find me if he thinks I've gone that far, not for the cash I took, unless it was from more than one night. But there were five of us working. It was probably just one night.

The dryer finished and I put the journal away.

I whispered to myself as I folded my clothes into the pack. "He won't bother. I'm not worth that much. He won't bother. I'm not worth that much. He will not bother. I am not worth that much."

Chapter 11: Charlie

After a good night's sleep, I ate a big breakfast in a diner and headed for the highway to hitch a ride west. But someone was there ahead of me. He grinned and held out his hand. He was a serious traveler with a frame pack and a sleeping bag tied on top. A floppy wide-brimmed hat added to the impression that he was a harmless, friendly person.

"Good morning! I'm Charlie."

"Hi." I still hadn't decided what to call myself.

"Saw you at the laundromat last night," he said. "You part of the Rainbow Family?"

I'd avoided looking at anyone last night or I would have noticed this guy. I might never want to have sex again, but I could still notice that he was cute ... borderline handsome.

"Uh, no. Someone just gave me that booklet," I replied.

"Oh. Well, if you want to check it out, they had to move it to Granby."

"Thanks, if I decide to go. So how does this work?" I waved at the road. "Do we stand far enough apart so we know who people stop for, or do you get the first ride because you were here first, or what?"

"New to hitching, huh?" He didn't wait for an answer. "We could do it either way, but since we're both headed west, the best thing would be to catch rides together. It's easier for me to get one when I'm with a girl and it's safer for her. Creeps don't usually pick up couples."

While I was considering his suggestion, thinking it was probably a good idea, a shiny new white and red Cadillac ambulance with an orange cross on it pulled over. I followed Charlie as he approached the driver's window.

"Where you headed?" The gray-haired driver seemed friendly.

"Denver." Charlie turned to me and smiled. "Right, Sunshine?"

"Yeah."

"I can get you a third of the way! I was hoping for some good company." The driver waved to the door behind his. "You better ride in the back so no one sees you. I didn't ask, but I'm probably not supposed to have passengers. There's two seats back there, and if you're careful not to muss it up, you can rest on the stretcher."

Charlie held the door open for me. It was higher inside than a normal car, but I still had to hunch some. Curtains all around covered the windows, but they were white and filtered light made it easy to see. I put my pack on the floor near the back door and sat down on a red Naugahyde seat. Charlie settled in closer to the front. A small window near his head slid open.

"All set?" the driver asked.

I nodded and Charlie answered, "Yup."

I pulled aside the curtain on the passenger window just enough to be able to watch the countryside as we drove along. It was new to me, lots of rolling green hills. We rode in that ambulance all day. Charlie offered gas money, but Derek wouldn't take any.

"They're paying me to deliver this to a hospital in St. Louis, and they're covering all my expenses, too. Besides, you're keeping me company with your stories."

Of course, I wasn't the one doing the talking. That was Charlie. He seemed to have no end of tales about himself, other people he'd met on the road, how the Grateful Dead had been touring for seven years with hardly a break, and, once he had sounded out the driver for his feelings on marijuana, how the best was grown in Northern California, up in the redwoods.

When we stopped for lunch, Derek turned his attention to me. "How about you, Sunshine? He hardly lets you get a word in. How long have you two been together?"

"A couple months," I lied. I had my new name, for the time being anyway.

"Yup, we met in Pittsburgh," improvised Charlie. "There was an art festival by one of the rivers and she was there with a friend selling these bracelets." He held up his wrist so the driver could see the braided leather around his wrist. "We've been together ever since."

"Traveling around whenever, wherever, no deadlines – must be nice." Derek sounded envious.

"Sure is." Charlie clearly loved his life. "Though there are slim times when we depend on the generosity of others, like you, giving us this ride and lunch. You are a kind spirit."

By the time we arrived in St. Louis, I was comfortable with Charlie as a traveling companion. I even slept on the stretcher after lunch, but I used my pack for a pillow. Though most of my money was in my pockets, there was still a wad of small bills in the pack. I wasn't going to risk losing any of it.

At Charlie's request, Derek dropped us off at a truck stop on the edge of St. Louis. A big orange 76 ball was the first thing I saw.

"We should be able to get a ride from a trucker," Charlie explained as Derek drove away. "You want any more food first? Don't know where we'll be at dinnertime."

"I might want a candy bar or something later, but mostly I'm tired."

"You just woke up."

"Yeah." I didn't look at him as we walked quickly to the building. It seemed to be both a diner and a store.

"Guess you're sleeping off whatever you're getting away from. If you want to talk it out, I'm actually a good listener."

I laughed. The sound shocked me. I couldn't remember the last time I laughed.

Charlie protested. "Really I am! I listen. I could tell you didn't want to say much. That's why I talked so much today, though I do usually tell stories to people who give me rides. It's kind of payment."

"Before I met up with you, I was asking people about themselves and letting them do all the talking." I smiled.

Charlie chuckled. "That's probably a good way to pay them back, too, making them feel important. I'll have to try that when I'm tired of telling stories."

Less than an hour later, we were in the cab of a tractor trailer, just by going around and asking for a ride west. It was definitely safer with Charlie and easier, too. The driver was only going to Kansas City.

"I plan to get into K.C. before eight. May be pushing the speed limit a bit, but it's my kid's birthday and I want to be there before he goes to bed. I'll drop you at the last truck stop before I head home. There should be plenty of truckers leaving for an overnight run to Denver."

That seemed to work for Charlie, so I figured it was fine. Two days and I'd be far enough from Nick that I wouldn't have to worry anymore.

Charlie sat next to the driver and spun a tale that had us trying to get to my older sister's place in Denver because her husband had work for Charlie. He let on like we were married without ever saying it.

I leaned against the window and pretended to sleep, but watched Charlie through my eyelashes. He didn't look as tough as Nick, but he'd be able to talk his way out of most situations. He'd gotten into the truck first, saying it was so I could have the window, but I knew it was also so I didn't have to talk to the trucker.

Mostly I watched the trees and fields go by. There weren't as many cities and it was mostly flat now, but still a mix of farms and woods that reminded me of home. Maybe I'd have things figured out and be able to go back by harvest, when everywhere smelled like grape jelly. But that wouldn't really happen. There was no way to erase what I'd become.

That trucker – I never did get his name – must have been speeding a lot, because he dropped us off at another truck stop not much past seven. We grabbed some snacks at the store and were on our way before eight. The driver was hauling produce for supermarkets in Denver and said we'd only make the one required stop. Apparently there were rules about that stuff that he had to follow.

As soon as it was dark, I fell sound asleep. Charlie had made sure I had the window again. I woke up sometime in the night to find his arm across the top of the seat behind me and his hand on my shoulder, pulling me into him a bit. But his head was leaning straight back and his breath was almost a snore, so I drifted back to sleep without moving his hand.

We got to Denver as the sun rose. The trucker left us at another 76 truck stop.

"Are those the Rockies?" I asked. I could see mountains in the west, rising straight up off the plain.

Charlie grinned as if he'd made them himself. "Yep. So, Sunshine, are you coming to the Gathering with me?"

Deal with creepy rides by myself or go with Charlie? I chose Charlie.

We got a few short rides in the general direction of Granby, then squeezed into a VW bus headed for the festival. It was painted all over with flowers and full of people who were smiling and happy. They didn't even get grumpy when we had to leave the bus behind and walk through the roadblock miles down the road to the encampment.

We were in the middle of nowhere, then suddenly the woods were full of people.

We walked around, checking out camps. There were lots of girls with no shirts. Charlie happily accepted hits from joints that were offered; I politely declined. They offered brownies; we both accepted. We hadn't eaten much since lunch the day before, and it was late afternoon. Even when Charlie warned me they were hash brownies, I was too hungry to care. He finished a conversation with someone, then he led me away from the crowds.

"We could sleep right in camp, whenever we're ready to, but it'll be nice to put our things somewhere instead of carrying them around the whole time." He led the way along a narrow path until the drumming and voices weren't so loud. "This is good." He took his pack off and rolled out the sleeping bag.

"Are you sure it's safe to leave it here like that?" I asked.

"It'll be okay," he said cheerfully. "Will it bother you if I take my clothes off?"

"No, as long as you don't mind that I keep mine on." Sunshine wasn't going to take her clothes off in front of strangers, but she evidently wasn't as prudish as Peg, either. "Where are the bathrooms?"

"There aren't any." Charlie dug in his pack and held up a small roll of toilet paper. "Save this for number two. Just cover it with leaves or whatever you can to help it rot. I'm going back to the drumming circle. Want me to wait?"

"I think I'll stay here and catch a nap." It was probably the brownies. The guys in the band had given me some before Nick got me to try anything else. I got sleepy then, too.

"Okay. See you later."

I walked quite a ways before I felt private enough to drop my jeans and pee. Then I had to kind of shake it off the best I could. I went back and sat on Charlie's sleeping bag and took out my new journal.

September 1, 1972

So I've been traveling with this guy since yesterday morning and now he's walking around naked. Charlie looks good without clothes, which complicates how I'm feeling. I don't want to be a slut, but I'm not sure where the line is. I mean, I really like him. He's funny and he's been watching out for me without getting nosy. And from the way people are acting around here, he probably expects to have sex with me tonight.

Pyra would, definitely.

I'm not sure about Sunshine. Charlie named me Sunshine, but I don't know who that is yet. He hasn't made any moves, other than putting his arm around me while we slept in the truck. He may not even have done that on purpose.

I don't want him to see the bruises, either.

The marks from when Nick beat me are mostly gone, but I heard Julian tell one of those men that he had to pay extra because he'd left marks on the last girl. Then he left me alone with the guy. I don't want to have to explain any of that to anyone. So I guess that answers my question.

I'm not going to have sex with Charlie.

I stretched out and dozed in the sun. Charlie's cheerful voice calling up the trail woke me.

"Hey, Sunshine! Did you have a good nap?" He pulled his clothes out of his pack. "A little sun goes a long way on tender parts."

"I was wondering about that. I've seen some very red privates."

"They've probably had too much weed to notice." He didn't turn away as he dressed, but it wasn't like he was showing off. He just didn't think anything of it. "They've opened the kitchen. You ready for some dinner?"

"Sure. How much is it?" I asked.

"Free."

After dinner, I stayed with Charlie. I was too nervous to be on my own. There were thousands of people there. He ran into a group he knew not long after dark. We sat around a campfire while they talked about Humboldt Gold.

"I hitched out from back East," said Charlie. "So I don't have any on me."

"Not a problem," smiled one of his friends. "We drove in from Garberville with plenty."

They passed around a joint. I took one shallow hit. It wasn't as nasty as what the guys in the band had smoked, but I didn't want to be messed up, so I passed it without partaking after that. Charlie noticed but didn't try to get me to do any more. He also noticed when I started shivering as darkness cooled the air.

"Night all," he said, pulling me to my feet.

"Here, take a few," said someone. A hand passed Charlie three joints, which he put in his shirt pocket. "Thanks."

He was prepared with a flashlight and where the path allowed, he put his arm around me, trying to warm me.

"You should have said something, Sunshine. You're like an ice cube. Actually, I'm a little chilly myself. We should have worn sweatshirts, or at least brought them along."

I was nervous with the contact, but freezing when the path narrowed and we had to walk single file. When we got to the sleeping bag, I was relieved to see both our packs were still there. I immediately pulled out my Fredonia State sweatshirt. It was the only warm thing I had.

"You don't have a sleeping bag, do you!" Charlie said. He really sounded like he hadn't noticed before. "Use mine. I can crash in someone's van."

That would leave me alone in the dark, with all those strangers around. That frightened me more than being close to Charlie.

"Is it big enough for us both to sleep in it?" My uncertainty came through in my voice.

"It'll be snug, but it's been done before."

"Sleep," I repeated.

"Sleep," he agreed. "But I usually sleep naked. It's a warm bag."

I took a breath and nodded. "That'll make it easier to fit. You don't mind if I keep my clothes on?"

The next afternoon I slipped away to write in my journal.

September 2, 1972

I woke up with Charlie's arms around me. He was spooned behind me and I could tell he had a boner. But he didn't do anything except snuggle a little more for a moment, then, when he knew I was awake, he gave the back of my head a kiss and said he had to go take a leak.

While he was off in the bushes, naked, I got out of the sleeping bag with my clothes still on and started rolling up the bag for the day. He came back and got dressed and didn't act at all upset or surprised. He gave me another peck of a kiss, this one on my cheek near my eye, and told me not to worry about it, that I don't owe him anything. I don't know how he tuned into that, but he did.

He stayed with me today. We smoked a joint - well, I took a couple hits, Charlie smoked the rest of it. The little I had did relax me enough to enjoy the music, the drum circle, and the people at the core of the Gathering making decisions through consensus. No one person's in charge. That was pretty cool. Charlie left his clothes on, too, except for a little while in the afternoon when it got hot for a while, he took off his shirt.

Charlie's a hugger. When he runs into old friends they hug and when I laughed at a naked little kid covered in rainbow colors of paint, he hugged me. It felt good. A few times he's put his arm around me like a loose sideways hug, too, when we were watching something like the drumming together.

He told me all about the marijuana harvest in Northern California. That's where he's headed after the Gathering. But he's going to stay here and help clean up first. That'll take some time. There's thousands of people here so even if they try not to leave a mess, there will be one.

We're headed to dinner now.

After dinner, we went to the same campfire and people talked about travels and adventures – so many fascinating places, so many exciting experiences. And they discussed politics and philosophy. I didn't know anything, so I sat quiet and listened.

Life was an adventure beginning to unfold.

We had sweatshirts on, but as it cooled off Charlie put his arm around me. When I started getting sleepy, it felt comfortable to lean into him, and he tightened his arm to pull me close and planted a light kiss on the top of my head before he continued with the conversation. I was almost asleep when he said good night to everyone and half-lifted me to standing. He kept his arm around me most of the way back to his sleeping bag. He unrolled it and unzipped the side.

"Do you want to leave your sweatshirt on?" he asked. "It might get hot."

Sleepily, I shook my head. As if I was a little kid, he lifted it up and pulled it over my head for me. I grinned sleepily and wandered off into the bushes to pee. He was in the bag, naked, when I got back. I climbed in next to him and zipped the side shut. I could feel his arousal as he hugged me from behind, but he kissed my neck once gently and said good night.

"Are you okay?" I whispered.

He kissed the back of my neck again. "Don't worry about it." He snuggled closer, though. "This is nice. It's okay, Sunshine."

His breath came even and slow, though I was sure he wasn't asleep. Suddenly my tears started flowing and before I knew it, I was sobbing. Charlie rolled me over and held me and kissed my face and told me it was okay, it was going to be okay. I cried myself asleep and woke the next morning with his arms still around me. He peeked through his eyelashes and snuggled me closer. I could feel his erection. He felt me stiffen ever so slightly and immediately gave me a quick hug and kiss on the top of my head.

"Let me out of here," he said. "I obviously need to water a bush."

Again I got up and put the sleeping bag away for the day. This time he looked at it a little sadly as he pulled on his pants.

"I'm sorry," I said.

"You don't have anything to be sorry about. It's okay." He put on his shirt.

"I'm not a virgin."

He shook his head. "That doesn't mean you have to do anything you don't want to do."

"I'm not sure I don't want to."

That made him laugh. "Well good. I'm glad I'm not falling for someone who finds me repulsive. But you don't have to do anything you're not ready to do, either. It's okay, Sunshine. You can tell me all about what's got you so knotted up inside, or not tell me a thing. Either way, it's okay."

I relaxed and enjoyed the day with Charlie. I didn't flinch once when he hugged me or put an arm around me. I even gave him a quick peck on the cheek once, just because.

Before dinner, we went back for our sweatshirts and he saw my journal.

"Do you write every day?" he asked.

"Just when I have some privacy."

"Well, privacy it is," he said. "I'll be back in what, fifteen minutes long enough? Or longer?"

"Fifteen's fine."

I settled in to write.

September 3, 1972

I think I love Charlie. Not lust, though there's some of that, too. And not crazy in love, though we haven't known each other very long, so maybe it's that. But it feels like this is something that's growing out of "like" to "love" and I think he's feeling the same, and I think that's a good thing. If we have sex, I think maybe it will really be making love, not just having sex. He did say he was falling for me. If I was sure, I'd say yes right now.

But I wasn't sure. So I didn't say yes for two more nights.

Then, when it was only a few of us left, cleaning up the camping area to leave it as close as we could to its original state, I decided to sleep naked with him. I told him I still wasn't sure how far it would go, but I wanted that intimacy. He agreed.

"You won't get mad if I get aroused, though, will you?" he pleaded. "I can't really control that completely."

"Will you be okay?"

"Of course," he said. "Guys have to deal with that whenever they see a sexy woman. It might... leak? But it's my sleeping bag, don't worry about any mess I make."

I laughed. "I'm not sure this is a good idea."

"There's one thing I'd like to do before either of us gets naked," he said. He put his hands on my shoulders and looked into my eyes.

"What's that?" I asked, though I was pretty sure I knew and I wanted it and was terrified at the same time.

"I'd like to kiss you," he said. "Really kiss you."

Holding my breath, looking right into his eyes, I nodded my head and lifted my face. As he pulled me to him my mouth opened slightly to take in his air. When we finally broke apart, there was no question what would happen in that sleeping bag.

In the morning, I woke first and slipped out to get dressed before Charlie could see any sign of bruising that might be left. I hadn't told him anything and wasn't going to. It felt as though my history would poison anything good and should be left behind forever. I was sitting writing in my journal when he woke up.

September 5, 1972

We made love most of the night, here under the stars. Charlie was tender and loving in every touch. When we finally fell asleep, I was warm and safe in his embrace. This is what it's supposed to be like. Maybe this is what my parents have.

He asked me to go with him when we're done here. He said he's never felt like this with anyone before. He called what we were doing loving, not fucking or even screwing.

And he doesn't seem to think I'm a slut for not being a virgin. Maybe someone really can love me. Maybe Charlie does. I love him, but I'll wait for him to say it first. I'm still a teeny bit afraid, I guess.

Charlie stayed in the sleeping bag, head propped on his hand as he watched me write. "Are you regretting last night?" he asked.

"No!"

"I was hoping for some morning loving."

He still called it loving in the daylight! "I needed to pee."

He nodded, got up and went off into the bushes to do that himself. When he came back, some of his friends from the cleaning crew were there.

"We're heading back tomorrow. We'll miss the beginning of harvest if we stay any longer and there's not much more to do here. You want to ride with us?"

"Do you have room for both of us?" asked Charlie.

"Sure!"

That night, we again slept naked together after making love. In the morning, Charlie woke up first. Instead of slipping out of the bag to go pee, he unzipped it and saw the faint discoloration still showing on my boobs. I sat up quickly and pulled my knees to my chest. He put his arms around me, knees and all.

He stared straight into my eyes. "You have nothing to hide."

He kissed me on the lips gently and I burst into tears. He pulled me down, closed the pack over both of us and zipped it back up, then held me until my sobs slowed. He kissed me on top of my head and stroked my body gently.

I looked into his eyes and fell completely, utterly in love. No maybes about it.

We made love and he kissed those marks gently.

Later we headed out in a camper on the back of an old pickup. The cab had three people across the bench seat; there were four of us riding in the back. We'd been on the road for about an hour when they pulled over for a break at Rabbit Ears Pass, the Continental Divide. I'd always lived where all waters flowed to the Atlantic. I was about to cross over to the side where all waters flowed to the Pacific.

My life was changing direction, too.

While the others shared a joint, I wrote in my journal.

September 6, 1972

I told Charlie I don't want to talk about the bruises he saw and he said that's okay. He says living in the present is good.

He hasn't said he loves me, but he's always giving me hugs and kisses and smiles.

I'm so happy. Sometimes I wish I could let my parents know how happy I am, how wonderful Charlie is, but I can't. They'd want me to come home and I can't do that. They'd want to know everything I want to forget. They might even have Charlie arrested.

Charlie doesn't know I'm fifteen. I look older and I'm sure he thinks I am. But that wouldn't matter to them. They'd say he should have asked me, but I didn't ask him either. I'm pretty sure he's twenty or twenty-one. I don't need to know how old he is; I'm not going to risk ruining everything. And I'm not going to call home, either.

I'm moving forward.

One of the guys had worked at the ski resort in Steamboat Springs and talked everyone into taking a break there so some of us could ride the gondola up the mountain. Charlie had never done that, either. We stood holding our breaths and expanding at the same time. You can see so far from the top of a mountain. We didn't say a word. We just stood there, holding hands.

The camper felt cramped after that. I was glad they stopped every hour or two for a break. There was some discussion late that afternoon about going to see dinosaur bones, but then someone pointed out it would be too late in the day by the time we got there.

It was getting dark when we made it to Provo, the first big city we'd seen. We took a break there. No one wanted to stop to eat, though. We were all sharing nuts and stuff.

Charlie took over driving across Utah, so I got to sit up front. Suddenly in the dark there was a great fireball in the sky, a meteor according to a newspaper we saw the next day, but it seemed like another sign that I was crossing over into a new beginning. I was part of a couple now, with a guy who was always tender and loving.

Charlie pulled over for the night at a gas station in Ely, Nevada. We needed gas and they wouldn't open until morning. Everyone slept wherever they were riding. I asked Charlie why we didn't get out of the truck and use his sleeping bag.

"Some places aren't very friendly to long-haired fellas. When in doubt, stay together and maintain low visibility."

In the morning, everyone pitched in what they could for the gas. I hadn't let even Charlie know how much money I had. I wasn't sure when I'd need it, so I just contributed my small change.

When we got to Reno, everyone spread out to panhandle to get enough to finish the trip. We came back together at five. I felt so guilty about hoarding my stolen cash that I pretended I'd found four fifties on the sidewalk.

"Farm out!" was the general response.

September 7, 1972

With the money I "found" Charlie rented a cheap motel room and everyone took turns slipping in to take showers. We all invaded a seafood buffet for dinner, then met back at the motel at nine. So Charlie and I are in a bed surrounded by people in sleeping bags on the floor. Everyone's drinking and telling stories. Oh well, it's more comfortable than the truck.

We got a late start the next morning and decided to eat a good breakfast at one of the buffets before we headed out, so it was late afternoon as we came out of the foothills into Sacramento. Since I'd treated everyone, we were riding up front with the driver, Mike. Charlie had been quiet for an hour. I hoped he didn't realize I'd had that money all along.

He took my hand and gave me a serious stare, then said, "Mike, drop us off near Sac State. I have some friends for Sunshine to meet before we head north." He squeezed my hand and smiled.

Chapter 12: Family

Mike insisted on driving us all the way to Charlie's friends, then waved goodbye as we stood in front of an apartment complex.

Charlie stood there quiet and serious, looking at the place, then me. He had just taken a breath, like he was about to say something, when a lady came around the corner of the building carrying a basket full of folded clothes.

The little girl with her squealed "Daddy!" and ran and jumped into Charlie's arms.

He grinned and looked like the Charlie I was used to seeing as he blew a raspberry on her neck and hugged her tight. The girl had to be six or seven, and I didn't think Charlie was that much older than me. He shifted her to one arm as the woman approached.

Maybe this was an ex-girlfriend and her daughter called him Daddy. *She* looked old enough to be the girl's mother. She shifted the laundry basket to one hip and smiled. "Hey, Charlie. How was your trip back East?"

She opened her free arm to hug him and they kissed on the lips. The little girl giggled and kissed Charlie on the cheek. He beamed at her, then answered the woman with a shrug.

"What you'd expect from my family. But Suzy looked beautiful on her wedding day. The guy's a stockbroker, but he didn't seem like a total jerk." He nodded in my direction. "This is Sunshine. We've been traveling together since Columbus. We went to that Rainbow Family Gathering I told you about."

"Nice to meet you, Sunshine. I'm Cheryl and this is Amy."

She held out her hand and I shook it, not sure what was going on, wondering how this woman fit into Charlie's life and who was Suzy? Charlie carried Amy on his shoulders as Cheryl led the way up some steps to an apartment loaded with books and kid stuff. A pot of soup bubbled on the stove.

"I thought maybe you'd go straight to harvest," Cheryl said.

"We could have," said Charlie, "But I missed my favorite girl."

He tickled Amy until she squealed and ran over behind me for protection and hugged my legs laughing.

"You can't get me now!" she taunted.

"Oh yes I can," he roared in play.

He threw his arms around my legs and tickled her again until she broke away and ran off into another room. She came back almost immediately with a stack of books and grabbed my hand.

"Sunshine, can you read me stories while Mommy and Daddy have their tickle time?"

Charlie gave me a worried smiled as Amy dragged me to the couch and made me sit. She curled up next to me, opened one of the books, and put it in my hands.

"This is my favorite story."

"The soup is on low now," said Cheryl. "It'll be fine."

Then she and Charlie disappeared in the same direction Amy had gone for the books.

Amy pulled a ragged stuffed rabbit from a corner of the couch and placed it on her lap. "This is Snuggy Bunny. He likes hearing stories, too."

I read to the little girl, fighting back tears when laughter drifted into the room from wherever they were having their tickle time.

Amy was sweet and charming like Charlie. I could see him in her eyes and her smile, so I had to accept he was really her father. Charlie hadn't actually said he loved me, but he'd treated me like he did. I should have known anyone so kind and gentle would already have someone in his life. Then I wondered how Cheryl would feel if she knew Charlie and I had been sleeping together. She probably thought I was just a friend.

I should leave, but I wasn't sure where to go. I'd felt so safe with Charlie. Maybe I could pretend we were only friends long enough to make a plan.

Amy and I read the entire stack of books, then she got restless and wanted to go to the playground.

"I don't know if your Mommy would want me to take you outside."

"It's okay," she said. "It's right in the middle of the apartments." She dragged me over to a window. "See?"

"Find something for me to write a note, so she knows where to look for us."

"Okay."

She stuck the note on the refrigerator with the A from the alphabet magnets that littered it along with finger paintings and a worksheet with a big A+ on it. She pointed to that proudly.

"A is for Amy and that's the grade I always get. I'm in first grade now. We're learning how to read."

On our way outside, I broke down and asked, "Does your Daddy live here? He didn't say."

"He travels a lot but he always comes home."

I took that as mostly a yes. Why had he brought me here? Maybe he was lying, maybe he did really think I was just a slut. But he wouldn't want me near his little girl if that was true. Maybe it had been mercy fucking and this was his way of telling me not to be so serious about it. But he said he was falling for me. Maybe he was trying to decide how to break it off with Cheryl, but that would make me a home-wrecker. Maybe he wanted me to meet Amy so I'd understand why it was over.

I should go now. I could figure out a plan at a motel. If I could find my way back to the highway, there had to be one there. I still had money.

But I didn't think I should leave Amy alone, either. My backpack was in the apartment. I could leave her there in the living room. But she was having so much fun, and what would she do by herself? I hadn't noticed a television. They had to have one, didn't they? But maybe it was in Cheryl's bedroom, which was Charlie's bedroom, apparently.

Amy grabbed my hand. "Let's go upstairs. I'm done here."

"Okay."

I let her lead me back up the steps and into the apartment. She dramatically pulled on a sheer paisley covering in the corner to reveal a television set. I laughed. As horrible as I felt, she made me laugh – so much like her daddy.

She shrugged her shoulders. "Mommy doesn't like it staring at us all the time, but she lets me watch when she's busy."

"Good," I said, picking up my backpack. Tears were filling my eyes, threatening to spill.

I blinked them back. The smell of that soup was filling my stomach. Just to be sure it hadn't started sticking while we were outside, I went into the kitchen and stirred it. Then I checked on Amy. She was glued to the tube.

"You'll be okay by yourself, right?" I asked.

"You can watch cartoons with me."

"I really need to get going." I didn't want to be wandering around a strange city by myself after dark, looking for a motel. I started for the door. "Tell your Mommy it was nice to meet her and say goodbye to your Daddy for me."

"Okay."

The tears started flowing as I went down the stairs and by the time I got to the edge of the parking lot, I was sobbing. I stood there, trying to stop, trying to remember which way we'd come from, so very frightened, hurt, and alone. Then I heard Charlie shout. He came running down the steps to me while Cheryl stood at the top, waving her arm as if to beckon me back. I stood there dumbly. Charlie pulled me into a hug and kissed the top of my head.

"Don't leave," he begged. "It's okay. Cheryl and I have an open marriage. She likes you already."

"You're married? She knows? That we..."

He nodded. "It's okay. Really it is. Come on, eat with us."

I still hesitated. He stroked my face gently, like he did before that first time.

"I didn't mean to hurt you. I was going to explain, but then there they were. Cheryl knew you were special right away or I wouldn't have brought you home. I'm sorry."

At that point, my stomach betrayed me by rumbling loudly.

He laughed. "Come on."

I let him lead me back into the apartment where he showed me into the bathroom. I closed the door and washed the tears off my face with cool water. I looked in the mirror.

Charlie was married, with a little girl. I wasn't going to break up his family. I loved him too much to do that.

I'd leave after dinner.

Amy was setting the table with four sets of silverware and napkins while Cheryl dished soup into bowls.

Amy pulled me to a chair. "This is your spot." She patted on the seat and I sat down.

"Charlie, can you pour some wine?" asked Cheryl.

"I get milk," said Amy.

"I've never had wine before," I fake whispered to her. "I'll let you know if I like it."

Charlie filled the glasses half way and I stared at mine, then back at Amy with eyes wide like I was afraid to try it. It was easier to focus on her. I took one sip and made a horrible face. Amy and Charlie both laughed. He brought me a glass of milk with Amy's.

"It's an acquired taste," said Cheryl. "You'd probably like a sweeter one to start."

She didn't sound upset at all, but I didn't know what to say and I couldn't face her, so I mumbled a sound of agreement and took a sip of milk. It didn't taste good, either, after the wine. Cheryl put bowls of soup in front of Amy and me and came back with her own and Charlie's.

I focused on eating without slurping, wondering what I should do next. Maybe I could find another guy to hitchhike with and just be smart enough not to sleep with him. Except where would I go? Probably not after Charlie's friends. I was just glad no one was asking me to talk. I kept my eyes on my food and listened to them.

"How long will you be home?" asked Amy. "Can you go to the air show with us?"

"Air show? What kind of air show?" asked Charlie.

"It's something she saw on a poster." Cheryl sounded resigned to going. "It looks like it's a bunch of jets doing maneuvers, but it's not a military thing. It's the twenty-fourth."

"I'd only planned to stay a day or two," said Charlie. "They've already started harvest."

"It's *airplanes* and they do lots of fancy tricks in the air." Amy sounded determined.

"Well, if it's *airplanes* I guess I should go," said Charlie.

"Amelia Earhart flew a plane. Our teacher read us a book about her."

"Ah, so are you going to be the next Amelia Earhart?" he teased.

"Maybe."

When I finished, I cleared my plate. Cheryl got up too.

"Guys," she said, "Sunshine and I are going to take a walk while you two do the dishes."

Charlie put on an act like he didn't know what to do and Amy started instructing him.

"Come on," said Cheryl. "Leave your pack. There's a really nice walk along the river not far from here."

We didn't say anything until we'd been on the river trail a few minutes. Then she stopped and took a deep breath.

"I love it here," she said. She paused before she continued, "I'm sorry about earlier. I'd never have left you with Amy like that if I'd realized Charlie hadn't explained our relationship."

"I never even thought to ask if he was married." My voice was full of guilt.

"That wasn't your responsibility. I always tell guys I'm married, to be sure we're on the same page that it's just a fling, and normally Charlie does the same. But he says you were fragile and he didn't want to scare you off."

"If I'd known, I'd never have…"

"He wasn't talking about getting into your pants. He didn't want you out there on your own. Charlie really does care about you, Sunshine. You're not a fling."

"I can't believe he told you that."

"If you were still saying no, he'd still have you here with him."

I wanted to believe that. "But you actually don't mind?"

"I told you, we have an open marriage. There's a book back in the apartment if you want to read it. We're not the only ones."

She took my arm and started walking up the river. By the end of the walk, she'd convinced me Charlie genuinely cared for me and she was okay with that.

She asked me to stay.

"Where would I sleep?" I asked.

She paused to think. "The couch for now? Theoretically, I should just invite you into bed with us, but I'm definitely not into girls and I'm not sure how I'd feel actually being there while Charlie made love to someone else. And there's Amy to think of, how she'd react."

I slept on the couch. I stayed up late describing the craziness of the situation and everything she'd told me about Charlie.

September 8, 1972

Cheryl got pregnant in high school. She was a junior and Charlie was a senior. They decided on an abortion and Charlie went with her, but it was a dirty motel room with bloody bedding and the doctor reeked of booze. Charlie got her out of there and they drove to a state where they could get married without parents signing, then came back and told their families. Her parents disowned her. They haven't spoken to her since.

Charlie's aunt in a different city took her in before she started showing. His parents were hoping they'd come to their senses and give up the baby, get an annulment, and go on with their lives. But as soon as he graduated, Charlie got her and they came out here before Amy was born. His family's never seen their granddaughter, but they talk to her on the phone, and Charlie went back for his sister's wedding this summer. But he won't take any help from them.

Cheryl wants to be a lawyer. She's working at a law firm and taking college classes and taking care of Amy, so she doesn't have time for a serious relationship. She says Charlie had planned on being a lawyer, too, but he's been following the Grateful Dead and enjoying the freedom of his current lifestyle, so they really don't get along that great for more than a week or two at a time anymore.

She said the open marriage thing has worked because neither of them ever got serious about anyone, and their flings were always when they were apart. But she says she knows I'm really special to Charlie or he wouldn't have brought me here to meet them.

It would be easier if we were leaving right away, but Amy needs time with her Daddy. He told her he'd stay for the air show. I don't want to wreck their family, but it's killing me to know he's in there with Cheryl. I should leave, but where would I go? I don't really want to be on my own again, all alone.

The next day was Saturday. Cheryl didn't have to work, but she was happy to spend the day at the college studying without Amy having to be with a sitter. I wanted to talk to Charlie, but Amy didn't give us a moment alone. She was in seventh heaven because Charlie was home. We used Cheryl's car to take Amy to the zoo and Fairytale Town. Half the time Amy grabbed our hands to walk between us, swinging along as if we were both her parents. At dinner she chattered about the things we'd done and seen and how we went *two* places, not just one.

Cheryl laughed and told her to enjoy it while it lasted.

"I know," Amy replied. "We have to pack all our fun in while Daddy's here, because he's got to leave again soon. It's even more fun with Sunshine here."

That didn't seem to bother Cheryl.

They put Amy to bed at nine after stories with Snuggy Bunny on her lap. I'd hoped maybe the three of us could talk, or I could take a walk with Charlie, but Cheryl led him off to bed.

September 9, 1972

I'm alone on the couch again. Maybe that's why Cheryl's not worried about me. She's the wife and mother, I'm just the girl on the couch.

But I'm falling more in love with Charlie every minute we spend with Amy, and I love that little girl, too. I had to keep reminding myself today that she's THEIR daughter, a child Charlie and Cheryl made together. She is so much like Charlie... Cheryl doesn't seem upset when Amy gives me hugs or kisses.

I can't stand it. I don't know what I'm doing here. I need to make a plan and get out of here on my own. This is crazy.

Sunday Cheryl wanted to study again, so we took Amy tubing on the river. The sun and playing in the water all day wore her out.

September 10, 1972

Amy fell asleep in the car and stayed asleep when Charlie carried her into her room. Then he took me into the bedroom he shares with Cheryl. I hesitated, but he said they talked about it last night and agreed it would be okay for us to use the room if Amy was asleep. In fact, Cheryl was going to call before she came home, just in case.

She's never had guys over here that way. Supposedly she's got a guy from work who wants her to be more serious, too. Charlie says they've decided it's time to move on. They just have to figure out how to explain it to Amy.

When I pointed out he's still sleeping with Cheryl, he said that's all they're doing - that and talking things out. I told him good, because I thought their open marriage thing was nuts. I read that book and while parts of it sound better than my mother having to hide the fact she was working, the rest of it sounds dumb.

I love him. That's why I haven't left. He offered to leave sooner if I need him to, but I said I don't mind, it's his time with Amy.

We were careful not to fall asleep after we made love; we were dressed before Amy woke up. It felt like we were doing something wrong. I hope he was telling me the truth.

Cheryl did call before she came home. She brought wine and they're fixing dinner while I write this. Does she really know? How could she know and not care?

It was a sweet wine and Cheryl was right, I liked it much better than what they had the first night. I drank it like it was grape juice.

Before dinner was over my nose was a little numb. They laughed and when nine o'clock rolled around, Charlie tucked me in like he did Amy, with a kiss to my forehead. I grabbed him and pulled him into a hungry open-mouth smooch.

I heard Cheryl come into the room.

I stuck out my tongue at both of them and plopped back onto the couch.

Charlie tucked me in again, laughing and giving me the kiss on the forehead again, but retreating more quickly. He tweaked my nose.

"You know I love you, Sunshine."

That's the only time he ever said that.

Then he turned and went into the bedroom with Cheryl. She was still smiling. In fact, she blew me a kiss and said goodnight. I thought about getting up and following them, but I was suddenly too tired to move.

Thirst woke me up. I found my way to the kitchen in the dark. It was three in the morning. I drank three glasses of water to match the time, then I needed to pee. Cheryl poked her head into the bathroom.

"Are you okay? We shouldn't have let you drink so much wine."

"Just thirsty."

"That's normal. Wine dries you out."

"I'm not drunk anymore."

"You sound okay ." She smiled. "You're a pretty funny drunk."

"Charlie says you're just sleeping together, not doing anything anymore. Should I believe him?" I was terrified what her answer would be, but I had to know.

"Yeah," she said. "It's just not right for us anymore, neither of us. And don't think it's your fault. It's been headed this direction for the last year. I love Charlie, but he doesn't fit what I want out of life anymore."

"So it's really okay that we...?"

"Yes," she said. "I'm just worried about Amy, how to get her used to us moving on to other people, you know? She really likes you, so that helps."

Maybe I was still a little drunk. "He said he loves me. You heard it too, didn't you?"

"I heard. Don't expect him to say it often, but he'll show it in the way he takes care of you."

I went back to the couch, still a little drunk, but the next night, once Amy was asleep, Cheryl and I swapped places. We meant to change back before Amy woke up, but it didn't turn out that way.

September 12, 1972

Amy ran in with Snuggy Bunny and pounced on the bed. She didn't seem surprised to see me there in one of her daddy's T-shirts. Her only question was why Cheryl wasn't with us. Charlie told her it was too crowded for three grownups.

Amy got her mom and dragged her into the room and pushed her onto the bed to prove he was wrong, then climbed on top of us, bouncing and saying "See? See Daddy? There's lots of room," until we were all laughing. Cheryl finally told her that I'm Daddy's special friend and we'd like to sleep together, so Mommy's going to sleep on the couch while we're here.

Amy shocked her by asking if the Bruce guy who came to dinner once was going to be Mommy's special friend. She'd picked up on more than Cheryl had admitted to herself. Cheryl said Bruce is out of town, but she'll invite him to dinner if we stay a couple days after the air show. That way Charlie can meet him, since he may be around Amy a lot.

Everything's working out! I have a new family.

The next two weeks were full of love and fun, more than I'd ever experienced before. We'd drop Cheryl off at work each morning, take Amy to school, and then I had Charlie to myself for a few hours. We spent some of that time in bed, but he also had fun showing me Sacramento. I really liked the taffy in Old Town. Then we'd pick up Amy after school and play with her and make dinner together. The next Saturday, we all went back to the river and on Sunday drove up into the foothills to an apple farm for cider.

Cheryl enjoyed giving herself a weekend off.

"Charlie's good for me that way," she said. "He reminds me to stop and enjoy life."

That second week, Amy brought home the book on Amelia Earhart and other airplane books we had to read every night.

We were a loving family the day of the air show – an odd combination, but a family, happy to be together. Amy was bursting with excitement. She agreed we could watch from outside the grounds because the jets were so loud. We took a picnic basket and she lasted until after four. We were getting ready to leave when Amy saw a girl with an ice cream cone and started begging for one.

"Okay, we'll go over to Farrell's for an ice cream," said Cheryl.

"I'll go get the car," said Charlie.

"I'll help you carry everything," I said to Charlie, then asked Cheryl if she'd get me a plain vanilla cone.

"Sure," she said.

The car was several blocks down the street. Charlie had just closed the trunk when there was a burst of light followed by the sound of an explosion. We turned and saw the fireball reaching high into the sky over the buildings.

A jet had plowed through the fence into the ice cream parlor.

Charlie ran back and into the burning building. The heat and smoke were intense. I never thought I would see any of them again but a policeman dragged Charlie out. He was choking from the smoke and had burns on his hands.

The policeman kept going back to find more people. I don't know how he did it. When the firemen arrived he went into the building with them, too.

Charlie refused to show the medics his hands. Most of the people being brought out were in terrible shape and he didn't want to slow down their getting help.

"Promise me you won't go back into the fire," I pleaded.

"I'd only get in the way again," he said miserably.

I ran to the car and got an empty Tupperware bowl from our picnic. I filled it with water from a fire hydrant the plane had run over. It was shooting water to the sky right across the street from the inferno. I made Charlie put his hands in the cold water.

He was still watching for Amy and Cheryl. If they didn't get out right away, they weren't alive. But Charlie couldn't leave. I held him for hours while the fire fighters dragged bodies out of the flames, then the blackened ruins. I made him keep his hands in the water.

Amy and Cheryl were two of the twenty-three people who died that day.

Charlie called his family. They wanted to fly out. He told them not to, that there wouldn't be any funeral and he was leaving. They wanted him to come home. He had other places to go. They offered to break the news to Cheryl's parents. He agreed that was the right thing to do, even though they'd never answered her letters.

Charlie had their ashes mixed together and sealed in a beautifully carved redwood box.

"That way they'll never be alone and they'll always be with me."

As Cheryl's legal husband, Charlie was her sole heir. She didn't have much, but we had to get rid of everything we weren't taking with us because there was no way Charlie wanted that apartment anymore. Under the circumstances, they didn't give him any trouble about getting out of her lease. The whole city was reeling from the tragedy.

The hardest part was Amy's things.

Charlie couldn't throw them away or have someone resell them. Then a neighbor suggested giving them to the Sacramento County Hospital for sick kids. There was a whole room full of toys bereft parents had donated. We left most of Amy's things there, but Snuggy Bunny was too beat up. Charlie knew it would be thrown away, so we sat outside until we saw a little girl leaving. She was in a wheelchair with bandages on her legs, but we could see the less serious burns on her arms. Charlie walked up to the little girl with tears in his eyes, holding out the ragged stuffed toy. The woman pushing the wheelchair stopped and glanced over at me. I tried to smile, to let her know it was okay. Charlie didn't notice her. He spoke directly to the child.

"My little girl wanted to be like Amelia Earhart when she grew up, and she loved chocolate ice cream."

The girl blinked. "Me too."

Charlie held out the ragged stuffed toy. "Could you take care of Snuggy Bunny for my little girl?"

The girl nodded and Charlie placed the bunny on her lap, tears pouring down his face.

"Thank you." He looked up at the woman. "Thank you." Then he walked away.

I had to run to catch up to him.

That night, he drove us north in the car that had been Cheryl's, with more belongings than he'd ever carried before and a big gaping hole inside him.

Chapter 13: The Redwood Curtain

I don't remember anyone calling it the redwood curtain back then, but they do now. Maybe they did then. Time plays tricks on our memories and I didn't write very much in my journal those days. I was drunk or stoned with Charlie most of the time.

Some people say it's called the redwood curtain because everything's more expensive when it has to be trucked up into the redwoods with the narrow roads lined with trees that are centuries if not millennia old. I think it's because it's like a different world. Along the Lost Coast there are some folks who consider themselves a separate nation.

We were lost when we were there.

The marijuana harvest was already underway, but Charlie had worked for the same farmers for years, so we went to work immediately.

We had to camp out near the fields. Charlie helped cut the plants; I worked with the crew stripping them. Mostly we did that as the plants came in from the field, but when the cutters got ahead of us they'd hang some to dry a few days before we'd get to them. It reminded me of tying grapes; the days were long and the task repetitive. But we listened to music or joked around while we worked so it wasn't that bad, and the pay was good.

We earned enough in a few weeks for the year.

When the rains came, we moved into a house with several people Charlie had known for years. We did a little more stripping work for people who'd dried their crop in barns, then the season was done. When everyone else left, it was just Charlie and me at the house. I wrote my worries into my journal because there was no one to ask for help.

January 1, 1973

I don't think Charlie's smiled since that day - maybe a faint hint of one when people were joking and laughing during harvest, but his eyes are always sad, and the pain showing through is so deep. I'm worried about him.

The people we were working with have known Charlie a long time. Some of them knew Cheryl, too. They told me Charlie would head straight for his girls at the end of harvest every year, then later he'd join some of them in Baja for the winter. But he doesn't want to go anywhere.

The chilling rain seems to suit him.

He's not mean, but he's not really here with me. It's like there's this big chunk missing. And I don't know what to do. I'm not even sure he knew which day was Christmas. I figured it was probably a big deal, with Amy, so I didn't say anything. I didn't want him to feel worse.

I'm only fifteen. Everyone thinks I'm older, especially since I've started driving now Charlie has the car. I couldn't tell him I was too young to drive. I'm sure Cheryl thought I was older - she was planning on being a lawyer, it would have made a difference to her - but no one ever asks me. I wish there was somebody I could tell, because I need someone to take care of me, and Charlie can't.

He needs me to take care of him now.

He's tired of having to explain to people why he's changed so much, or people who know telling him how sorry they are. He just wants to be by himself. I have to tell people he wants to be alone, and some of them get mad at me because they don't know me or how things were with all of us like a family. And then sometimes I don't think Charlie even wants me to be here. But I'm scared to leave him alone longer than it takes to go for groceries.

That's the only time I get to talk to anyone, and it's only the people who work at the store, just how-about-this-rain kind of talk. Not hey, I'm scared to death for Charlie and I don't know what to do to help him. There's no one I can talk to about that.

Charlie was drinking or smoking himself numb every day. In fact, he was almost always drunk or stoned. It was easier to join him than keep worrying.

A lot of nights that winter, one of us would pass out on the couch or the floor and the other would go to bed alone. Once in a while I'd pull it together enough to make a journal entry.

March 13, 1973

I don't remember the last time we had sex, and it was like he didn't really want to do it, it was just something his body demanded. It's fine he doesn't want to do it that often - turns out I'm not really a slut or a nympho. But I wish it felt like he loves me or at least wants me when we do it, and it doesn't.

I was probably kidding myself when I thought he loved me. But I still love him and I'm scared he'll look at me one day and tell me to go away and never come back. Because he hates me. Because I asked Cheryl to get that vanilla ice cream cone. And maybe if I hadn't, they'd have been out of the store before that plane hit. If I just hadn't asked her to get that cone.

Cheryl said I was special to Charlie, that he'd never brought anyone else home. And I loved her and Amy like family. But even if he doesn't blame me, every time Charlie sees me he has to remember that day.

It also occurred to me that maybe he just didn't want to care about anyone ever again.

We both got really bad chest colds as winter ended, so bad that we had to stop smoking. In spite of being sick, Charlie seemed to start pulling out of the depression a little. Then in May one of his grower friends offered to let us stay in his summer camp above the Eel River with its beautiful green rocks, if we'd tend his crop. We didn't drink as much out there.

June 20, 1973

We're living in a yurt. That's a big tent on a platform with a real bed in it. There's a lean-to set up as a kitchen. That's separate so the yurt doesn't get hot when we cook, or smoky. There's an outhouse. It doesn't smell much with just two of us using it. It doesn't have a door, which would bother me except there's no one out here and it looks out over the river, which is beautiful.

We've planted a vegetable garden that would make my mother proud, and Charlie knows how to find food in the forest, too - mushrooms and wild berries and stuff to make tea. And he's teaching me how to fish.

There were fishing poles in the lean-to when we got here. I'm getting pretty good, but I still let him take it off the hook. He usually cleans them, too, so I do the cooking. It's just frying them in butter and they taste so good fresh like that, mostly trout. I never liked fish before.

Best of all, Charlie seemed to be finding some peace.

The first week in July, we went into town for basic supplies like flour and cheese and I talked Charlie into a cake. I said it was for the holiday, but it was really for my birthday. I turned sixteen the tenth of July that year.

July 10, 1973

I remember Jan's sweet sixteen. Her parents took a carload of us all the way to Sandusky to the amusement park. My parents wouldn't have done anything like that. So cake's fine. Besides, people ask your age when they know it's your birthday. Everyone thinks I'm like twenty or something and I like that. I'd hate to be treated like a kid again.

The year had aged me – and Charlie too.

He used tending the crop as an excuse to not travel that summer. Three of his friends came out to the camp when they were taking off for the Summer Jam at Watkins Glen. They couldn't believe it when he said he wasn't going. He'd followed the Grateful Dead for years, never missing a major concert.

"What are you, crazy? It's going to be massive, another Woodstock. Did you hear all the bands that'll be there?"

July 19, 1973

Charlie's friends left today. The driver pulled me aside and told me he was really worried about Charlie, that he didn't seem to be himself and it probably wasn't good for him to be out here. He was about to say more but Charlie came to say goodbye right then.

I'm wondering if he ever had Cheryl and Amy out here, if that's what his friend was going to say. But it doesn't matter. He's so much more himself than he was before. They didn't see him last winter.

We stayed the rest of the summer, just the two of us out there.

We had sex a few times, in the middle of the night, and it felt more loving again. But it was always in the dark and part of me was afraid he was making love to Cheryl. We hadn't mentioned either of their names all summer. As harvest time approached, so did the anniversary of their death.

September 12, 1973

Yesterday was our last day on the river. We were fishing side by side and I finally got up the nerve to ask if Cheryl and Amy had ever been out there with him. He said yes, when Amy was a baby, before Cheryl started working and went back to school.

He turned and put his pole down carefully, then looked at me with tears pouring down his face. He tried to say something and instead gasped and started shaking and sobbing. I dropped my pole and wrapped my arms around him. He held onto me, tight, and when the sobbing eased he gave me a kiss on top of my head, like he used to do. He reminded me how much both Cheryl and Amy had loved me, and I told him I'd loved them and how scared I'd been that I might lose him too.

We kept standing there like that until his tears stopped flowing and my pole started getting dragged into the river. I let go of him to catch it and pulled in a pan-sized trout for our dinner. After we ate, we sat together on a blanket watching the sunset, and in the twilight we made love right there in the open, and it was like it used to be.

He didn't say he loved me, but he promised I'd never lose him.

We moved back into Garberville, this time in a tiny cottage by ourselves. We worked with a lot of the same people from the year before, but with our own place we didn't spend as much time with them. I enjoyed our quiet evenings alone.

There were stacks of books another tenant had left behind in every room – a ton of mysteries and romance novels with steamy pictures on the covers, but Steinbeck and Hemingway were in there, too. Charlie was excited to find a hardback copy of *The Drifters,* by James Michener. He insisted I read it and it completely absorbed me for days.

We were snuggling on the couch one night, each reading our own book, when it suddenly occurred to Charlie that we'd been together over a year and I hadn't had a birthday.

"Of course I had a birthday." I laughed.

"But we didn't celebrate. When was it?" He looked so guilty. "You didn't even have a cake."

"July. We had cake." I nudged him, trying to make him smile.

"You said that was for the holiday." He smiled, but it was an apology. "I know I wasn't very good company, but you should have told me."

"It's no big deal. No one's ever made a fuss about my birthday."

"Not even when you were little?"

I shook my head. "We'd have cake with candles on it and my parents would get me a few presents, but no big parties or anything."

"My birthday's next week. We'll celebrate together. We'll need twenty-six plus how many candles?"

Twenty-six? Of course. He graduated from high school before Amy was born. First graders are usually six or seven. Another year had passed. But I'd never done the math. He'd never seemed that old. I couldn't tell him I was sixteen. "You don't want to know."

"Just because I never asked before doesn't mean I don't want to know."

I could have lied and told him I was nineteen. That would have made me eighteen when we met. But I didn't *want* to lie to Charlie. So I smiled and shook my head, then walked away.

That night when we were in bed, he asked again.

"I'm younger than you think."

He pulled back a little. "Now you've got me scared. You're not like a fourteen-year-old in disguise, are you?"

"No. I'm sixteen."

"Seriously?"

"And almost a half."

"Your birthday's in July."

"Yes. The tenth."

"So you were barely fifteen when we got together." He sat up. "Shit. I molested a child."

"It's not like I was a virgin. You didn't rape me or anything."

"I was almost ten years older than you. I *am* almost ten years older than you."

"So what?"

"Either you're way too old for your age or I'm way too immature for mine. Or both."

I tried to pull him back down under the covers, but he turned away from me and put his feet on the floor.

"I have to think about this," he said.

He got dressed and left the room. I heard the outside door close and cried myself to sleep, not sure if he was ever coming back. But he did, sometime in the night. I woke up with his arm around me and thought everything was going to be okay.

Everything seemed to go back to normal after that.

October 29, 1973

I was really afraid when Charlie first found out how old I am, but he hasn't said anything about it and we're still sleeping together and everything.

We did NOT add my candles to his cake, though. Everyone razzed him for being an old man, almost thirty and not to be trusted. He laughed it off.

He's staring off into space a lot, but he's not down like he was last year. He took Cheryl's car into a shop for new tires and told them to give it a good checkup because it hadn't been serviced in a year. Cars don't last long on the crazy rutted dirt roads here.

He told them he wanted it in shape for a trip. I asked if we're going to Baja this winter and he said he's not sure yet. I hope we do.

Except what if I need a passport? We didn't need them to go to Canada when I was a kid. I have to remember to ask him. He's asleep already.

But I forgot, and a few days later we were done for the season.

That night, Charlie started packing.

"Where are we going this winter?" I asked. "Do I need a passport if we're going to Baja?"

"I'm going back East to visit my family," he said.

Not we. He wasn't inviting me. He wouldn't want his family to know he had a sixteen-year-old girlfriend. I could understand why. "I could go and camp out while you were with them. You wouldn't have to drive across the whole country alone."

"It snows in the winter back there. You know that. You couldn't camp, and I can find a rider along the way." He stopped packing and looked at me. He opened his arms and wrapped me in a hug. "I'll be back." He gave me a squeeze. "I just need some time on my own, Sunshine."

"What about me?" It was so hard not to cry. He didn't love me.

"Have you thought about going home? Fredonia, right? I could take you there. It wouldn't be much out of my way."

I still wore that sweatshirt Jan gave me. "I can't go back,"

"Are your parents really that bad?"

"No. It's me."

"You don't have to tell them everything. My dad would probably have a heart attack if he found out how I've been making money all this time. They think I've got a sales job that has me on the road a lot and gives me time off when I visit them."

"That's you. And your parents." Anger suddenly flowed through me and I pushed him away. "You know, just go. You were always going to leave someday, I knew that. I'll figure out what to do."

He wasn't angry, just sad. "The winters here are depressing, but if you want to stay, I'll pay the rent through the spring. I'll be back by then, maybe sooner."

"I can take care of myself. I was taking care of myself before I met you and I can do it again." The words were like hot drops of lead spraying out of my heart.

Pain swelled out of my chest through my arms and legs to my fingers and toes. I couldn't stop the tears and the shaking that came with them. I lashed out at him with my words, hysterically sobbing, "You don't love me. You never did. You just want people who need you and I don't. I don't need you. I took care of *you* last winter. I can take care of myself."

With that I ran out the door. I walked through the dripping redwoods for an hour before I calmed down and returned to the cottage. He'd left a note for me. "I'll be back and I'll call you at Mike's on Christmas." Mike had a phone. Charlie expected me to wait around for him.

We hadn't been drinking much. All I could find was one beer in the fridge. I chugged it down, then headed over to Mike's. They always had booze. If Charlie was out on the road, he was screwing other people. He probably had while we were together and I was too dumb to notice. Two could play that game. Getting good and drunk helped.

Christmas Day, 1973

I came out to the beach to be by myself, relatively sober today. I've been drunk or stoned almost the whole time since Charlie left, and it still hurts. He doesn't love me, he never did. No one ever will. I really am nothing but a slut. I've been giving the guys at Mike's a good time. Why not? Charlie wouldn't care. No one would. No one's hurting me or making me do anything I don't want to. I was kidding myself that it was different with Charlie. There's no such thing as love. At least not for me.

But what about Amy? She wasn't pretending. If a little kid can love me, maybe someone else can, someday.

What am I going to do with the rest of my life? I can't get a real job with no identification and not even a full year of high school. I can make good money here during harvest, but then what do I do the rest of the year? Alone.

I could still feel her little hand in mine. Guilt washed over me. If only I hadn't asked for that ice cream cone... I nearly took a swim straight out into those icy waters that day. When I got back to the house, they told me I'd missed a call from Charlie. He didn't leave a number. When he didn't call again, I figured it was over.

I got drunk and stayed that way for the next week.

A slut never had to be alone. I threw myself into the role.

Chapter 14: Growing Pains

New Year's morning I was sleeping it off at Mike's. There was another guy in bed with us, all of us naked and still drunk from the night before. Charlie walked in as if he couldn't even see them and gave me a tender kiss on the tip of my nose.

"Hey, Sunshine," he said softly. "It's a brand new year. Come on home with me."

I burst into tears. Mike woke up and looked at Charlie through one eye.

"We okay?" he asked.

Charlie waved off the question and Mike closed his eye. I climbed out of bed while Charlie found my clothes. He gave them to me one piece at a time. When I was dressed, we walked downstairs in silence. Everyone else was asleep. He led me to a new little car that was parked in front of Mike's house.

"You got rid of Cheryl's car?"

"This is a rental. I flew into San Francisco. I was worried about you."

"I'm sorry," I sobbed as he drove. "I didn't think you were ever coming back."

"There's no reason for you to be sorry. I don't own you."

"I'm such a slut."

"Stop beating yourself up," he said.

When we got to the cottage, he went straight to the bathroom and cleaned out the tub. I'd let it get pretty gross. Then he started running a bath and poured in some shampoo for bubbles.

"You think I'm dirty because I was with the two of them."

"Mike's house reeks of pot, stale beer, and cigarettes, and so do you, Sunshine." He smiled to take the sting out of telling me I smelled bad. "Plus, a nice warm bath might make you start feeling better."

"You cut your hair." He looked even cuter with it short.

"I'll tell you everything later." He kissed my nose again.

I let him undress me, then took his hand as I stepped into the tub. He was right. It did feel good.

"I'll get you some tea," he said.

The kettle whistling hurt my head and I was glad he brought a big glass of water along with the cup of tea. He set them on the toilet lid where I could reach them and started to leave.

"Wait," I said. "You're not mad?"

"No. I told you. I don't own you."

Part of me wanted him to be mad. Could he really care about me and not care I'd been screwing around? He smiled and left me in the tub. If he'd gotten in the tub with me, I'd have known he wasn't mad. But he did fly back to see me. That had to have cost him a bunch of money.

Did it make him think of the crash?

Then I smelled bacon cooking. He must have bought food. I'd been over at Mike's most of the time and hadn't brought many groceries into the cottage since Charlie left. I let the tub drain and rinsed off the suds, then searched for some clean clothes in the bedroom. Mine were all dirty, but Charlie's backpack was there with a clean pair of jeans and a sweatshirt that smelled a little like Charlie. They were too big, but it was like wrapping him around me. When I walked into the kitchen, he broke out laughing.

"I was afraid you'd prance in here naked, and I'm starving." He turned back to the food cooking on the stovetop.

"I'm hungry, too. And I am sorry."

"Please, stop." He held bacon over the frying pan, letting the grease drop off before putting it on plates he must have washed. "Unless you're apologizing for having no paper towels to soak the grease off this bacon."

The kitchen was a disaster of dirty pans and dishes and I hadn't bought paper towels, either. I suddenly realized the place smelled bad, too. I couldn't remember washing dishes since Charlie left. I'd just rinsed off something if I needed it.

"I'm so glad you're back. I'm kind of a mess on my own."

"So I see." He smiled and fixed plates with omelets and the bacon. "That's why I'm not mad about..." He tilted his head in the direction of Mike's house. "That's just part of you being a mess, isn't it?"

I mumbled an affirmative as we sat down to eat, but my mind was racing. Charlie was different. It wasn't just the hair. He was happy, but it wasn't the laid back kind of happy he'd always been. Something had changed.

We ate in silence, measuring each other. It was easier to talk as we started to wash the breakfast dishes – and everything else I'd left dirty while he was gone. That way we didn't have to look at each other the whole time.

"I like your hair short. It was nice long, too, but why'd you cut it?"

"I needed a change. I'm twenty-six years old, Sunshine, and I haven't done a thing with my life. Cheryl always had enough plans for both of us. I could keep being a kid chasing after a band. Now I wish I'd been there more." He sighed. "I always thought there was plenty of time."

"So, you're settling down?"

"I interviewed at Dickinson. It's a little college my uncle graduated from, a good one. My dad's happy to help me and with a degree from there I'll be able to do something worthwhile in the world. *Really* make a change instead of talking about it with other stoners. I start in the fall."

I couldn't go there with him. The guy who gave me my first ride went to Dickinson. It was near Harrisburg, too close to Nick.

"Is this where you want to be, Sunshine?" he asked. He watched the water draining out of the sink.

"No." I didn't know what I wanted but having drunken sex with a bunch of guys who didn't care about me was not part of it. "I can't go with you, though."

He looked up at me, his eyes sad. "I'm glad you see that we can't be together."

I sighed and waved my hand at the dishes. "I do so well on my own."

"What's the last year you finished in high school?"

I blushed with shame. "I didn't. I left right before exams my freshman year."

"I was afraid of that when you told me how old you are."

"Cheryl said she didn't have to have a diploma for community college, and it was free."

Maybe this would be a good thing. I used to look ahead. I used to have lots of plans for my life. College would make things possible. It would be scary without Charlie, but I still had most of my harvest money. Charlie had paid the rent on this cottage ahead of time before he left, someone else provided the alcohol and drugs at Mike's, and I hadn't spent much on food, either.

But Charlie said, "Cheryl finished her junior year, so she was mostly ready for college. You aren't. But I have a plan that would help you get there, if you're willing to work hard."

"I was always good at school. But don't they ask for birth certificates and stuff to go to a high school? Besides, I don't think I could do that now."

"I have some friends down in Marin County, an older couple. I stopped there when I got in yesterday. They have an apartment under their garage. They'll let you stay there if you'll watch the house for them when they're traveling. I promised them you're not a thief and wouldn't have wild parties or anything."

I ignored the implied question. No, I wasn't a thief and I would have respect for someone helping me out. Instead I asked, "*Under their garage?*"

"They live on the East Ridge in Mill Valley, so their house is built that way, too. Their bedrooms are under the main floor of the house."

"How would staying there help me get into college?"

"For starters, you wouldn't be here anymore. Not that there's anything wrong with the people up here, but most of them will never change. And you're smart, Sunshine. You can have a lot better life than this. Lynn said she'd help you. She's on the board of the community college, so she's finding out what you'll need to know."

"What did you tell them?" I asked defensively.

"I told them you're a wonderful young woman I care about who has had some hard knocks and never got to finish high school."

"Would they expect me to be like some little virgin girl? What would they say if they'd found me like you did this morning? Having a drunken orgy?"

"Drunken orgies are probably out, because the apartment's right next to their house. But that's not really you, Sunshine. They won't set a curfew or anything. And they travel a lot."

"I guess I could at least meet them."

If Charlie still said I wasn't really a slut, maybe I could convince myself.

Before we headed south, Charlie said I needed to get some identification papers so I could go to college when I was ready. He convinced me to tell him my real name so my college work would count if I ever decided to go home. I told him the truth, that the name on my birth certificate was Margaret Lewis.

"Maggie? Meg?" he scrunched up his face at the names.

"Peg. They called me Peg."

"That's not any better. You're still Sunshine to me."

January 6, 1974

Charlie knows someone who knows someone who got me a birth certificate, social security card, and a California driver's license that say I'm Margaret Lewis from Chicago. I turned nineteen July first and my Great Lakes accent fits. I'm glad my birthday's still in July. It'll be easier to remember, though my real birthday's the tenth.

Charlie thought I should be Margaret Lewis in case I go home again. That won't ever happen, but he thinks it may because going home has been good for him. Anyway, it doesn't matter. Unless I want them to, no one's going to connect Margaret Lewis from Chicago with the younger one from New York State.

I've made up this whole background, with some help from Charlie. My family moved when I was four, so all I really remember about Chicago is making snowmen and the wind off the big lake all the time. After that, we were always moving from one dumpy place to another. I'd start to make friends, then we'd leave again. When I turned eighteen, I left. They moved again and I don't even know where they are now.

I practiced saying it with this depressed kind of voice so no one will ask me to say more. Charlie says I have it down perfectly.

He took me shopping for clothes. He said to save my harvest money, he wanted to buy me some things. He paid for the identification, too. Cheryl said I could tell he loved me by the way he'd take care of me, so I guess maybe he does.

I wish he'd say it, though.

I threw away the Fredonia sweatshirt—it was pretty ratty and I didn't want anyone connecting me with that part of the country. It was too close to what used to be home.

We ran into Mike once. He asked Charlie again if they were cool.

"No problem, man. But we're heading out and probably won't be back next year. We're going new directions."

"Where?" asked Mike.

"Wherever life takes us."

Charlie made it sound vague, but he had every detail planned. In less than a week, we were driving down the coast. We stopped at a little store and Charlie bought me some earrings. I took out the gold studs I'd gotten in Fredonia and slid the hooks through the holes. Abalone shell and silver glittered against my hair.

"They're perfect," I said.

"Whatever color you wear will bring out that color in the abalone," said the store clerk.

Then we headed inland and I was surprised by more redwoods – not as large as the ones up north, but still incredible. We wound down out of the forest into a beautiful little town.

"Mill Valley's probably the richest place in the country," Charlie warned me as we were driving through the center of town. "A lot of musicians live here, like David Crosby. So don't freak out if you see someone famous."

"Are your friends rich?"

"They have to be to live here, but they're not snobby or anything. They both worked for what they've got."

We drove up the ridge on the east side of town on narrow winding roads where cars had to find places to pull over if they met. The glimpses of houses I caught were intimidating, with expensive cars in every driveway. I didn't really belong here. But my nervousness disappeared when Lynn greeted us in paint-spattered clothes.

"We've been freshening up the office," she explained. "We did the apartment a couple days ago and left it open to air out. There shouldn't be any fumes."

The apartment was smaller than the bedroom I'd had as a kid, but there was a tiny refrigerator under the counter, burners built into the counter, and a sink all in one short space of wall and a bathroom where you could turn on the water in the stall shower while you sat on the toilet, if you really wanted to. The apartment was definitely compact, but it had a sliding glass door out onto a little deck that overlooked the valley, so it didn't feel cramped. There was even a closet for my new clothes. A flowered walkway ran between the apartment and the main door of the house.

Lynn's husband John was as nice as Lynn and he gave me a hug when we first met that night. Charlie offered to go get Chinese, but Lynn put on a real dinner, treating us like special company even though she'd been painting all day. She even set the table with good china and candles. But they were so easy-going, it was comfortable. Then Charlie asked if they'd mind if he slept out in the apartment with me, to make sure I settled in okay.

John and Lynn exchanged a knowing look. There was only a twin bed out there.

"Charlie," said John. "We are not your parents, or this young lady's. What the two of you do in private is your own business. Frankly, we rather assumed the nature of your relationship when you first talked to us about her. However, as one of your father's friends, I know he would want me to remind you, while this young lady may be old enough to make her own decisions, she is still young enough to be very impressionable. You are considerably older and you must keep her best interests in mind."

It was neat having someone talk like I was something precious, but I was glad that Charlie still slept with me until his plane left later that week. We made love every night like we had at the beginning, back in Colorado and at the apartment in Sacramento, before the plane wreck.

I didn't write in my journal until he left.

January 12, 1974

Charlie really does love me. Like Cheryl said, he won't come out with the words, but he's taking care of me. It's not just everything he's done to get me set up to have a better life here, it's the tender way he made love to me each night. He makes me feel as if I really am something special.

I'm never going to get drunk again. I don't like myself drunk and I always act like a slut. I told Charlie that and he agreed that if we have to be drunk to do something, it's probably something we shouldn't do.

I watched his plane until it was nothing but a spec in the sky, then Lynn brought me home.

I'm calling this home, isn't that neat? It feels like home.

She gave me a stack of books and tests in all the high school subjects and explained what I really needed to know to succeed at the community college. She thinks I might as well get my GED, too.

Lynn discussed the literature with me and critiqued my essays and other writing. John explained some of the math that I couldn't understand on my own from a book. I did as much learning in seven months as I would have in three more years of high school.

They went skiing in Aspen a few weeks in February and took a cruise in June. I watered their plants and fed their cat while they were gone. Each time, Lynn left me with a long list of assignments. I kept up with my studies and wrote to Charlie every week. Most weeks he wrote back, asking questions about whatever I'd written.

Charlie flew out the thirtieth of June. Lynn and I met him at the airport. He was carrying a package wrapped in birthday-balloon paper with a huge bow on top. He insisted I couldn't open it until after midnight. He let me carry it to the apartment while he brought his suitcase.

The birthday package was soft.

"Some kind of clothes?" I asked.

Since we were alone he teased, "I should make you wait until the tenth, but Lynn and John think your birthday is tomorrow."

"And they think I'm almost twenty, not seventeen."

"You could get in touch with your family and ask them to send you your real birth certificate. Did you have a social security card yet?"

"I had to have one for my bank account, and when I worked in the grapes."

"So call them," Charlie said.

"I can't. I told you before. I've changed too much. That's some other life."

"Okay," he said reluctantly. "It's just things are working out so well with my family, I wish you could have the same."

We joined Lynn and John for dinner and sat and talked with them for a while, then Charlie pointed out that his body thought it was three hours later and we went to the apartment. He wasn't really that tired. We made love until midnight, when I begged to open my present.

He laughed and gave it to me. It was a red hooded sweatshirt with Dickinson College written across the front. I gave him a big hug and a kiss.

"It's the best birthday present I've ever gotten," I said. "I'll wear it all the time. That'll be okay, won't it, even though I'll be at a different college?"

"College of Marin's a two-year school, so it should be okay. People will transfer from there to different places." He paused, then put on a very serious tone. "Lynn says you haven't been doing anything but studying. Promise you'll make friends once you start school."

"I will," I promised. "But I'm going to tell them I have a boyfriend at Dickinson."

"No," he said, using that serious tone again. "I can't be your boyfriend, Sunshine. I know coming out like this and sleeping with you is confusing, but I can't help it. I really care about you, and I love making love with you. But you should find someone closer to your own age."

I flashed on a moment when Amy had been complaining how stupid a boy at school was, and Charlie had used that same voice to make her promise to be nice to the boy, even if he was annoying.

Amy had crumpled her mouth and scrunched her nose, then sighed and said okay. He was talking to me like a six-year-old!

"That's silly," I pouted. "I'm not a child, and the older we get, the less important the age difference is."

"I've never pushed you to explain anything, but where you were, whatever happened to you, that's why you ended up with an old guy like me." He gave me his most charming face.

I laughed. "You've never seemed that old. When we met, I thought you were like twenty."

"But you needed someone to take care of you."

I stopped laughing. He was serious, and he was right. I had needed someone desperately when we came together.

He continued, "You need to find out who you are without me, Sunshine. I need to give you space to do that without me."

"Stop saying *without me*!" I snapped. "I don't want to be without you. I love you."

He looked pained, the same face that followed those days after the crash.

"I don't want to hurt you, Sunshine."

"Then don't."

He paused and just looked at me forever, and then strangled words came out of his mouth. "I've been seeing other people."

The blood drained out of my face down into my feet. I sat without realizing it and stared at him with tears in my eyes. I had to know. "We were together for more than a year. Were you sleeping with other people the whole time?"

"No!" He looked horrified that I'd asked.

"In Sacramento, you... when we started sleeping together, you and Cheryl..."

"No, it wasn't like that. But I'm too old for you, and we're far apart now, and it's going to be that way for a few years. I don't want you to miss out. These are supposed to be the best years of your life. Try having a healthy relationship with someone your own age. It's okay for you to have a boyfriend. Just make sure he deserves you."

Charlie stayed until the tenth, my real birthday.

July 10, 1974

Charlie doesn't love me. He flew back to his other life this morning. He wants me to find someone else. He told me his first night here.

My heart was breaking and I turned away from him, but then I let him spoon with me. I felt his protective affection again, the same as I had that first night in the sleeping bag at the Rainbow Gathering, when I kept all my clothes on. In the middle of the night, we ended up making love. In fact, we made love every night he was here.

He apologized before he left - apologized, for making love to me. Then he asked me to believe he wasn't using me, that he really does care and he'll always be there for me, whether we're together or not, whether or not we ever make love again - that it's never been just sex, that he really does care about me.

He means as a friend. A close friend. That's all I am to him.

Chapter 15: Margie Goes to College

I passed the equivalency exam easily.

Lynn helped me get set with Monday-Wednesday-Friday classes at College of Marin, so I wouldn't have to hitchhike over the mountain as many days. I couldn't afford a car. There was a bus, but it took so long going around Mount Tam and stopping in small towns that it was way faster to hitch. People would line up where the road over the mountain started and drivers knew to stop by the one closest to the mountain because that's who got there first.

I only had one bad ride, when I was running late and got into the car even though my instincts were saying to wait for the next one. The guy started to mess with his fly.

"What do you think you're doing?" I demanded. My mother's voice echoed in my head. I sounded just like she did when she caught me picking some of her flowers.

He fumbled around closing his pants, apologizing and making excuses. "Some girls want more than just a ride," he said.

I stared ahead silently. I could feel my mother's grim face on mine. He'd offered to get me as far as the hospital, but instead took me all the way to school. As he drove away, I glared at the back of his car as if I was making note of his license plate number. He probably was in a panic all day, wondering if the police were going to come for him at work. That was the worst thing that happened during my two years at College of Marin – not bad, considering how my life had been going before that.

At the college there was a job board where I could find part-time work catering for someone's party or babysitting or cleaning. That way I could work more when my classes were easy and less when I had exams. I had to stick with places I could get to by hitching or riding the bus, though.

I'd never seen such beautiful homes. But I didn't have to work much. Besides house sitting while they traveled, I helped Lynn and John with housekeeping and stuff, so they refused to take any rent. Half the time I ate with them, too.

I started with basic freshman classes I would need to transfer to a four-year school. I decided on Astronomy for science. The first day in each class, when they read "Margaret Lewis," they asked me what I preferred being called. I decided on Margie because that's what Lynn and John had been calling me.

I wanted to keep Sunshine for Charlie.

Lynn got me to add a counseling course called Career Planning, too. That class had me really thinking through everything with this book called *What Color Is Your Parachute?* At first I thought it was silly, but I began to know myself better through all the crazy exercises. By the end of that first semester, I decided to major in English and be a writer of some kind.

I had direction again and was making plans. I was writing in my journal more often, too.

October 21, 1974

I had my first real date! Isn't that a kick and a half?

Whenever anyone asks about my Dickinson sweatshirt, I tell them my boyfriend's going there. I know Charlie isn't really my boyfriend, but I don't want to get involved with anyone else until I'm sure who I am, what I want.

There's this guy Al who plays the piano in the Student Union between classes. He can't read music, but once he's heard a song he can play it. That is so amazing. He plays mostly songs that are on the radio, but he does a lot of jazz and blues, too, and it reminds me of the station Dad listens to in the car. I don't know why I always hated it. Anyway, I told Al my boyfriend followed the Grateful Dead for a few years before he started college and Al said they always give a great performance and that he had tickets to see them at Winterland.

Then I had a class and when I came back, there was a girl there. He introduced us, but I've forgotten her name. I was surprised when she gave him a peck on the lips and left. He said she was his ex-girlfriend. She moved on to someone new last summer, but they're still friends. I admitted my Dickinson boyfriend is also an ex- and we're still friends.

Though I'm not sure how true that is. I haven't heard from Charlie since he was here in July and it's almost December now. Half a year. If I didn't believe him before, I guess this makes it crystal clear that he doesn't love me.

Anyway, when Al realized I don't really have a boyfriend, he asked me to go to the concert. He'd bought an extra ticket, hoping to find someone to go with him and figured he'd scalp it if he didn't. I offered to pay for it, but Al said it was his treat.

I wrote Charlie to let him know I was going, with a guy, and that it might be the last chance to see the Grateful Dead perform because they're taking a break from touring. I thought he might come to see them, and check out my date, but that didn't happen. He didn't even write back to me. If Lynn didn't have the same address for him, I'd think my letters were going into outer space or something.

It was a real date, too. Al picked me up and took me to a fancy Indian restaurant before the show, which was almost as great as the concert. I hardly even thought about Charlie at all, except a little during the show. He spent years following this band, so it was kind of a way to get to share that with him. But mostly I stayed focused on the fact I was there with a guy I liked. Not sexually. I don't think of Al that way at all. But I like him. I like talking to him. I like who he is.

Overall, we had a wonderful time, and when he drove me home, he got out and walked me to my apartment door and gave me a sweet kiss, then said goodnight and walked away without trying for anything else.

I don't have any girlfriends and Lynn doesn't know that much about me, so I wrote Charlie about it.

My very first date!

It wasn't long before Al and I ended up in bed, always at his place because I wanted to keep the apartment for myself, and Charlie if he ever came back.

Al and I agreed we were "in like" rather than "in love" so the sex was fun but not emotionally charged. Today we'd call it friends with benefits. I didn't explain that to Charlie. I was afraid he'd think I was selling myself short again. I wasn't. My relationship with Al fit my needs at that point. Of course, I was still in love with Charlie, though I was in denial because I knew it was hopeless.

Lynn and John met Al one day when he picked me up to go for a hike in Muir Woods and Lynn invited him to join us for Christmas dinner. He was the only person who knew where I lived, so they'd probably noticed him come by for me other times. They may have realized I'd spent nights away from the apartment, too.

I got a Christmas card from Charlie, with a note saying he was doing well in school, Lynn had told him I was too. He said the date sounded great and asked me if I liked the Dead. He wished me a merry Christmas and said he would be spending the holidays with his family.

I was disappointed but relieved that I wouldn't have to deal with the feelings I still had for Charlie while Al was there.

That was the best Christmas I'd ever had. Lynn and John really got into the holiday. They had two kids who were both living abroad and couldn't be there, but they still decorated the whole house with me helping. On Christmas day, Al came over and played their piano while we sang carols. Then we shared gifts. Everyone had gotten something for everyone else. I still have the yin-yang necklace Al gave me. We hadn't shared much history, but he seemed to know intuitively that mine was a combination of light and dark.

My relationship with Al kept me out of trouble as I started meeting more guys who would have liked to screw me without caring. I made more friends, but didn't have sex with anyone but Al.

January 4, 1975

I am so proud of myself! Someone in my Career class threw a party. Al wasn't there and I had too much to drink - not on purpose. I didn't realize at first that the punch was spiked. But that's not why I'm proud.

A really cute guy caught me in the hallway outside the bathroom, pulled me into an incredibly hot kiss, and started walking us into a bedroom. I said, "Hell no!" and pushed him so hard he almost fell down. I held my head high and walked away haughtily. He left me alone.

I am so not a slut! Even drunk!

Whenever I was home at mealtime, Lynn and John would invite me to join them. They routinely discussed current events as they ate, and I realized I'd been so wrapped up in myself that I hadn't even noticed while major changes happened in the world around me. I'd left home the spring of 1972. A lot had happened in three years.

While Charlie and I were stoned or drunk, abortion had been made legal and we'd finally finished getting out of Vietnam. Patty Hearst was kidnapped and then helped her captors rob a bank. Charlie and I were living on the Eel River with no electricity while people were glued to the Watergate Hearings on television and I'd barely noticed when Nixon resigned because I was getting ready to start college.

As a kid, I'd wanted to be a journalist or work in the Foreign Service! So my second semester I took a political science class on current affairs.

January 24, 1975

I feel so stupid. I need to keep my mouth shut in class. There's this guy Jason that I used to talk to at the Student Union and now he thinks I'm appallingly ignorant—he's from New York City with a Russian Jew father and an African mother, so he's completely aware of the racial and ethnic issues of both. Almost every minority group on campus has asked him to join them. And this girl, Sarah, is Lakota, what we call Sioux Indians, and she's so informed about all the stuff going on with the occupation of Alcatraz and Wounded Knee. She had family killed there and says there will never be justice for Native Americans while the federal government controls reservation politics.

I'd grown up in a small town. There were a couple Puerto Rican kids in my classes, but their skin wasn't any darker than mine with a good tan. I didn't think of them as any more different than the Greek or Italian kids. However, my parents probably wouldn't have wanted me dating any of them, even though they talked about civil rights as a good thing. My world was becoming larger.

As I became more informed I participated in heated discussions.

February 28, 1975

I remember what I was like in eighth grade social studies, when we were studying current events in relation to world history. I was really smart and a good debater. I'm starting to feel like that again.

We've been discussing whether Nixon should have faced criminal charges along with his key aides and whether the use of force by the Weathermen or the I.R.A. can ever be justified when innocents are often killed, and whether the beginning of construction on the Alaska Pipeline is the beginning of independence from Middle Eastern oil or a death knell for the environment.

I am so good at this! I can make convincing arguments for either side, which is such great exercise for my brain, but I'm also giving my opinions based on facts I've researched. And people listen! Jason and I continue the debate over lunch half the time, too. He doesn't think I'm hopeless anymore.

Sarah said she's going back to the reservation at the end of the semester. She says there's too much work to be done there to play in school.

I was still seeing Al when classes ended. Everyone thought I turned twenty-one on the first of July. Lynn and John took me to a nice dinner where I ordered a glass of wine with them. Al was only twenty, so we had ice cream earlier that day.

Charlie was the only one who knew my real birthday and age. If I'd never run away, I'd have just finished high school. Instead, I had a year of college already.

Thanks to Charlie, my life was coming together. I longed to see him, but the letter he included in my birthday card explained that he'd be busy all summer, earning as much as he could for his school expenses by working in his father's law firm.

"I don't want to owe him any more than necessary when I'm done with school," he wrote. "His firm deals mainly with big business and contracts, so I know I'd never want to join them, but learning what they do is an education in itself. Next summer I'll find a different kind of firm to intern with." Then he asked, "How's your boyfriend? You haven't said anything since your first date, but Lynn said he came for Christmas. She liked him. Is he good to you? Don't settle for less, Sunshine."

I hadn't heard from Charlie since his Christmas card and I'd stopped writing him regularly. It was hard to think of him as just a friend. I curled up with my journal after I answered his letter.

July 10, 1975

At least he didn't talk about anyone. WHY does that still matter to me!? He'll probably never be satisfied with one woman. I never could have done that open marriage thing. Even with Al, we've agreed it's mutually exclusive and if that changes, we let the other person know immediately.

Charlie's life is coming together too, and it's not going to include me. I have GOT to accept that. I sent him a short note that turned into a long letter. I told him how good I was at debating in current affairs class and how good it feels to be informed and looked at like a smart person. I told him Al and I are still seeing each other and that he's good to me. I told him it's mutually exclusive and I like that, so he was probably right that I'm not a natural-born slut. I did NOT explain that Al and I are just close friends who sleep together.

Al might be a good person for the kind of relationship I thought I had with Charlie, but the risks outweigh the benefits. It's better the way it is.

My analytical side was flourishing and I felt good about myself.

The second year at College of Marin I took as many classes as they would let me. Tuition was free there and a four-year school would cost money, so I wanted to be sure I'd only need two years when I transferred. That didn't leave much time to work. While my expenses were low, I still had to buy books and other things.

In September, Al suggested applying for financial aid. "You'll need it when you transfer anyway."

Unfortunately, even with the three years my identification added, I was still young enough that I needed to include parent information for financial aid.

"But I don't even know where my parents are," I told the woman, sticking with the story that matched my identification.

"I'm sorry, but you are required to include their information to get any assistance," she explained. "Unless you're married. Then they consider you independent."

I told Al I needed to get married to finish school.

"My parents are helping me," he said. "And there's this girl I've been talking to a lot in my music classes? I asked her out today and she said yes, so we should probably cool it for now. Are you okay with that?"

"Of course," I said. "It's what we agreed on."

"Are you sure?"

"Yeah," I said.

There was a sinking feeling in my stomach, because our relationship was an anchor in my life and I wasn't sure what this change would bring, but it wasn't painful.

"Good," Al was saying. "But about needing to be married? My friend Arnie might help you. His parents disowned him for dating a black girl. Then she dumped him for cheating on her, but he won't tell his parents."

"He cheated on her?"

"Yeah, but if you guys get married just for show, that won't matter, will it?" asked Al.

Arnie was all for the idea. He was struggling to stay in school.

Since Charlie had gone back to his plan to be a lawyer like his father, I wrote to him and explained the situation, how Arnie was willing to get married without strings so we could both get financial aid. I was hoping Charlie would make the same offer, but he didn't. What really surprised me is that he phoned me at Lynn's. She took a walk to give me privacy.

"Hey, Sunshine."

I hadn't heard his voice in over a year. It brought back the old feelings immediately. I forced myself to stay calm and businesslike as he asked questions about Arnie and our plan.

"It's not really legal if it's not a consummated marriage," he said. "But no one's going to demand pictures or anything. You should share the same address for at least a few months, though. That should satisfy any inquiry into the legitimacy of the relationship."

"Lawyer talk," I teased. "You aren't even in law school yet. I'll crash on his couch for a few months."

"I destroyed your letter. Don't put anything else in writing that makes it sound like the marriage is fake. And make sure you keep track of him until you finish school, so you can get a divorce and not be stuck with a missing husband."

"I hadn't thought of that. I will." That's why he'd called, to make sure I wouldn't get caught. He'd do that for any friend.

There was a pause and I thought he was going to say goodbye, but he asked, "How's your boyfriend?"

There was another pause while I tried to decide what to say, and then another question from Charlie, "Why didn't the two of you get married?"

It needed to be the truth. "Um... actually, we weren't ever going that direction. And we've broken it off because there's someone he wants to date now."

"So you're not serious about anyone?"

"No. It's okay. I'm pretty busy with school. I'm not doing the slut thing, either."

"Good," Charlie said. "It sounds like you're happy with yourself."

"Yeah," I said. "I am."

The call left me confused, though.

September 27, 1975

Charlie almost sounded happy, or relieved, that I'm not serious about anyone. But I haven't seen him in over a year, and he's the one who insisted I should find someone my own age, or at least closer to it.

One Christmas card and one birthday card—he hasn't been missing me much. Of course, when he stopped writing, I did too, mostly.

I looked it up at the counseling office. If he's going to be a lawyer, he's got to finish the four-year degree, then do three more years in law school. So maybe he stopped writing because he's working as much as I am, maybe even more.

No. I'm doing it again. Trying to convince myself he does love me. I've got to get over it. He's probably just happy that I'm doing well on my own.

Arnie and I got married at city hall right away and I started using his address for everything. For a couple of months, I crashed on the floor at his place most nights, until he got a new girlfriend. Then I went back to staying in my own apartment every night.

I didn't tell Lynn and John what was going on. It was kind of embarrassing. They probably assumed I'd been staying with Al all those nights and it hadn't worked out. When Christmas came around, Lynn didn't ask if I wanted to include him.

Charlie called their house while I was there for Christmas and I let him know I was following his directions about the phony marriage. He said he'd hoped to come out, but his mom was having some health issues. He sounded like it was serious but didn't say what.

With Lynn's help, I applied to Sonoma State. It would mean moving off on my own, but she insisted I should still consider their place home. I got a long letter from Charlie with my birthday card that year.

July 10, 1976

Charlie's doing an internship with a law firm that does lots of pro bono work (that means they do it for free). He sounds happy with that. He said he'd planned to fly out for my birthday, then his mom had to have emergency surgery and she's okay now, but he can't take more time off.

He didn't mention any girls, so he's probably keeping it casual.

Typical Charlie.

Sonoma State was almost an hour north of Mill Valley, in Sonoma County. Coming in as a junior, I could live off campus, which was a lot cheaper than the dorms. Lynn drove me there and, through one of the bulletin boards, we found a girl with a two bedroom apartment.

Cindy was a sweet and naïve twenty-year-old. I was really nineteen that summer, but felt much older, and was still claiming the extra three years. Her boyfriend was in his thirties. Cindy explained up front that if he ever got around to proposing, she'd move in with him and I'd have to take over the lease and find another roommate. But she went on to tell me she spent most nights at his place, so I figured that he liked things exactly the way they were and I'd be done with school and moving on before he ever proposed. When I met him, I could tell I was right.

Of course she wanted to know about me, too. Cindy assumed Lynn was my mother and I was single and away from home for the first time, like she was. I'd never mentioned my bogus marriage to Lynn, so I didn't say anything about that to Cindy, either. Since Arnie had headed south to Los Angeles to finish college, she would never meet him. Arnie and I had shared new addresses and agreed to inform each other of any changes. He didn't want to get stuck in a not-real marriage, either.

I didn't have much time to write in my journal, but I did over Christmas.

December 27, 1976

As a married person, I've gotten some grants and work-study jobs that cover my school costs and most of my rent. Fifteen units make you full time, and you don't have to pay for extra units you take on top of that, so I'm taking eighteen every semester to get the most I can out of this place.

There's no time for real dating, but I've had a few casual encounters with classmates, guys in the same situation as me, with no time. I'm still not doing the drunk thing, so it's always with mutual respect but no expectations.

I went to Lynn and John's for Christmas. Their whole family was there this year, but I had some time alone with Lynn. I talked to her about relationships and Charlie. Lynn agreed the two of us could never have a casual relationship, which is how she described what I've got at school. She is so different from my mother. I think I could be fifty and still not have that kind of talk with Mom.

Anyway, Lynn said it's not just me, that Charlie cares too much about me to be casual, too. She didn't say it, but the reality is he cares too much for that but not enough to have a real relationship. While I was there, he called their house to wish everyone a Merry Christmas. He talked a long time with their son. I talked with him last. He said he'd wanted to come out and see me, but he was working multiple jobs and couldn't get away.

He probably has a new girlfriend.

Why did I say that? I really need to move on with my life.

Aside from the call from Charlie, which left me off kilter for a few hours, spending Christmas with Lynn and John and all of their family was great. It was the first time I met their son and their daughter, and their spouses and kids, and everyone treated me like part of the family. Such a warm feeling.

It made me remember that last tense Christmas with my parents as if it happened in a previous life. I was so stupid not to catch on that Dad had given me the wrong gift. I didn't even realize it was a diamond necklace. As far as I knew, it was glass. I'm glad they worked past that, though. I was really childish to be upset with my mom for forgiving him. I'm glad they're happy together.

I've been thinking about calling them, but what I would say? I'm nineteen now, they couldn't make me come home, but how would I explain never calling them before? And I don't know if they could still get Charlie in trouble. If I didn't mention him, I'd have to make up a whole different life. And I don't want to. I want to enjoy this wonderful Christmas with this family that makes me feel so welcome.

What kind of daughter would call to tell her parents she was happier away from them? It's better to stay in my new life and let them have theirs.

Chapter 16: Independence

I worked full time every day that summer, off the books so it wouldn't hurt my financial aid, at a restaurant where I made good tip money.

July 10, 1977

Happy birthday to me! Twenty and I'll graduate from college before my next birthday! I'm a real hotshot!

I worked all day, except for my dinner break. I treated myself to abalone, the most expensive dinner on the menu. Aside from that, I've been saving like crazy.

As soon as I graduate, I'm going to move down to Marin and get a job in the City. That's what they call San Francisco. If I have enough to last through fall, I can always go north and work harvest if I have to, but I'd rather have a job by then.

I got a postcard from Lynn and John wishing me happy birthday from Rome. They plan to stay in Europe at least a year. They want to spend some time with their grandkids and John wants to see more of the historical sites and cathedrals. They've got a new renter in the apartment house sitting for them.

So I'll need to find a place to live when I graduate.

Charlie sent me a birthday card, with a note telling me how much he's studying and working. He doesn't want to owe his dad or anyone else any money when he graduates, and the school he's in is really expensive. He'd hoped to finish in three years, but it's taking him the full four. We'll both graduate next spring! So much for the big deal about age difference.

I'm borrowing a little bit because this English major demands so much time reading. I'm enrolled in a fiction writing course, too. Hopefully my work-study will be enough to pay my rent and stuff. If it's not, I'll pick up something else.

In the end, I took a job restocking a store at night so I wouldn't dip into my savings. When my roommate realized I would be alone for Christmas, she offered to have me spend the holidays with her family in some little inland town. Cindy spent so much time with her boyfriend I didn't really know her all that well and she was kind of annoying when she was at the apartment, so I was glad I had a good excuse to turn her down.

"I have to work," I said, doing my best to sound disappointed.

"It's Christmas. You'd only be gone two or three days."

"I have to restock the store. They depend on me to be there every night except Christmas itself. This is their busiest time of year. I'll be okay. I'll treat myself to dinner out."

So I had my first solitary Christmas.

I did go out to eat, but there weren't any nice places open. The little dive I found served seafood, though, so that was a special treat, until I spent the next twenty-four hours in the bathroom throwing up and miserable.

That last semester I focused on my studies and saving money because I knew I'd be moving as soon as I graduated. I had no time for dating, but took some time out each week for a romp in bed with my current buddy, Jake. Part way through the semester he already had a job waiting for him in Seattle. He shocked me by asking me to move there with him.

I explained that I had my own plans.

It made me reassess my relationships.

March 28, 1978

I had no idea Jake was going to ask me to move to Seattle with him. I thought he was as detached as I was, but he made it clear he was not. I haven't slept with many people these last two years, but I realize there were a couple others that I brushed off because they got too serious.

It's not about Charlie. Not anymore. Aside from notes with Christmas and birthday cards, we haven't even been writing. I haven't seen him in four years, and we've talked on the phone twice. The last time was Christmas before last. He called while I was at Lynn's. I'm not even sure that was to talk to me as much as them. No, it's not about Charlie.

I'm not going to depend on anyone but me. I'll have my English degree and with that I'll get a job and take care of myself. I won't have time for a major relationship because I'll be writing in all my spare time.

I didn't consider the possibility that I was afraid to care.

My identification said I would be twenty-four that summer, but I was actually twenty when I graduated. Arnie had filed for divorce and it was final in April, so that was done. He was going on for more school, but had found someone he wanted to marry for real.

Charlie would see the humor in the fact I'd never had sex with my ex-husband. I couldn't share that joke with anyone else without sounding like a slut. Charlie had never thought of me that way, even when I was acting like one. I missed him, but it was time to say thank you for everything he'd done and move on.

I bought Charlie a graduation card and wrote a long letter to enclose with it. I told him the sexless marriage joke and my plans to move to the Bay Area and work in the City at any job I could get to support myself and spend my spare time writing. I stressed that I was ready to be totally independent, and thanked him for everything he'd done that made this happen. I told him he'd been a true friend and I'd learned so much from him. I apologized for trying to make more of our relationship than there'd ever really been. I admitted that he'd been right – I'd been too young. Despite everything, I'd been a silly little girl with her first serious crush.

June 1, 1978

I got a graduation card from Charlie today with the longest letter he's ever sent. I just mailed mine yesterday. He probably hasn't gotten it yet.

His whole family's going to his graduation. His father's really proud that he got accepted into law school. He'll be busy studying and clerking in law firms the next three years. He sounds a lot different from the Charlie I met hitchhiking. Of course, I'm different, too. He said he wished he could come out for my graduation, but it's the same weekend as his. He thinks Lynn and John will come to mine. I guess he doesn't know they're still in Europe.

It's funny. He sounds different and the same.

He signed it "Love, Charlie." But he was probably writing a lot of cards and did that without thinking. He didn't say "I love you" or anything like that.

People sign cards and letters like that all the time.

But Charlie had never signed a letter to me that way. I tucked it into my journal to save it, even though I knew better than to believe it meant anything special.

I graduated with honors a few days later.

June 7, 1978

I've got my degree. The piece of paper is what's important. The whole cap and gown thing's expensive, so I didn't do it. There wasn't anyone coming to watch me graduate anyway. I did get two cards, though. Charlie's and then Lynn and John sent one with a check, which was awfully nice of them.

I haven't seen them since Christmas before last. I was kind of a project for them, I guess. I wonder if their new renter's a project, too. Probably not. It sounds like they may stay in Europe near their grandkids another year. The renter will be house sitting.

I haven't heard from Charlie since I sent him that long letter telling him thank you. He's probably been busy with finals and graduation, too.

When I saw Jake in his cap and gown I had a twinge of regret. I'm not sure if it was because I didn't do the ceremony thing or if it's because I didn't realize how he felt about me.

I'm feeling pretty alone right now.

But that's part of being independent, I guess. It's time to make my own choices, decide on my own future.

I used the ride board to get down to Marin last week and I'm set to move in with a girl a few years older than me in a Tiburon apartment complex. It's a two-bedroom. She was leery of me because I don't have a job yet, but when I gave her first, last, and two months up front, she decided to give me a try.

All that extra work and scrimping paid off, but I better get a job soon because I only have enough left to eat and get back and forth to the City for a month or so.

The day after I moved in with Joanne, I signed on with a temporary agency to do office work in the city. My school work had prepared me to type and file, but it wasn't really using my English degree. I didn't care. I was independent.

In mid-June I temped in a two-girl office in San Francisco and they hired me full time. The job wasn't challenging, but it was fun because the other girl and the guys we worked with were all nice. My roommate Joanne drove into the city every day, but she started later than I did so I couldn't ride with her.

I didn't care about that, either.

I loved taking the bus to the ferry, then the ferry to the cable car that dropped me off right by my building in the financial district of San Francisco. I could have walked, but taking the cable car was fun. Every Monday, I'd buy one rose from the dark-eyed guy selling them on the corner by my office, except for the days he flirted and gave it to me for free. For lunch, I'd get a sandwich from The Haven or another deli. It was always something loaded with sprouts and other veggies. Then I'd sit in Union Square to eat it.

Getting a regular paycheck made me feel rich. The other girl in the office, Rhonda, had been a stewardess, so she took me shopping at Macy's. She had me wearing makeup for the first time in my life and I got a haircut at an expensive salon that made me look more professional, too. I was so busy working and having fun, I didn't write in my journal for weeks, not even on my birthday.

August 1, 1978

I actually have girlfriends to do things with! Joanne and Rhonda. When Rhonda realized they'd missed my birthday, they took me out to dinner and made a big deal about it. The funny part is, they think I turned twenty-four on the first, but they took me out on the tenth, when I was really turning twenty-one. I'd tell them, but there's too much I'd rather leave in the past.

We go out every Friday after work. There are a bunch of bars that serve free hors d'oeuvres during happy hour. Our favorite place serves all-you-want seafood and Swedish meatballs, along with finger foods. I guess they make their money on the people who booze it up. We each get one drink and then eat our fill of the food.

Once happy hour is over, Rhonda heads home. She lives in the City and can take a bus. I ride back to Marin with Joanne in her car. We change, then go to Sausalito to dance. My favorite bar has backgammon tables, too, but sometimes Persian guys are using all of them, playing for money, I think. At least that would explain the intensity.

Neither of us drink much - we're too busy dancing. It's so weird to do the bump with strangers, but that's the music they play. We leave before the last song of the night, to avoid guys who think bumping means more than it does and the really creepy ones who just watch all night, then try to glom onto someone they never even talked to before last call.

So I was out and talking to guys and dancing with them, but I wasn't dating and went without sex for months. I still had no interest in a serious relationship and I didn't want to hurt someone like I had Jake, but one-night stands did not appeal to me either.

Then one Friday a guy I was talking to over Swedish meatballs asked me to dinner the next night. He wanted to go to some fancy restaurant way out in the boondocks of Marin County. It wasn't even in a town. When I told Joanne I'd accepted a date in the middle of nowhere with a guy I'd just met, and told him where I lived, she thought I was nuts.

"He could be some kind of psycho!" she cried. "Or a rapist!"

I knew she was right, but I argued anyway. "He could also be a nice guy who wants a date because he wouldn't go eat at a fancy restaurant by himself. Or maybe he found my conversation scintillating and wants to get to know me better."

"Fine," she said. "He could be a nice guy. But wear a one-piece pantsuit with the zipper up the back and a light jacket on top. That'll make it difficult for him to try anything and send the message that he better not."

"I don't have anything like that."

"I do," she said. "You can borrow it."

I shook my head. "I'll be fine."

"You *will* borrow it," said Joanne. "And I *will* be at the apartment when he arrives and I *will* get the name and address of this restaurant. I'll get his license plate number, too."

I had a real friend watching out for me. I borrowed the outfit.

As my date walked me to his car, Joanne shouted, "Don't forget we're going on that hike tomorrow morning with the guys from downstairs, so don't be out too late."

There were no such plans and we barely knew the gay guys downstairs, but I was home by eleven. All my date got was a closed mouth kiss goodnight.

October 14, 1978

The poor guy was really trying to be nice, and the dinner was insanely expensive, but he was so incredibly boring, and he didn't know when to stop talking. We were the last people in the restaurant. He didn't notice them getting ready to close or the looks they were giving us until they started putting the chairs upside down on the tables!

When he asked me, I was thinking of my first date, when Al took me to that Indian restaurant that was so fancy with a whole dessert tray and everything - that's why I didn't brush the guy off like I usually do. But it was the company that made that first time so memorable. Okay, the Dead might have been memorable anyway, but not as much as they were WITH good company.

I haven't really had many dates. In college it was mostly hopping into bed with a buddy whenever you had a few minutes to let off steam together. Dating takes time, and it might not even lead to sex. I've been brushing off people when they ask me out. I'm going to stop doing that. I might find out someone's better company than I expect, and if I don't, well, I don't have to give them a second chance.

After that, I started going out more often, usually ending it after one or two dates and seldom ending up in bed. It opened my world to the good restaurants, museums, theater, and everything else available in San Francisco. I was just another girl enjoying my independence in a beautiful city, enjoying being treated like a lady. I stuck to the short version of having no family and having put myself through college.

I still sent Lynn and John a Christmas card that year, with a very short note saying I was doing well and staying busy. I'd never heard from Charlie after my long letter, but he didn't have my address, either, so I sent him a card with a simple "Merry Christmas, Hope you're doing well" note on it.

Joanne didn't have enough time off to fly home for Christmas that first year, so we put up a tree in the apartment and decided to have a turkey dinner. She invited a couple of friends from her work who didn't have anywhere to go; I invited one of the guys I'd been dating. I bought a cookbook because neither of us had ever cooked a major meal like that. Fortunately, pies and a side dish were coming with the guests.

Once the turkey was in the oven, Joanne called her family and they talked for an hour.

Christmas 1978

There's nothing to do in the kitchen right now. I'm in my room trying not to listen to Joanne laughing and chatting with her parents and brothers and nieces and everyone else who's gathered for the holiday. I never had a holiday like that. The closest was when Lynn and John's kids came home, and that was borrowed family.

When our guests arrived, I managed to shake off the gloom. We had a good time together and the guy I'd been dating stayed over that night. That made him special. On the rare occasions I decided to have sex with someone, we'd normally do it at their place. That relationship lasted a couple months, but he started getting serious and I broke it off.

March 10, 1979

He really is a nice guy, but he makes all these assumptions that aren't true. He'd be horrified if he knew about my teen years. I don't think I'll ever find a guy I can be completely honest with.

I still went out on some dates, but sex was not going to happen. I threw out my pills and bought some condoms to carry in my purse, just in case I had an uncontrollable urge or stumbled into the perfect man or something.

We'd gotten friendly enough with the gay guys downstairs to joke about my lonely condoms.

The guys downstairs told Joanne she should get some condoms, too. The pill doesn't protect you from disease, and they said there are rumors that something new is killing gay men. In the Bay Area, there's no way to be sure who's straight and who swings both ways.

I know bad things can happen to me. I'll stick with condoms. IF I ever have sex again.

When I'd been working for almost a year, Rhonda got married. I was invited to the wedding, but her sisters were the bridesmaids. She stayed on a few months, then she got pregnant and quit when she started to show. The last time I saw her was at the baby shower. We were on different paths. The woman who replaced Rhonda had kids in college.

November 14, 1979

Betty's nice, but she definitely won't ever go out with us on Friday nights. She's working to help her son and two daughters pay for college. She has no idea what it's like to be twenty-something and single. She married her high school sweetheart at eighteen and she believes her children (at least her daughters) are virgins and going to stay that way until they get married. She doesn't know what college and dorms are like and I'm not going to be the one to tell her.

That year Joanne flew home to be with her family for Christmas. I invited the gay duo from downstairs for dinner, but they canceled.

Christmas, 1979

My second Christmas alone. No puking seafood this time. I went ahead and bought a turkey and cooked it with all the trimmings, like my mom used to. We'll be eating leftovers for a month, but at least it smells like the holiday.

I thought about calling Lynn and John, but I haven't heard anything from them since last Christmas, and there wasn't even a note on their card. They're probably still in Europe. Besides, I'm not really their family or anything. I don't belong anywhere, but I never did.

Joanne will be back for New Year's Eve. We've already planned where we're going and we got new dresses. I've got a good roommate and friend. I shouldn't be upset that she has family to go visit for Christmas.

She's normal.

Joanne ran into her high school boyfriend while she was home and the flame rekindled. She came back for a month, long enough to end her job on good terms and to pack up everything to leave for Chicago permanently.

We had fun New Year's Eve, but it was bittersweet, knowing it was the last time. Her boyfriend drove out with his truck so he could help her pack and move everything back for her. I offered to pay her for the couch and dining room table that were hers before I moved in, but she didn't want them anyway and refused to take the money. The boyfriend, fiancé I guess, was a really nice guy and I didn't mind the noises that came from her room in the night, except that they reminded me that I was alone.

January 6, 1980
Joanne left today. They didn't need a trailer because she left all the big stuff - even her bed. Hopefully that will make it easier to rent out her room. The lease is mine now. We said we'll keep in touch, but we were friends because we were here together. People move on.

I kept the apartment and from February to December went through six roommates. The apartment was nice enough, especially since Joanne left so much furniture. But I discovered good roommates were hard to find. The night before my birthday, the girl who'd just moved in on the first had a fight with her boyfriend.

July 10, 1980
That asshole punched a hole in the wall and my new roommate broke a window. I kicked them both out. She came back this morning and I made her take her things. She actually complained when I told her I was keeping the whole security deposit. She's lucky I gave her the rent - I probably won't find anyone else until the beginning of next month.

I've had it. I'm making a list of rules and if they don't like them, they can find somewhere else to live.

No guys over. I'm not going through a repeat of last night's drama! And no drugs. Not even pot. They can do that somewhere else.

I should say no alcohol because I'll kill the next drunken weepy roommate wailing over some jerk. Or maybe just limited wine drinking at home. And don't drink mine! Or eat my food! For that matter, how about quiet after ten? That would be nice since I have to get up for the commute every day.

And don't keep asking me to go out and do things with you. I don't want to make temporary friends who'll move on when something better comes along.

They're just looking for husbands anyway. You'd think it was the 1950s. They only move in because they're from out of state and no one else will take them until they prove they're going to stay. Most of them have temp jobs for the same reason - businesses don't want to hire someone who may get homesick and leave as soon as they're done training.

I don't care if they go home or move on to a better place. Being a temporary situation is fine with me - everything in life is temporary.

It's no wonder I couldn't keep a roommate. I did have them sign a list of rules before moving in, and when they annoyed me, my rants were blasted straight at them. I stayed home every weekend, reading my journals and remembering the things I'd never recorded. In a new notebook, I filled in the worst details I'd glossed over at the time, especially Harrisburg. That darkness spilled over into my present.

Work kept me sane.

October 19, 1980

I still love my commute.

The current roommate had a major snit because I called her the wrong name this morning. She went into a laundry list of all the reasons I'm impossible to live with. But her bitching washed off me as I rode the ferry across the bay.

Betty's not as much fun as Rhonda was, but she's more efficient, so the work goes smoothly and everything gets done on time. We both got bonuses last week. And she is funny, without meaning to be: She keeps telling me I need to be more open with men.

If she only knew!

But she only sees me in the office and our boss is an old guy, his assistant is married, and the salesmen just annoy me when they come in and try to flirt. Even if they were cute, I like my job and Rhonda told me how she lost one by having an affair with a co-worker. Betty just wants to see me meet a nice young man to marry. She of course assumes I'm a virgin, and if six months of celibacy could restore it, I would be. The last roommate complained my problem is that I need to get laid. I don't think so. I'm kind of done with sex. Maybe if Betty's nice young man materializes I'll change my mind.

I was between roommates again when Christmas rolled around. There was no one in my life to share the holiday. I hadn't bothered sending cards out. I bought some deli turkey and crab and curled up with Stephen King's new book, *Firestarter.* I imagined Betty cringing at my selection on any day, but particularly Christmas. Good thing she'd never know. I didn't like it as much as *The Stand* and decided to take it back to the library unfinished.

Joanne had left her little TV behind. I wasn't sure if she simply forgot it or if she thought I'd need it for company. Usually it gathered dust, but I turned it on to tune out. The only movie that would come in was *It's a Wonderful Life.* I turned it off, thinking it was the worst of the awful cheery movies shown at the holidays, sure my guardian angel would give me a shove off the Golden Gate if I was about to jump.

I tried to read *Firestarter* again, then put it down and looked at the phone. I still knew the number, of course.

Christmas, 1980

I called my parents today - my real parents back in New York - but when my mother answered it was clear she was irritated. It reminded me of our last Christmas together.

I hung up without saying a word and stayed on my bed, hugging my pillow and crying about everything that's ever happened to me and how no one's ever really cared about me and no one would miss me if I was gone. How Lynn and John were nice to me because Charlie asked them and this year my Christmas card from Charlie didn't even have a note.

And I didn't send cards to any of them. Cards don't count anyway. People send cards to their dentists.

My last real contact from Charlie was the note on my graduation card and that was mostly about him.

I was a charity project, that's all.

I'm alone in the world and always will be.

I could cease to exist and no one would notice. I've been out of college for two and a half years and I'm still working in a job a high school graduate could do. The world wouldn't miss me either.

God, I'm a whiner. Chocolate. I need chocolate.

I made cocoa. It got me through the day and I managed to slog through the rest of the month. It helped that I didn't get many days off work. And I got a new roommate in January.

We both knew it was temporary; Patty planned to land a lawyer or a stock broker for a husband by the end of the year. I told myself that was fine for her, but I wasn't the type of person who needed other people.

Then the spring of 1981 I met Dylan.

Chapter 17: Dylan

It was a beautiful March Tuesday, unusually warm and sunny. I was eating my sandwich in Union Square when this incredibly handsome guy asked if he could sit on the bench by me. He was in jeans and a western-cut white shirt, but they were clean and neat and he had an air of confidence that made it clear immediately that the only reason he wasn't in a suit is that he didn't have to be.

March 10, 1981

I met someone today. His name is Dylan.

He engaged me in conversation - saying we chatted does not describe the way he drew me out. I stuck to my standard story that glossed over my lack of family or roots, but I told him all about working in the City, Joanne and the string of roommates after her, and even how I studied English to be a writer but the only thing I write now is business letters for my boss and a journal for myself. When it was time for me to go back to work, he'd barely told me anything about himself, but he asked to meet me at the office after work.

He arrived with a dozen roses a few minutes before the day ended. The cylindrical vase I had on my desk held my one flower for the week, but there was room for three more. Betty went and got water in the pottery jug one of her kids had made when they were young. We put the rest in there.

"Keep it on your desk," I told her. "You have the spot for it and I can still enjoy them."

"Why thank you." She turned to Dylan with a smile. "Both of you. Well, I've got a bus to catch. I'll see you tomorrow, Margie. Nice meeting you Dylan." As she walked out past him, she turned to give me an approving nod and a wink. She obviously thought he was husband material.

"Are you ready?" he asked. "I thought we could go to dinner."

I thought he meant one of the restaurants there in the financial district, a short walk away, but he flagged down a taxi and told them to take us to the Cliff House. He almost sounded like a tour guide, explaining how the original building survived the 1906 earthquake, was destroyed by fire a year later, then rebuilt.

I'd heard of the Cliff House but hadn't ever been there.

"It looks out over the ocean and the seafood is excellent," he finished. The taxi was moving slowly across the city at rush hour.

"I love crab, but I live in Tiburon." He was so suave it made me uncomfortable. "I'll need to get back to Van Ness in time to catch the last bus home. It shouldn't be a problem; they run pretty late."

"I live in Marin, too. I'll make sure you get home. Tell me more. What do you write in your journal?"

"It's too personal," I replied. "Besides, you haven't told me anything about yourself."

"Ah, true. You're going off to dinner with a stranger." He smiled. "Okay. What would you like to know?"

"Everything."

"I was born on a dark, stormy night," he said melodramatically.

I laughed gently. "Maybe not everything."

His laughter joined mine. "Actually, I was born on a sunny afternoon, or so I've been told. I don't really remember the day myself."

"Where did you grow up?" It might make him ask about my childhood, but I was curious.

"Ah, a good question. My parents divorced when I was six. They spent more time fighting over custody than actually having me, so mostly I lived with my grandfather, until they put me in Andover."

He sounded as if everyone knew what that was, so I resorted to, "Really?"

"Yes. I lived and studied with a bunch of randy boys until I went on to Yale, which was a slightly more mature version of the same lifestyle."

"Oh." If he went to Yale, Andover must be a boarding school. He was obviously rich, way out of my league, even if I'd never left home.

"I was supposed to go on to medical school, but my senior year, my grandfather died and left me his place in San Rafael, his boat, and enough money to avoid working. For the time being, anyway."

"That must be nice." I might as well get a good meal out of him before he decided to stop slumming with the little secretary.

He told me more about his boat and places he'd sailed and then we were at the Cliff House. It was a cool-looking old building. They knew him and seated us right by a window. He ordered for both of us.

If he hadn't still been in his jeans, I would have felt out of place in my secretarial skirt and blouse. They get me wolf whistles from construction workers and they're fine for the after-work bars we used to go to and regular restaurants, but for a dinner date at the Cliff House, I'd have dressed up. Most of the other customers looked like they were ready for the opera or symphony after dinner - something formal. But Dylan didn't seem to notice. He looked at me the whole time he talked and I focused on him and what he was saying.

I relaxed and enjoyed myself. Betty will be proud.

As we ate, he told me stories of sailing with his grandfather as a kid, all along the coast of California and even down to South America.

"Gramps always wanted to sail around the world with me," he said. "But my parents forbade it. It was one thing they actually agreed on. They put me in Andover partially because they were afraid he'd take off with me in spite of their protests."

"That's such an amazing way to grow up." My discomfort was forgotten. I was entranced by his tales. "I always dreamed of traveling and having adventures, but I've never been outside the United States, except we went to Niagara Falls once when I was little." It had been a school trip, but I didn't want him asking for details. He didn't.

"Have you ever sailed?" he asked while we waited for desert.

"No. I've been in a canoe a few times."

"You do know how to swim?" He sounded concerned.

"Of course. We lived by the Great Lakes and I learned to swim in them."

"Which lake?"

I tried to remember which lake was by Chicago but my mind went blank with panic. I avoided a direct answer. "We lived by a couple of them, at different times. I was too little to really remember much except being warned about undertow and playing in the waves."

"Well, then. I have a special surprise for you when we're done here."

Betty will NOT be happy with what I did next. Instead of telling the taxi driver we were going across the Golden Gate, he gave the man an address in the City that turned out to be a marina not far from the Ferry Building.

Dylan explained that he'd brought his boat in for some engine work that morning and they'd agreed to leave her docked where he could get her after dinner.

"You're going to sail across the bay at night?"

"If you're not comfortable with that, I can still get you a cab."

It sounded as if he had plenty of sailing experience and aside from having to get used to the way he talked, nothing had happened to make me worry about being alone with him, so I said, "I love being out on the bay. I usually ride the ferry to and from work."

He grinned. "Well come on, then."

"I guess you could drop me off near the ferry in Sausalito. The bus will still be running from there to my apartment complex."

"Don't worry about that. We'll sail back to my place, and then I'll drive you home."

His boat was a forty-foot sloop, the kind with one mast, as I learned. We went into the cabin and he found a pair of jeans and a sweater for me.

"They'll be a little big, but you'd freeze in that skirt." He opened a drawer, pulled out a piece of clothesline, and held it out. "Is this long enough to use as a belt?"

I took the clothesline and wrapped it around my waist over my work clothes. It was just right, enough overlap to tie, not so much it would be hanging down too far. "It's perfect," I said.

He lifted a bench seat and pulled out an orange life vest. "Put this on over the sweater. By the time you've changed, I'll have us under sail."

I was a little nervous. All his talk about traveling made me realize how boring my life is, how much I want to travel and have adventures. Not horrible experiences I want to forget, but exciting tales to share with the world. I knew it was a risky choice, sailing off with someone I'd just met. But a rapist would have left me in my short skirt and fitted blouse.

Still, I did leave the skirt on while I pulled up the jeans, just in case he came back into the cabin, even though I'd heard the quiet motor start. I was figuring out the straps on the life vest when the motor stopped. We were still moving, and the boat tilted to one side. I yanked on the jacket. It was secure.

I made my way up to the deck. The sail soared above me, gently curved with wind. Dylan stood behind the wheel, a silhouette backed by the Golden Gate Bridge and the last faint wash of sunset - somewhere between pink and purple.

"Sit right there by the cabin," he said. "I'm going to catch more wind once you're settled. The boat will pitch harder, so hold on."

I sat with my back against the cabin, holding onto the entrance as instructed. He turned the wheel slightly with dramatic effect – the sail filled with air and pulled that side of the boat toward the water as we picked up speed.

"Are we going to tip over?" I asked as I planted my feet so I didn't slide toward the water.

"No, I won't take her that far," he assured me. "I can back off a bit if this makes you uncomfortable, but it will take longer to get to my place."

"No, I'm fine."

Once I knew we weren't in trouble, the quiet speed of the boat was thrilling. There was no sound but the slap of boat against water as we cut through waves. We kept on in that direction for several minutes before he warned me to hold on and keep my head down. He turned the wheel and the sail swung across the boat to the other side, then snapped full of wind again. The boat tilted the opposite direction.

I'm in love - with sailing!

"That's called tacking or coming about," he explained. "We'll have to do it quite a few times. My place is north of Richmond Bridge, on San Rafael Bay. The tide is with us, but it'll still take a good bit to get there."

"Okay." I was mesmerized by the entire evening.

As we approached Richmond Bridge, he dropped the sail and used the motor.

"It's safer to motor through here, especially at night," he said. "Come help me steer."

He stood behind me with his hands over mine on the wheel as we went under the bridge. He nuzzled my neck lightly, just once. When we'd left the bridge well behind us, he turned off the motor and turned me away from the wheel and pulled me into his side. Instead of moving in for a kiss, he tilted his head back.

"Look at the stars," he said softly.

We stared at the sky with nothing but quiet lapping of water against the sides of the boat disturbing the silence.

"It's like being in the mountains," I whispered. "I never knew you could see so many stars this close to the city."

Then he kissed me, a gentle, dry meeting of lips, not the least demanding, but it tingled all the way to my toes. Just one kiss, then he looked back up at the stars.

"I love it out here. The only place better is out in the ocean, away from everything."

It felt as though I'd always known him, somehow.

After the kiss, he started the motor and kept an arm around me, steering one-handed as we slipped quietly through the night, gazing at the stars above and the lights along the shore. We didn't talk until we were close to his dock.

"You can find a bag for your clothes to the left of the sink, unless you want to change," he said. "It'll be warmer to keep mine on. I can get them later."

I decided to leave his clothes on and put mine into a brown paper grocery bag. I returned to deck just before we reached his dock. He handed me a heavy rope.

"I'll tie her off up front. Grab the dock if you can, then toss this to me for the back cleat."

He turned off the motor, ran to the front of the boat and jumped out onto the dock with another heavy white rope. I grabbed at the edge of the dock as he leaned down near the front, but the boat was pulling the boards out of my grip as he ran back to me. I threw him the rope, a line, as I learned to call it, and he quickly pulled the boat to the dock and wrapped the rope around a metal cleat.

"Not bad for a first-timer," he said as he held out his hand to help me off the boat.

He pulled me to him for another kiss, this one with our bodies pressed together. He continued to hold me close when he lifted his head. "What time do you have to get up tomorrow?"

"Six," I groaned.

He pulled my hips closer and I could feel the warm lump in his jeans. He sighed, gave me a quick peck on the mouth, then moved back and took my hand.

"Come on. I'll take you home." He began walking us to shore. "But I need your phone number. I have to get my duds back somehow."

It was late when we got to my apartment. I wanted to invite him in, but knew I wouldn't get any sleep if I did. We kissed again outside the door, passion building as we pressed more closely together. When he broke off the kiss I was trembling inside.

"Lunch tomorrow?" he asked.

"Yes."

"Noon?"

"Yes."

"I'll be there."

I was so excited.

I helped dock the boat! And he wants to see me again!
I really need to get some sleep—if I can. Lunch tomorrow!

The next two days, he drove into the city, had sandwiches with me in Union Square for lunch, then picked me up after work. We went to a different marvelous restaurant each night, always overlooking the Bay. Then he drove me home with nothing more than passionate kisses.

He came into the apartment Thursday, but only far enough to see the living room. My latest roommate, Patty the husband-hunter, was there. He politely engaged her in conversation for a few minutes before he left. She watched from the door as we said goodbye at his car.

When I came back into the apartment, Patty regarded me with new eyes. "A Porsche? You've caught a rich one. And he looks great for an older guy, too. Is the sex as good as the package?"

I just smiled.

"That better mean you're in orgasm heaven."

I kept smiling and went to bed, hoping the rest would be as good as his kisses.

March 15, 1981

On Friday Dylan picked me up at my apartment after work, so I could change and pack a few things for the weekend. By sunset, we were anchored in a sheltered cove enjoying a light supper of deli crab and salad with a white wine. We stayed on deck until the stars were out, then we kissed and he led me into the cabin.

The rest is definitely as good as his kisses. He is so patient, and makes sure I'm satisfied first, every time. There was an awkward moment when I pulled a condom out of my pocket. Even though I was so ready to go, I didn't get careless. He was surprised I'm not on the pill, but didn't fuss about using it. The only bunk in the cabin is small, but I like how we have to sleep entwined.

We stayed out until sunset tonight, Sunday, and then he drove me back to my apartment so I could get enough rest to get to work on time in the morning. He's so thoughtful!

We ran out of condoms, but he was careful to pull out every time.

While Dylan didn't have a job, he kept himself busy. We slipped into seeing each other for dinner or lunch just once or twice a week, but we spent every weekend on the boat, anchoring out in one sheltered spot or another. Even when it was too foggy to sail, we'd stay on it at his dock until it cleared enough to go out. Once we anchored somewhere, we'd often sit in companionable silence.

June 7, 1981

It really is like we've known each other forever.

I love sailing, and I'm turning into a good crew member. He tacked a lot that first night, so we wouldn't heel too sharply, but I love hanging out as ballast on the top side so we can go as fast as possible. He's even let me take over steering in the bays, but when we go out past the Golden Gate, I just help. Still, I'm getting so I know what to do before he says it.

By my twenty-fourth birthday that July, Dylan declared I was a competent sailor. Of course I was still living my lie—pretending to turn twenty-seven. Dylan was thirty-four, but he was so full of life and took such pleasure in little things that the age difference didn't matter.

July 19, 1981

Patty keeps saying how I've caught a rich one, but I don't care about Dylan's Porsche or his beautiful home. The boat is part of him and our life together. We both love sailing and I can't imagine him without it, but it could be a junky old thing for all I care. It's the sailing and the way he makes me feel.

There's no way I'll ever share my journal with him, but he respects that. I can even bring it with me on the weekends and know he won't look in it. He's a very private person himself. But he encourages me to write in it because he knows writing is what I want to do, and everything I put into my journals will help me write stories.

I liked writing fiction in college. Eventually I'll get back to that. For now, I'm collecting material. Dylan says we need to LIVE our lives, not just drift through them, that we need to do things that make us feel alive, like sailing full out.

Betty noticed my hair was noticeably lighter every Monday and I told her we were spending the weekends sailing.

"It's the combination of sun, salt, and wind."

"Has he proposed?" she asked.

"No. It's too soon for that." But I'd found myself thinking of Dylan as my happily-ever-after.

"Is anyone else out on that boat with you?" she asked.

"No, it can actually be sailed by one person, though it's easier with two."

"The sailing's not what I'm worried about," she said. "You need to be careful things don't go too far out there, alone with him so much."

"It's okay," I said. "Sailing keeps us busy."

July 20, 1981

Betty's so out of it. There's no point trying to explain it's not like it was in her day, that most people live together before they get married now. She'd be so shocked if I told her how I got drunk and lost my virginity at fourteen! That seems like another lifetime.

I trust Dylan. We haven't discussed being mutually exclusive, but we're together every weekend all weekend. We're not even using condoms except when I'm mid-cycle. He always pulls out.

When Dylan told me I was a good mate, I knew he meant mate as in shipmate, but still found myself hoping he meant more.

Then he added, "You don't talk about your family."

"No. I don't really have any." He'd taken so long to ask, I'd hoped I'd never have to tell him my lies.

He lifted an eyebrow, questioning without words.

"We moved a lot when I was growing up. I left home at eighteen and when I tried to contact them, they'd moved again. I've been on my own since then."

This had become my reality over the years. Still, it felt wrong to lie to Dylan.

He reached over to stroke my cheek gently. "That explains why you're so independent. Do you want to find them? I could hire someone."

"No. It wasn't a good situation. I'm better off on my own."

"Or with me?" He smiled. "You don't want to be completely alone, do you?"

"No." I laughed, relieved that he seemed ready to let the issue of my family go and happy that his words promised a future together. "I love being with you. But I have to admit, I really enjoy knowing I can take care of myself."

"So you wouldn't want to give up your job?"

I thought he was about to propose marriage. Part of me wanted him to, but my stomach tightened because I wasn't ready to give up my job and depend on someone else. But it was a different kind of proposal.

July 26, 1981

He was so casual about it. He said he'd been planning a trip and was hoping I'd crew for him. I said I was sure I could take some time off. I was disappointed and relieved at the same time that he was suggesting a trip, not marriage. I asked how long we'd be gone. He teased me along, saying it could be quite a long time, before he came out and told me.

"Well, I'm planning to take several months to sail south to the Galapagos Islands off Ecuador, then next March head for the Marquesas, then on into the South Pacific and spend at least one cyclone season exploring New Zealand and Australia."

"You're going to sail across the South Pacific?" I was stunned. "All the way to Australia?"

"Around the world." He grinned broadly. "Like my grandfather wanted us to do. Do you think they'd give you a few years off?"

I couldn't speak.

Dylan continued. "We can check out whatever parts of Southeast Asia are safe by the time we're there, and India. Then we'll sail through the Suez and visit the Pyramids, stay in the Mediterranean for as long we like. Then we'll time the season to cross the Atlantic."

"Yes!" It was my dream of adventure, wrapped up in the loving relationship that was developing with Dylan. "Yes! When do we leave?"

"Do you have a passport?"

"No," I cried.

"It's not difficult, but it may take a few weeks for them to process your application. We could still leave before the end of August. If we start hitting dicey weather anywhere, we'll dock in the nearest port for as long as it takes to clear. We won't have any time schedule except the seasons of the ocean."

July 27, 1981

I'm going around the world with Dylan! It's really going to happen!

I applied for my passport during my lunch break today. It was the first time I'd used my birth certificate since I needed it to start college. I was terrified they'd somehow see it was phony and arrest me, but none of that happened. They said I should have my passport in a couple weeks.

I floated back to the office and gave them three weeks' notice.

Betty's so upset. She knows I don't have any family, so she's acting like she's my mother. I think she would have anyway, but she said that's why she had to have her say. Basically, I haven't known Dylan long enough and he could be planning to sell me into the white slave trade!

Dylan is nothing like Nick. I know the difference, but I couldn't explain that to Betty. So I just told her that, while he hasn't come out and said it, I know he's beginning to love me. It shows in the way he treats me.

That didn't satisfy her. She was still suspicious, even though she'd liked him at first.

"Have you met his family?" she demanded.

"No, they live back East."

She didn't think that was any excuse, but when she realized it wasn't making me come to my senses, she tried one more angle. "At least he could marry you first. What if he decides to break it off with you when you're heaven only knows where?"

"He won't. But I was saving for a car, so I'll have enough for a plane ticket home from anywhere in the world, Betty." I wasn't sure if that was true, but I'd have a thousand dollars to take with me. "I'll be fine. I'll send you postcards from all the exotic ports we visit."

She humphed. "At least I'll know where to tell them to start looking when you disappear."

Then she typed up a letter of recommendation detailing everything I did in the office and had our boss sign it. "Take care of that," she said as she handed it to me. "If this fellow doesn't ever propose, you'll need it."

Patty-the-husband-hunter's reaction was much more to my liking. "That is so amazing! God, you're lucky. When do you leave?"

"As soon as my passport comes. Probably three weeks."

"One of the girls I work with has been looking for a new place. She's renting a room from a little old lady who walks in on her without knocking. I'll tell her tomorrow. I bet she'll move in the day you move out."

August 14, 1981

Today was my last day at work—and my passport's here, so we can leave tomorrow! Patty took over the lease on the apartment. I sorted through my stuff. I got rid of most of it, but some's in the guest bedroom closet at Dylan's house.

His gardener's keeping an eye on the place this fall, then Dylan's cousin is graduating from college in December and she'll come out in January to house sit while she gets established here. He says I'll like her, though it will be some time before we meet.

We're really going to be gone for a year! At least a year! I'm going to see the world!!!

Chapter 18: Sailing Away

We sailed under the Golden Gate the next morning, out into the Pacific past seals lounging on the rocks ashore. The swells rolled gently and the wind was perfect – not too strong and not so weak we had to use the motor. It was a beautiful mid-August day.

"We'll stop in Half Moon Bay tonight," he said. "It will be a short day if these conditions keep up, but it's always a good idea to take it easy at the beginning. If anything's going to break, better while you're rested and close to home."

We'd stocked some food, of course, but had dinner ashore that evening. We got back to the boat before dark and made love until we both fell asleep. The next morning, the lurch of my stomach woke me in time to roll out of bed and vomit in the sink. The boat wasn't moving any more than it usually did when we anchored out in the coves off San Francisco Bay.

"Are you okay?" worried Dylan.

"Yuh," I said as my stomach settled. "I'm fine now. It must have been something I ate last night, probably the chicken. You were right, I should have had fish in a seaside town."

"No, you were right," he said. "We'll be eating fish most of the time. It's too bad it made you sick, though. Will you be okay to sail?"

"Sure. I think I'll just eat a few of those soda crackers we brought, though, instead of a big breakfast. Give my stomach a chance to settle."

"Good idea. We're going to hit some rougher water today – nothing dangerous or we'd stay put until it passed, but not as easy as yesterday. Let me know after we eat if you're still feeling sick and we can wait a day."

August 16, 1981

I brought my journal topside along with the crackers. I hope he'll think I just wanted privacy to write, but the smell of bacon cooking made my stomach clench. Why does this have to be happening? I shouldn't have eaten that chicken last night. Now Dylan thinks I'm a landlubber.

Once I ate the crackers I was fine. We headed for Santa Cruz, twice the distance we'd covered the day before. Dylan was right about the waves being larger. They were the biggest I'd been in, big enough to be exhilarating but not frightening. We made good time and arrived in Santa Cruz before dark.

"You did great out there," Dylan said as we tied up for the night. "Your stomach didn't bother you anymore?"

"Nope. Once I got rid of that chicken, I was fine. The sandwiches we ate for lunch didn't bother me a bit."

"We could have sandwiches again for dinner if you want to play it safe, but I'd really like to eat at the Crow's Nest while we're here. You'll love the view."

"I'll get fish tonight."

We ordered two different kinds and swapped plates half way through dinner. So when the next morning had me leaning over the sink miserably, we both knew it wasn't the food. In spite of the instant realization that a baby would make this trip impossible, I felt a flood of joy. Dylan's reaction squelched that.

"How late is your period?" he demanded.

"Let me look at my calendar."

I dug under the clothes in my drawer. I'd been so careful to monitor my cycle since we stopped using condoms, but with the rush of getting ready I hadn't thought about it. As my hand reached the small notebook calendar, I realized I hadn't had a period since before Dylan first mentioned the trip. I lurched to the sink again. Dylan grabbed the book from my hand.

"Seven weeks," he said with disgust. "When were you going to tell me? Is it even mine?"

An icy fist gripped my heart and squeezed tears out of it.

"You needn't look so wounded," he said. "We haven't been together every night. It's a reasonable question."

"Yes, I'm sure. It's your baby." Hurt and anger raged within me.

He shook his head. "No child of mine should ever live."

"How can you say that?"

"I'm not cut out to be a father, Margie. Not ever. And we definitely can't take a newborn on this trip. What were you thinking?"

"I wasn't thinking anything. I was excited, busy getting ready to leave. I didn't notice I was late."

"Well that was irresponsible. At least we've found out in time to deal with it while we're still in the states. We can sail to Monterey today and go to a clinic there tomorrow."

"Take care of it?" I didn't want to understand him.

"Seven weeks is early enough to get an abortion. It'll actually be safer than going through with the pregnancy."

August 17, 1981

We're sailing to Monterey. Dylan wants me to get rid of the baby. I was so happy that first moment I realized I was pregnant. But he said no child of his should ever live, and he keeps saying how he never wanted any children, how dead set he is against adding to over-population, how he has no interest in being a father, ever.

How can I bring a child into the world with a father who feels that way?

I could leave him in Monterey.

They probably still have a temp. I could go back to work until I have the baby. But how could I take care of her by myself? Somehow I'm sure it's a girl. What kind of parent would I be on my own? I've made such a mess of my life.

And how would I support her? Women do it all the time. I could figure out a way. Somehow.

But how can I bring her into a world where her father hates her existence?

I let him take me to the clinic in Monterey the next day. We had to stay over. They wouldn't do it without giving me time to reconsider.

There was no getting away from him on the boat. At the same time I couldn't stand being touched by him I needed to be held, and he was the only one there. He made a gentle attempt to have sex. It was the first time I refused him.

"It'll be for the best," he said.

"It's right for you, but so wrong for me," I whispered. "You have to be there."

He stayed in the room and held my hand as they vacuumed his child out of my body. He looked panicky when I started bleeding profusely. My body was fighting to keep the child and losing. As I slid into shock, they put a needle into my arm with an intravenous sugar solution.

"She'll be okay now," said someone in white. "But she should rest for a few days – and bring her back immediately if the bleeding doesn't keep slowing."

I didn't want to be near Dylan or feel his touch, but I needed someone to take care of me and he was my only option. We stayed docked in Monterey. He slept on the deck at night and nursed me attentively during the day. Conversation was limited to questions about my comfort. Once it seemed like he was going to bring up the abortion. I closed my eyes and pretended to doze off. He let it drop.

After he left me each night, I'd let the tears flow silently.

By the third day, the bleeding had slowed to a trickle.

"I think I want to go back to San Francisco," I said. "I don't think they've replaced me yet."

Betty had said she'd insist on using temps as long as she could; she'd been so sure I was making a mistake.

"The doctor said you might have some depression. It'll pass. Don't give up the adventure of a lifetime. You'll see – this was the only choice." He sounded so sure.

I shook my head listlessly.

"You'll start feeling better soon," he insisted.

"No," I whispered. "I'm never going to feel better."

August 24, 1981

He ignored me and resumed our journey this morning. I should have gotten off in Monterey, but I just want to sleep.

There's no physical reason, but I feel so weak.

The bleeding is less than I get with my period. That's not right. I shouldn't recover so easily. I just want to get away from him. Maybe Dylan is right, it's depression that will go away. Maybe I can forgive him - and myself - and go on with our adventure.

If I go back, Betty will want to know what went wrong so soon. She's got that mother's sixth sense thing. She might guess.

I'm sure she doesn't approve of abortion. Neither do I. Not for me. Not for my baby. But I did it anyway.

Because I'm a coward? Or because I couldn't bring my child into the world knowing someone hated her so much?

I don't know.

I forced myself to get out on deck that afternoon.

It was so calm we used the motor to make our destination before dark. That was a good thing. If it had been rough, I might have let myself be lost overboard.

We continued sailing south, stopping to anchor in safe harbors each night. He didn't dock at all – he was probably afraid I'd leave. And I might have. Dylan took it slow, changing the itinerary to make the days shorter. At first he did all the work. I'd come up for a few hours each day, but sat curled up, looking out to the horizon.

Then we anchored three days in San Simeon Bay to wait out a storm. Dylan sat playing solitaire while I huddled in the bed. Walking past the table after peeing, I finally decided it was time to stay up, even if it meant interacting with Dylan. I sat down across from him.

"Rummy?" he asked.

I nodded and we played without talking.

September 1, 1981

Dylan's simply not the person I thought he was, and he doesn't really know me, either. He still thinks everything is going to be okay. He's treating me lovingly, as if I'd been injured accidentally. He came back to the bunk last night and I pretended to be asleep. He spooned behind me gently and made no attempt to start anything else. Maybe it's sick, but the cuddling actually did make me feel a little better.

There was no one else to give me any support or warmth.

I started helping again and we sailed as a team, few words necessary, the way we were supposed to go around the world.

The hours in the sun with the salty wind on my face were healing. I used the time to think everything through - not just the abortion, but my whole life.

By the time I was up to leaning out as ballast again, I knew I would leave him in Los Angeles. I decided to enjoy my last days sailing and avoid ending with an ugly argument.

Some mornings we had to wait for fog to lift, but aside from that, we had unbelievably perfect sailing weather.

When we got to the Channel Islands, we anchored and used the dinghy to go ashore and hike. We stayed there several days as Dylan enthusiastically shared caves and other places from his childhood sailing the coast with his grandfather.

It made me smile and I let him hug and kiss me like he did the night we met. He didn't push for more; he was confident it would happen soon.

It was a temptation – the adventure of my dreams.

But when we docked at Long Beach, I packed my money and other things into one of his duffle bags while he tidied things up on deck. I took a moment to look around the cabin that was supposed to be my home for the next couple years and sighed. It had been a wonderful dream, but I needed to make peace with myself and what I'd done.

When he saw me with the duffle bag in my hand, his body sagged. "You're leaving?"

I nodded. My throat was full and if I tried to talk, I would cry.

"Where are you going to go?"

He actually sounded worried. Maybe he did care, but I couldn't stay. The lump in my throat seemed to grow as I stood looking past his hip.

"You left things at my house," he reminded me. "There's a key wired to the gate on the dock. Remember? You asked me about it once."

I nodded.

"You can stay there until you decide where you're going," he offered. "My cousin isn't coming out until January."

"Thanks." The word let loose the tears I'd been holding back.

He came forward and hugged me. "You're sure?"

"Yes."

He hugged me again and sighed. "I'll go to the airport with you and buy you a ticket back to San Francisco. I'll give you cab fare to get out to the house, too, and a note so the gardener knows you're supposed to be there. He comes once or twice a week, depending on what needs to be done."

I didn't really want to drag out the parting, but his plan made sense. We didn't talk in the cab to the airport. My gaze was locked on the cabbie's neck.

Dylan paid for my ticket, walked me to the gate, and handed me an envelope. "I put extra in there to help tide you over."

"I have savings from when I was working."

"A couple thousand won't last long."

He was right. I shoved the envelope in my pocket without opening it. If I didn't need it, I could leave it at his house. I sat down.

He stood in front of me, hands in his pockets. "I'll miss you."

"You'll find someone else to crew for you," I replied leadenly. I wanted this to be over. "My flight doesn't leave for hours. There's no reason for you to stay."

I could feel the relief pour off of him, but he mustered the right words. "Are you sure you'll be okay?"

"I'll be fine." I managed a weak smile.

Once he'd left, I found a pay phone and called work. A new voice answered the phone.

"Is Betty there?" I asked. "This is Margie."

"Margie! No, she had a dentist appointment this morning. She'll be so glad you called, though. She's worried about you every day."

"Are you the temp, or have they hired you full time?"

"I'm officially hired, as of Monday. I'd been temping ever since you left." She sounded like a perfect fit – bubbly and innocent.

"Well, would you tell Betty that she doesn't have to worry? I had second thoughts and got off the boat in Los Angeles. I'm going to find work here."

"Oh, you're calling from Los Angeles? I'm sorry for talking so much when it's long distance."

"That's okay. Just let her know I'm fine." Maybe I really should stay in Los Angeles.

As I waited for the flight, I pulled out my journal. I thought seeing my options in writing might help me make a better decision.

September 10, 1981

I could stay in Los Angeles, but I'd have to find a place to live as well as a job, and I don't know anyone here so it wouldn't be easy.

I have the plane ticket and I left things at Dylan's house. No one will bother me there for months. I can take my time and make a good plan.

I suppose I could try to stay with Lynn and John, if they're in the country, but I didn't even send them a card last Christmas. That would really be imposing. I can hear Mom chewing me out for even thinking of it.

And I can't go backwards. They're part of the past.

I need to look forward to survive this. At Dylan's I'll be able to think things through at my own pace.

That evening I sat on Dylan's couch with a bottle of wine from his special collection, staring out the sliding glass door across the lawn to the empty dock on the bay.

September 11, 1981

Three o'clock in the morning. I can't sleep. The house is full of him. The bay and empty dock remind me of him even more. Am I crazy to have left him, to walk away from my dream trip?

I understand now. That first day we met, Dylan was looking for an adventuresome crew member who would also be fun in bed. I told him I wanted to write more than business letters, that I wanted to have experiences worth writing about.

That's why he invited me to dinner, and why he wanted to know if I could swim. Sailing with him on the bay that first night was a test.

We never spent any time at this house. Everything happened on the boat. And once he knew the sex was good, he made me a sailor. When he first mentioned the trip, it was clear he was going with or without me.

I should have paid more attention.

We never talked about a future together, let alone children. He thought I agreed to go around the world with him because it was the adventure of a lifetime, which was part of it.

But he never realized I wanted him to love me, so it never crossed his mind that I thought he did.

I wasn't the only one not paying attention.

That fleeting moment of joy when I first realized I was pregnant came back to me.

The pain of what I'd done stabbed me in the chest and I crumpled onto the floor crying, barely able to breathe. I'm not sure how long I stayed that way—huddled in a ball unable to do anything but weep, my brain turned off. I was vaguely aware of the sprinklers running several times. I must have slept, but had no real sense of time.

Then one morning I woke up, still on the floor but uncurled and breathing more easily.

Thirsty! My body demanded liquid immediately.

I made my way to the kitchen and drank glass after glass of water. There was no food in the house except a few cans of peaches. I ate them all before I caught a whiff of my armpit and headed for the shower. I knew the depression would return, but if I took care of myself I'd be able to deal with it. I scrubbed every inch of me and put on fresh clothes.

I walked several blocks to the nearest grocery store and bought food for two or three days, only what I could carry. I shouldn't waste my cash on cabs until I had a plan. The receipt said it was the fourteenth – I'd been out of it for three days!

Back at Dylan's, I pulled out my journals. First I reviewed everything that had happened since I left home. There wasn't any point in going back further, or so I thought. Then I wrote down everything I'd done to make a living, except working for Nick, and every skill I had that I could use on a job. That list made me feel less helpless.

September 14, 1981

I am a college graduate and I've landed a job before. I just have to decide what kind of work and where. It might make sense to get something close and stay in this house until his cousin comes. But would I want to keep the job and stay in this area when I know Dylan will eventually come home? Should I get a job knowing I may walk away from it in a few months?

Do I even want to stay in the Bay Area? So many happy hours sailing, do I really want to be reminded of that every time I see the Bay? It will make me remember the baby, too.

I don't even know who I am. Until he got angry about my being pregnant, I can't remember Dylan ever calling me Margie. Early on, he said it didn't suit me, but he never called me anything else, either—not even Honey or any of those other things guys call you instead of your name.

He was right though, I never did get used to people calling me Margie.

Betty called me Peg when she first started working with me, until the boss corrected her. I kind of liked it, though. It's the name I grew up with.

The answers eventually asserted themselves. I wanted to leave California. I wanted to use my degree. I wanted to stop living a lie. I wanted to be myself.

I wanted to go home.

Thanks to Charlie, I could. My degree and all of my identification were in my real name, Margaret Lewis. I could say the birth date was a clerical error and fix it eventually.

To be sure, I thought about it over a week.

One night I dreamed of burning piles of red and gold leaves, the smell of grapes in crisp fall air, Jan smiling, and my mother in her garden. I heard my dad calling my name. When I woke up, I walked to a payphone and tried to call Jan, but it had been ten years and the number I'd called every day as a child belonged to strangers.

I dialed home.

Chapter 19: Going Home

It was almost noon their time, so I wasn't surprised when my mother answered. She'd be back from the breakfast shift, assuming she still worked at the diner. I couldn't imagine anything had changed for my parents.

"Who is this?" she asked when I didn't speak at first.

"Peg," I whispered.

"You're alive?" She sounded shocked and happy, but she recognized my voice. "They told us you died in that flood, right after you disappeared. A woman from the Red Cross said a Mac Nicholas had seen you drown and get swept away by the river. They had a list of victims."

"I didn't know. I'm sorry, Mom."

"Where are you? Where have you been? Why didn't you come home? Or call us?"

There was the anger I'd expected.

I'd planned my responses. As much as it pained me, I had to live with new lies. I could never tell anyone everything that had happened over the last ten years. I had to leave behind all the lives I'd led since leaving home and all the people, though that had already pretty much happened.

"I'm in California, like I told Jan. I went to college out here."

"You went to college?" She sounded proud.

That's why she'd been working at the diner, to pay for my education. At least I'd done something right, something I could talk about, thanks to Charlie.

"I have a degree in English."

"That's wonderful! When Jan finally admitted you'd run off looking like a hippie, we were afraid you'd gotten into drugs. She didn't say anything until they told us you were dead. Then she thought you'd lied to her about where you were going."

Tears were pouring down my face and my nose was filling. I hoped she couldn't hear that in my voice. "After Jan left me at the bus station, I was talking to a girl who was running away to Harrisburg. She watched my stuff while I used the bathroom. She must have gotten my name and address and used them for herself. It must have been her who drowned."

"That poor girl's family," said Mom. "They must still wonder what happened to her."

"I'm sorry," I sobbed, sorry for both the pain I'd caused and for my new lies.

"Are you still with the boy Jan met?"

"No." That was Nick, only Jan met him as Joe. "At first I didn't call because he was older and I didn't want him to get into trouble. When it didn't work out, it had been too long and I was ashamed." At least my new lies had elements of truth.

"Well, you're probably right we would have had him arrested. I'm just glad you're okay."

"Can I come home?" There was no way she couldn't realize how hard I was crying.

"You *need* to come."

Something in her tone warned me.

"What's wrong, Mom?"

"It's your father. You need to come as soon as you can."

October 4, 1981

I'm at the San Francisco airport, waiting for my flight to Buffalo. I'm going home, thanks to Charlie. Without him, who knows what would have happened to me. I wish I could give him a hug right now. I can't believe it's seven years since I last saw him, and I'll never see him again. I always thought I would. At least I wrote that letter to thank him.

They thought I was dead all this time. Mac Nicholas must have been Nick, making sure no one would look for me. He must have looked in my journal and known my real name and address. I wonder if he reported my death before or after I left? He may have looked for me after all.

Mom says Dad is in the hospital in Buffalo. I was lucky to catch her at home.

I hope he'll be okay.

I don't like lying to them, but even healthy it would be hard on him to know my whole story. I'll have to live with it. But from now on, no new lies.

I was wearing one of my best secretarial outfits and regretted the heels when I had to race across the airport in Chicago to catch my connecting flight.

Mom was waiting for me at the gate in Buffalo. She looked tired, grayer, but otherwise pretty much the same as she had ten years earlier. My outfit and the heels were worth the look on her face when she saw me – a combination of pride and relief that I wasn't a grungy hippie. She greeted me with open arms. The hug surprised me. She'd never been a hugger.

"Goodness, you're beautiful, Peg," she said. "And you grew more, didn't you?"

"It may be the heels," I said.

She shook her head. "It's not all your shoes."

"Where's Dad? Is he okay?"

"He's at Roswell," she said.

"Isn't that the cancer hospital? You didn't say it was cancer."

"I didn't want to scare you off. He's not doing well." Mom was blinking rapidly. "You must have luggage. Come on."

With those heels on, I had trouble keeping up as she raced to the baggage claim area.

"I have a huge suitcase and a box with all of my things," I said as suitcases began to come out of the chute.

"All of your things?"

"Yes. I'm not going back."

"Don't you have a job?"

"I quit. I was thinking I'd find something near home, when you said Dad was so sick."

"We put up a stone for you at the cemetery. Everyone knows you died. The gossips will go wild if you come home."

If. She said *if.* "You haven't told anyone I called?"

"Not yet. I wanted to see if you really came."

"Not even Dad?"

"Especially not your father." The stern voice was familiar. "He was heartbroken when you disappeared and shattered when they told us you were dead. Now he's holding on by a thread and if you hadn't come home after you called, he'd be done right then and there."

"He's holding on by a thread?" The words stuck and kept ringing in my ears.

"This last operation didn't help. As soon as he's stable, they'll send him home to die."

Her face remained as stiff as I remembered, but tears washed across it. She pulled back from my hand when I went to comfort her and shook her head. I backed off. She kept blinking until the tears slowed and stopped.

I pulled my suitcase off the conveyer belt, and then the cardboard box in which I'd put my journals and the other small things I wanted to keep. The suitcase had a strap I could sling over my shoulder. I picked it up first, then the box.

"That's it?" Mom asked. "That's your everything?"

The judgment stung for a moment, but she'd lived in the same house for decades. Of course she'd expect me to have more things.

"I sold the rest. It didn't make sense to bring more."

"Okay, then. Which is lighter?" She held out her hand.

I put the suitcase down and let the strap slide off my shoulder so she could take it. I could carry both, but I knew it would make her feel useful. It might help her think about something other than Dad for a few moments.

In the parking lot she led me to a new old car. Of course they didn't still have the same one they'd had ten years ago. I was silly to think their lives had frozen while mine had gone through so many transitions.

We didn't talk much on the way to the hospital. Mom was still tense driving in the city – that hadn't changed – so I quietly looked out the window. I hadn't realized how much I'd missed the bright reds and yellows of maples in the fall.

At the hospital, she led me to the intensive care unit. She explained in a hushed voice, "He's still in here because of the surgery."

Mom told the nurse I was family – she didn't specify long-lost daughter – and then she led me to a spot near the wall and held a finger to her lips. She pulled the curtain back an inch or two so I could see the top of his now-hairless head and a skinny arm connected to machinery by tubes. Tears poured down my face. Mom pulled me away so he wouldn't hear.

"Go rinse your face. The restroom's down that hall," she ordered in a whisper. "I'll tell him you're here so it won't be as much of a shock, but don't let him see you cry."

It took several minutes to compose myself. I walked back down the hallway and peeked in from the same spot. My mother saw me and with a tilt of her head indicated I should come in from the aisle, near the foot of the bed. She didn't want him to realize she could watch him without his knowing. I followed her silent directions and started by poking my head in the curtain.

I'd decided to pretend I wasn't appalled by his condition.

If my mother could do that, so could I.

I smiled and timidly asked, "Okay if I come in?"

The yellowed skin of his face was stretched thin over his skull, but I recognized the smile that lit up his eyes. I was home.

October 12, 1981

I've been sharing my mother's motel room for a week now. She actually dozed off watching an old movie tonight. I'm not sure she slept at all the other nights. That's why I haven't pulled out my journal sooner. I don't want her to ask to see it—I'd rather she doesn't know I have one because I definitely don't want her reading the others.

What if I'd gone on with Dylan instead of coming home? I can't believe I've been gone so long - more than a third of my life! Dad didn't even ask why I never called. He's so frail. He hates being in the hospital. He knows he's dying and wants to go home. He's changed so much.

In many ways Mom hasn't changed at all, like her concern for appearances. I understand it better now I've spent so much time pretending to be other people, hiding so much of myself. But when we're alone here at the motel, Mom lets herself cry a little and even lets me hold her.

They're going to send Dad home tomorrow or the next day and today, on the way back to the motel, Mom said she'd like me to come with them, that people can just gossip, they always do anyway.

She seems to be listening when I talk to Dad. There are so many things I'd like to tell them that I can't. It would hurt them to know how Lynn and John were like parents to me, so I said I got my GED while I was still with the phantom Joe. As far as they're concerned, we rode the bus straight out to California where he got a job and supported me, until he got hooked on drugs and I decided to leave him. I made myself sound strong - never a victim.

I'd love to tell them about Charlie and how he protected me and got me to Lynn and John so I could finish my education, but there just isn't a place for him in the new story. How can a white knight save someone who's not a victim? Besides, they'd expect me to keep in touch with someone that special and we've gone separate ways.

I told them I worked my way through school, so I didn't have time to build close friendships. I didn't explain my phony marriage or financial aid, because they wouldn't understand, but working my way through makes sense to them, and my not having friends does, too. Jan was my only friend when we were little. I was just beginning to develop a social life when she had me start covering for her trips to Fredonia.

I told Dad, with Mom listening, about working in San Francisco after graduation and sharing an apartment with one girl after another because they didn't stay. That way they don't expect me to have old friends from that period, either.

When Dad commented on my hair being so blonde, I explained it bleached out while I sailed on San Francisco Bay with a co-worker and her husband. That way I can talk about sailing as much as I want to, and as long as I remember the wind and salt spray and the waves slapping the hull, Dad can see how happy it made me.

Dylan is not allowed in my thoughts while I'm with Dad.

Chapter 20: Building a Life

I found my way home at twenty-four, almost ten years after I'd left. The gossip mill accepted the tragic romantic story that I'd run away to California with an older man, ended up on my own, worked my way through college, and finally found the courage to call home just in time to help my parents through their dying days.

November 8, 1981

Mom takes care of Dad while I make sure they both eat, and I take care of bills and anything else that needs to be done. Today I went to the cemetery and had my headstone removed. I didn't want Mom having to look at that when it's Dad's turn to be mourned.

I didn't even know the guy who worked there, but he'd heard the story of how I ran away and died in the flood. I pretended I hadn't known anything about Hurricane Agnes, that I'd already been in California with my fiancé.

That's what I told Jan, too. She's still living here. She and Steve got married when she graduated from high school and their kids are already in grade school, so she has a lot of time on her hands. She started asking a million questions about my life in California and "Joe" who was really Nick, but it was easy to get her talking about herself, complaining that she never went to college because she got pregnant and now she feels trapped and wants a career, and she wants to travel to Europe like we talked about when we were young.

Same old Jan.

Dad made it through Christmas and died two days later.

Half the town came to the funeral, including my old English teacher, who had become principal at the high school. She was excited to hear I'd majored in English and asked me to come work as an assistant for the English department.

"And we'll draw on you as substitute whenever one of them's out." She glanced around to be sure no one was listening. "Don't quote me, but the only decent English teacher I have wants to retire. I might get him to stay until you can get a credential."

Mom encouraged me to take the job and see if I liked teaching. By then, we had gotten closer than we'd ever been and it seemed natural to continue living with her. At first I was mainly grading papers and doing other paperwork, but then I started helping out in classes with unruly students. I had a knack for getting them to work, and I discovered I enjoyed teaching.

When I found out it would take two years to get the additional coursework required for my credential, I almost gave up. But Mom told me not to worry. Dad had actually had a life insurance policy that paid off the house and left Mom with a nest egg.

"And Louise has been asking me to work part time at the diner."

"No, Mom. You don't have to work for me to go to school. It's enough letting me live here for free."

She put her arm around me. "I miss it. I kept working after you left, until your father got so sick. My regulars are my friends. It'll just be the morning shift. That's all I want."

She finally convinced me she meant it. I could still work at the school, too, because most of the courses were in the late afternoon or evening. I took one that summer to get a head start. We slipped into a lifestyle where we were both centered on our own activities. Weekends we'd play Rummy for hours and chat about odds and ends of nothing. My class was over a couple weeks before I had to report to the school to help teachers ready their classrooms.

August 19, 1982

When Mom got home from work, she pulled out the cards to play Rummy. As she dealt, I burst into tears. It was one year ago today. I can't tell her about that, but I told her I'd just broken up with someone when I called home and found out how sick Dad was. She knew.

She didn't press me for details, but she told me not to give up on men. "They're not all rotten. Your father had his flaws, but he did his best. I was the love of his life and he was mine. You'll find yours. You're only twenty-five."

However, school and work kept me busy for the next two years. I made casual friends in my classes – we'd cram for exams or work together on a project at the library or student union, but I wasn't interested in having a social life or getting close to anyone. I was intent on my goal. There was a job waiting for me as soon as I had that credential.

My last semester I did my student teaching with Mr. Roberts, the teacher who had put off retiring for me. In June he gratefully submitted his retirement paperwork and I was hired contingent on my certificate of qualification coming through as expected by the beginning of the school year.

Mr. Roberts made Shakespeare come alive when he taught it, whereas the other teachers showed a dull movie and approached it as a dreaded requirement. He recommended a drama class in Shakespeare that was offered over the summer.

That's how I met Tom Wilson.

July 10, 1984

There's this ridiculous boy in my drama class. He says he's twenty-two but he acts younger. He keeps asking me out, saying he's falling in love with me, throwing Romeo lines at me. He does make me laugh. But this is my twenty-seventh birthday and I start a real job, one using my education, this fall. He's cheerfully described himself as a professional student. He's on his third major.

Mom may be right I should try dating again, but Tom Wilson is definitely not the sort of man I'd want to marry.

However, he was the right person to make me lighten up and have fun. He finally talked me into a day at the beach. That seemed safe. But it wasn't. When he rubbed lotion on my back, he caressed my hips right above the bikini bottom and let a finger slide along inside the top edge, saying it was an area that burned easily.

We stayed for the sunset, then he found a deserted spot to park on the way back to my house. When I told him I wasn't on the pill and we couldn't go any further, he grinned and pulled a condom out of his wallet.

July 30, 1984

I think I've lost my mind. Tom has roommates and I'm living with my mother, so we're screwing our brains out in his car every night. How did I go without sex for THREE YEARS?

Mom noticed, of course. "So who is he?"

I tried to convince her it was nothing serious, but she was convinced I'd found my true love. I finally agreed to bring him to a Sunday dinner. She pulled out Dad's old barbeque and had Tom take charge of the hamburgers.

August 5, 1984

I'd expected Tom to be charming with Mom - he is with every woman - but he tuned into her expectations completely. If Dad had been there, they'd have been sharing a beer like old buddies. She's going to expect us to get married now, and he's simply not marriage material.

We told Mom we were going to a movie. Actually his roommate was out so we went to his apartment and had sex. Then I told him it was the last time. I start teaching in a couple weeks and will be too busy for any kind of relationship, and I definitely can't risk getting caught in a parked car! Time for some sanity.

He took it well. In fact, he got another condom ready and came back for one more time with a grin on his face.

My intentions were good, but Tom was charming and we both had two weeks free. He kept finding ways for us to have privacy. I told Mom it would end naturally once I was working and he was in fall classes, but she just smiled, sure I'd found my true love.

August 24, 1984

Mom didn't wake up this morning.

Yesterday was Dad's birthday. We stayed up late, talking about him. She told me about when they were young and first together, stories I'd never heard. She said she was glad I had Tom, even though she knows I've been trying to break it off. Then she gave me a hug and went to bed.

She died in her sleep. The doctor said her heart just stopped. He said he was surprised she'd lasted this long after Dad, as close as they were.

I couldn't get hold of Jan at first, so I called Tom. He came immediately and stayed through everything. He helped me make the funeral arrangements, find her will, and sort through her finances. She was in better shape than I thought. She'd put my name on the house already and had me as beneficiary on insurance and savings.

September 9, 1984

Tom's been a godsend. He was solemn and mature where it was required and gently pulled a smile out of me whenever we were alone. I've been thinking back to when I was a kid, when things were not good between my parents, and when their relationship first rekindled, and how they were those last months Dad was alive.

But Tom's still not even settled on a major for college. And while it was great for him to be there for me, he had to have missed his first classes. That's never good.

Our relationship will probably die a natural death now. I worked all weekend on grading and lesson plans and there've only been three days of school! Tom was here, but I told him to work on his own schoolwork and ignored him most of the time.

Tom came the next weekend, too, and Jan called to let me know there was gossip that he was moving in with me. I told him he'd have to stay away. That's when he let me know he'd lost his apartment. He said his roommate had been collecting his share of the rent, but hadn't paid the landlord in three months. So they had to be out by the end of the week.

"I was going to ask if I could stay here until I find another apartment, but not if it's a problem for your job. I can always crash on a dorm couch for a couple weeks." He gave me his most charming smile. "But could I keep my things here? It'll probably only be a week or two. "

It was all in his car, parked in my driveway, no doubt the reason for the gossip. But he'd helped me so much, I couldn't say no.

"Okay, you can put it in the garage, but you can't stay over. Once you have a new apartment, I'll spend weekends with you instead. I really have to be careful how things look."

"Okay." He cheerfully emptied his car into the garage and thanked me for storing it loud enough for the neighbor sitting outside to hear. Then he gave me a chaste peck and left.

October 6, 1984

I'm pregnant. We've used condoms faithfully, so I'm not sure how it happened. But it did. I am going to be a mother. I told Tom it's my baby and I'm keeping it, with or without him.

He shocked me by proposing marriage on the spot! I said yes. Maybe our relationship will deepen as we live together with our child.

We got married on the beach the next weekend. The Methodist minister who'd let me be part of MYF officiated. Jan and her father stood up for us. No one else was there. Tom was done with his roommate and he said no one else could come on such short notice. He was estranged from his family.

The rules had changed since I was in school – I could work as long as my doctor and I saw fit. I felt fine, but decided to leave at the beginning of May – I didn't want to chance my water breaking in front of a class of teenagers! Maggie was born the twenty-ninth.

I had until September to be with her all the time. Tom went to summer school, then in the fall arranged all late afternoon and evening classes so he could watch Maggie while I worked.

Christmas 1985

Maggie's starting to pull herself up already and she crawls all over the place. We went a little crazy getting toys for her - all wrapped up from Santa. Jan and her kids stopped by this afternoon. They're getting so big! Sally absolutely adores Maggie - kept playing with her the whole time. She's almost old enough to babysit. Jan's going to watch Maggie this semester - Tom's changing to an accounting major and most of those classes are during the day.

I tried convincing him to call his family for Christmas, at least let his parents know they're grandparents. When he refused, I demanded to know why. He snapped at me for being nosy, then apologized. He said his parents are alcoholics and he doesn't really want anything to do with them. Like me, he's an only child. That's so sad.

But that argument took just a few moments.

Overall, this is the best Christmas I've ever had!

Tom said he needed study groups that met in the evening. It got so we only saw each other a few minutes each morning during the week. He'd get home after I was asleep. Jan was suspicious, but he was his normal loving self on the weekends.

May 29, 1986

My daughter's first birthday! Maggie's not just walking, she's running. It's a funny drunken-sailor run, but still too fast to call it walking. I'm so looking forward to being with her every day this summer! That is not why I went into teaching, but it's certainly a plus.

Now he's settled into a business major, Tom's taking school much more seriously.

I only worry how little time he has with Maggie. But he had her giggling like crazy today.

When Tom switched to accounting, he said he lost his financial aid – something about changing majors too many times. So I paid for his classes and books that spring and summer. Then in July I realized I was pregnant again. When I told him, I asked how long he thought the accounting degree would take, because I'd like to stay home with the kids once he was an accountant.

He laughed and walked away.

Stunned, I followed and watched as he got his stereo and carried it to his car, then came back for more of his things.

"What are you doing?" I finally choked out.

"Leaving."

"But... I'm pregnant."

"That's your problem."

It turned out he hadn't been taking classes at all, not since that one where I met him. He'd only been with me for the sex and, after Mom died, the money. He had no interest in seeing Maggie, let alone the "other" one. He had a new woman to take care of him.

I remembered Charlie's advice for my phony marriage and made sure Tom kept me informed of his whereabouts for the divorce proceedings. Once it was final, I never heard from him again. He was barely a footnote in my life and the girls' despite having provided half their DNA.

Chapter 21: Me and My Girls

Jan made life possible. That fall she watched Maggie and when I went back to work after Lizzie was born, she watched both of them whenever I was working, until Lizzie started kindergarten in 1992.

I built a solid, respectable life as a single parent and teacher and lived that way as if it was the only life I'd ever known. Sex was not part of it. I didn't realize I was still running away – from myself. Once in a while a discussion or news article would make me feel guilty or worried that if anyone knew I had been a prostitute, my life would be ruined. But I knew rationally that was not likely to happen and let myself forget my past most of the time.

Everything revolved around my girls. When I wasn't teaching, I was with them, working, playing, or camping. I made the kind of family I'd always wanted and we didn't need a man to complete it. My co-workers never tried to set me up; it was clear I wasn't interested in a relationship or anything more fleeting.

When the girls were old enough to wonder why they never saw their father like their friends with divorced parents, I said Tom had died in a car accident. When Lizzie was ten, she asked why she didn't have a photo of Tom holding her as a baby, like Maggie did. I expanded on the car accident story and told her it was before she was born.

"Not on the way to the hospital?" she gasped, horrified at the possibility.

"No, weeks before that, right after the divorce was final."

She looked at me pensively, nodded like an old lady and walked away. Neither of them asked about him after that. We had too much fun together.

The years flew by, and then suddenly Maggie was a teenager and Lizzie almost there. As their interest in boys grew, so did their concern about my lack of a partner.

February 14, 1999

The girls talked me into putting up a profile at an online dating website. They helped me fill everything out. It's supposed to find compatible matches. We looked through pictures of men and some of them aren't bad. I specified it has to be someone who's okay with my having children but doesn't want more. I'm in my forties! It all feels a little silly.

But the girls are going to be off on their own in a few years and I'll be here all alone. And Maggie, always right on target, asked if I hadn't used them as an excuse to avoid the chance I'd make another mistake and get hurt again, like I did with their father. I had to admit there was some truth to that. And they only know about Tom. If they knew the rest of my history with men? I'm going to be very careful.

I quickly learned to chat back and forth before bothering to meet with someone. The internet and email were still new. MySpace didn't exist yet, let alone Facebook, so an online search wouldn't have produced much, if any, information on non-famous people. Conversation was the best way to figure out if they were honest in what they'd posted about themselves and whether or not we might be compatible. It wasn't foolproof, though. Several unsuccessful face-to-face meetings later, I was ready to give up. Then Richard popped up as a match and he sounded charming.

But as I got ready for our first date, I told the girls, "If this doesn't pan out, I'm done with online dating." I met their eyes in my mirror. "You'll just have to start scouting for an eligible man here in town."

Maggie scrunched her face. "It'll have to be someone who moves here. All the nice ones your age are married, except Mr. Landers."

I shook my head and smiled. Chris Landers hadn't come out, but he'd never been interested in women.

March 10, 1999

All this focus on finding me a man has made me realize how lonely I'll be when the girls are gone.

Not to mention worried about them, though they're not naïve and ignorant like I was. Lizzie was the first to insist I meet people in a public place - smart girl. And I've talked with them about sex, too. I didn't want them to learn the way I did.

Of course, they think I'm terribly inexperienced, based on their lifetimes. I'm not about to disillusion them.

I didn't realize how vulnerable I was. Not only was I dreading being alone after the girls grew up, I'd been their only parent, their only family, all their lives. Jan had been there when they were little, but they were still in elementary school when her youngest child graduated and Jan took off for Italy. She never came back. She sent me a photo of her new man, but we'd gradually lost touch.

While I loved my girls, it was sometimes exhausting to be the only one to deal with every small and large crisis and monitor homework and everything else.

Richard was looking for someone exactly like me. He swept me off my feet, treated me like a queen. Those first few weeks were a whirlwind of concerts, museums, and fine restaurants. It reminded me of the good days in San Francisco. The only negative was that he lived more than an hour away.

When Maggie started being mouthy, I realized I'd spent hardly any time with the girls since I started seeing Richard. I decided it was time for a girls-only camping trip to Rehoboth Beach. Richard was worried about us going alone, but I told him we'd camped all their lives, that we'd be fine, that we needed to renew our connection.

June 30, 1999

The ocean tried to kill me today. I got taken off the beach on a backboard. The hospital insisted on calling someone, so I gave them Richard's number.

He flew out to take care of me. He rented motel rooms so I wouldn't have to sleep on an air mattress in our tent with my wrenched neck and broken nose. He got me situated there and took Maggie to get our gear while Lizzie stayed to help me.

It feels so good to have someone else take charge.

By August we'd married. Richard lived in Buffalo. It made more sense for us to move up there than have him drive through the snowbelt every day. It was easy for me to get a teaching job, though changing to middle school meant developing plans for a new curriculum. Between that and having a husband, I had little time left for my girls.

Richard manipulated each of us and damaged our relationships to the point that Maggie thought I'd believe him over her if she tried to tell me what he was doing. When she ran from Richard's abuse the next spring, she left her diary for Lizzie, in case she ever needed it. Bless Lizzie for showing it to me right away.

Truthfully, I didn't want to believe it at first, that I'd brought a predator into my girls' lives. It was actually when I confronted Richard that I realized it was true. Then I knew Maggie would never come back, that I had to find her or risk losing her forever. When I realized my first journal was missing, Lizzie and I headed to Harrisburg, hoping Maggie was following my path. I prayed she hadn't run into her own Nick.

If you've read Maggie's story in *Running Away*, you'll know we found her just in time. When she got out of the hospital, we went to Buffalo just long enough for me to file for divorce and get our camping gear out of storage. Then we headed for Rollins Pond in the Adirondacks. We rented a canoe and spent our days paddling and hiking, enjoying life and each other.

I had my journals and skimmed through all of them. Each evening by the campfire, I told the girls more of my story. Maggie had read most of my first journal. I was glad she hadn't taken the notebook where I filled in missing details.

When I got to the entries about their father, I realized it was time to be honest about that, too. I admitted he had not died in a car accident, that I had no idea where he was because he had no interest in them. "I'm sorry. I obviously have terrible taste in men."

Maggie gave me a hug. "Hey, we're great. His genes were good."

"And Richard had me fooled, too, Mom." Lizzie poked the fire. "At first I thought he was creepy, but then when we moved to his house, he was all nice to me and got you to treat me more like a grown-up. I thought Maggie was just jealous. I was so stupid."

June 23, 2000

I hope it wasn't a mistake to tell the girls my whole story, or at least the outline of it. I didn't go into graphic detail and I may never let them see those journals. And I hope it wasn't a mistake to come camping instead of having Maggie go back for the last two weeks of school. She's been through so much, but she could have taken finals. On the other hand, she wasn't doing well in school this year anyway.

At least Lizzie finished all her work and finals long distance, while Maggie was in the hospital in Harrisburg. Eighth grade is easier than high school.

There are so many choices ahead, so many options.

One decision has been made. None of us want to go back to Buffalo. We were only there because of Richard. All of our things are in storage there. We can move wherever we want to. The girls are definitely going to have input on that.

When I called to let the schools know we found Maggie, I also let them know we won't be back. My principal said he'll have a letter of recommendation ready for me as soon as we have an address. He assumed I'd be looking for another teaching job. But I'm not even sure about that.

Another night, Lizzie sat curled up on the blanket, warming her toes by the fire. "Is there any way we can go back to our old house? I liked our rooms, and we have friends there."

I smiled sadly. "I checked with the realtor. The new owners have already done a lot of renovations. Even if they would sell it back to us, it wouldn't be the same. But we could go back there and buy a different house."

"No!" Maggie spoke directly to Lizzie. "Everyone would stick their noses into our business. You know how it would be."

Lizzie grimaced. "Yeah. And I did kind of like going to a larger school, just not the same one." She turned to me. "Do you want to teach, though? Couldn't you get some kind of writing job?"

"Actually, I could."

Thanks to their father, the one thing I did right with Richard was keep our finances separate. I'd never borrowed against the house after Mom died, so not only did I have the money from selling it, every month we lived in it, I had put the equivalent of a mortgage payment into education funds for the girls. College was covered and I had cash to buy a new home. I had a healthy savings account, too. We didn't really need the stability of a teaching job.

My mind started spinning with plans. I could find part time work while the girls finished school and work on my own writing. Four years, then they'd both be in college and I could take a job that involved travel abroad.

"How about somewhere near Harrisburg?" Lizzie looked at Maggie. "I mean, a lot of bad stuff happened there, but Joe and his family are nice. You'd like to live near CJ, wouldn't you?"

If it weren't for Joe's nephew CJ, we might never have found Maggie. CJ was too old for her, but he was a nice boy. Joe, the real Joe, had the family restaurant, with his dragon in the window, and he was still married. They'd had Lizzie and me stay at their home while Maggie was in the hospital. It would be nice to be close to them, but I waited to hear Maggie's feelings.

She took a few moments to consider it, then nodded as she spoke. "CJ's going away to college this fall. But yeah, it would be nice to be somewhere there are a few people we know. And what about that friend of Joe's, Mom?"

I rolled my head back. "You've got to be kidding."

Patrick Murphy was a policeman who moved quickly to rescue Maggie when Joe called.

"Yeah, Mom." Lizzie grinned. "He said he wanted to take us all to dinner when Maggie comes back to testify, but it was totally obvious he was interested in you."

"And Joe grew up with him, so you know he's okay."

"I'm not moving anywhere for a man. Never again." I got up and put more wood on the fire. "However, Harrisburg would make sense. We can find a nice place outside of the city, but close enough for the trials *and* counseling, Maggie."

"Okay. If you go, too."

We got a weekly rate from the Hampton Inn in Camp Hill. I joined a support group with Maggie in the city right away – I wanted to make sure that was in place before the first trial – and we looked at houses from Carlisle to Hershey.

August 12, 2000

We moved into our new home today. It's a short drive into Harrisburg, but feels like we're in the country.

A wide yard slopes down from the deck to Conodoguinet Creek. The house is high enough above the creek, it shouldn't flood unless there's another major disaster, and we fell in love with it. We've already bought three kayaks.

The girls have their own rooms and are taking some time deciding how they want to decorate. Lizzie was talking about murals like they had at home, but Maggie said she thinks she might want something more neutral.

They will both go to Cumberland High, which has an excellent standing. The principal is the only one who knows why Maggie didn't finish school last year. He arranged for her to take the local equivalents for the exams she missed and gave us textbooks for Maggie to review. She's cramming hard.

Last week, Maggie testified against the young man who nearly killed her here. He'll be in prison for years.

Richard's finally out of the hospital, but still locked up. His lawyer's delaying as much as he can. Patrick says that's a typical trick; they're hoping Maggie will change her mind about testifying.

She won't. The counseling group isn't just working us through the abuse; they're providing moral support for the aftermath, dealing with the legal system and figuring out how to move on in her life.

Maggie managed to pass all the core subjects, so she didn't get held back. She started school with a positive attitude, ready to study and make new friends.

At first I went to the counseling group just for her. I thought I'd gotten over being victimized by Nick on my own, but it had taken years. I didn't want it to take that long for Maggie. However, as they got me talking about my own experiences, I realized I needed the counseling as much as she did. We also came to understand Richard had been grooming Lizzie to be next, so we decided to include her, too.

Between group and the girls, and Joe's recommendation, I decided to take a chance and date Patrick Murphy. I told him part of my story. He found out Nick was eventually arrested and sent to jail when another young girl got away from him and went to the police. At first I felt guilty for not doing that myself. How many other girls could have been saved from that trauma?

But I talked about it at group. You do what you can at the time.

September 20, 2000

Group's right. I got out. That's what I could do then.

Patrick's a nice man, but he can't get past seeing me as a victim. As the girls say, I gently but firmly put him into the Friend Zone. We've learned that most people only need to know who we are now, not how we got here. TMI, too much information, will make most people uncomfortable.

But for a close relationship I don't want to keep secrets.

I may very well be single the rest of my life. That's okay. I like how my life is coming together now.

As a safety net, I registered for the tests I needed to take for a teaching credential in Pennsylvania and signed up to substitute teach. However, I'd found part time work with *The Patriot News* in Harrisburg and, with the girls' encouragement, started writing fiction again. Not starting a full time teaching job also gave me time to focus on helping Maggie and myself heal.

October 4, 2000

In group last week, Maggie challenged me when I blamed myself for what happened in Fredonia, and everything that followed. I finally read those journal entries again, closely. She's right. I was raped. When I went back to fill in my journals, I never went back to before I left home. I always believed I'd chosen to get drunk that night and had wanted something "more than kissing" to happen. When I read back through all of the entries, I remembered how awful the beer tasted. I had no more than a few sips the entire night.

I'd never realized how the argument between my parents had left me adrift, either. Once I understood those events better, it was easier to understand my behavior in Erie.

I've done massive research on acquaintance rape for Maggie, but now I realize it's for me, too. Self-blame and sexualized behaviors are common reactions. Predators pick up on that, so many of us are victimized repeatedly. We tell ourselves we deserve it. Sometimes we seek out the punishment, just like that quiet girl said my first day in the whorehouse. We might as well have targets painted on our foreheads, until we forgive ourselves and accept our past not as defining us, but as informing who we are now.

Tonight at group, I acknowledged I've been a victim of both rape and a pimp. I told them it happened so long ago, I'm already feeling more comfortable with myself, history and all. Then they asked me, what about Richard?

I immediately blurted out my self-accusation. "I brought a predator into my daughters' lives!"

All those years being good, not letting any man get close to me in any way, and the first one I picked . . . Maggie and Lizzie spoke up and forgave me. Everyone knew our story. They pointed out that he manipulated each of us, that I'd been his victim too, not just my girls.

I'm working at feeling sad instead of guilty.

Once I started to accept myself, stopped hating myself and being ashamed of every poor choice I ever made, I could read the rest of my old journals more objectively.

I am amazed at how incredibly strong I was. While I was still a mess myself, a scared fifteen-year-old, I pulled Charlie through the violent death of his wife and daughter. I repeatedly let myself be used, but there were so many good people along the way, too.

I survived and built a good life with my daughters.

October 28, 2000

It's not what happens to you, it's what you do with it.

Clinton signed the Victims of Trafficking and Violence Protection Act today. Trafficking. It's amazing what a difference a word makes. Prostitutes are people who choose to sell sexual favors. The word trafficked makes it clear that the sex workers have been forced or coerced into it. Runaways, on the street, hungry and alone, their self-esteem already damaged, make great targets.

All those years I was teaching, there was a kernel of fear festering inside, fear that someone would find out I'd been a prostitute. I'm not carrying around a sign that says I was trafficked, but I'm not ashamed or afraid someone will find out. It's something that happened, I survived, and it's done.

It is not something I chose. It does not define who I am.

I've finally stopped running away from my past. It has less power over my present and future now that I can look at it clearly and accept that it's helped form the person I am today.

I like who I am. I also like who my girls are becoming. They're both happy in school, making friends, joining clubs.

The night before Maggie had to testify at Richard's trial in Harrisburg, I knew she was ready, but I still worried. After the girls went to bed, I pulled out my journal to write about anything except the trial.

November 6, 2000

My editor is pleased with the quality of my writing. He says I'm a true journalist, sticking to the facts, writing my news articles in inverted pyramid form so people get the most important information first and he can trim them easily. But I really want to write more in-depth stories, so on my own time I researched and wrote a feature article on the history of our creek, addressing larger environmental issues in the context of something close to our readers. Then I gave it to him.

He not only chose to put it in the Sunday paper, he sent it to a friend of his on the Washington Post, suggesting they might want me to do a feature for them now and then! He's having me do a similar article on the Susquehanna now. This is my chance to establish myself as an environmental writer and by the time the girls are done with school, I'll be ready for a job that will have me traveling the world. Or I may fund the travel on my own and pitch articles to multiple papers.

Climate change is beginning to be recognized as an issue, so the timing is right. However, what really has me on fire right now is my trafficking research. It's a worldwide problem and, in places that might not realize it, a local issue as well. So I'm going to work on features about that, too.

At least Maggie didn't get pulled into the sex trade.

My life took so many detours, but hers is already back on track. Thanks to frank discussions at group, she's decided not to have sex until it's the right person, place, and time. Then she'll tell him that, while she's technically not a virgin, she's never made love before.

She told me she would have had sex with CJ, but he knew she was too young. Having seen them together, I think she may wait for him. When she's a freshman in college, he'll be a senior. The age difference won't be a problem then.

I hope she'll be okay tomorrow.

Maggie did fine. She was the last to testify and the jury didn't take long to find him guilty. The girls and I were standing on the courthouse steps, discussing where to eat, when a man in a suit rushed by on his way into the building. He stopped, spun around, and stared at us.

"Sunshine?"

"Charlie?" He's aged well.

"I thought that was your voice. It's really you. What are you doing here?"

He gave me a hug, his briefcase bumping against my back. I could feel my grin reflecting his. Maggie interrupted to introduce herself and Lizzie, and then explained much more than I would have about why she ran away and what happened after and how court here was finally done but the hardest was yet to come, Richard's trial in Buffalo for molesting her.

She finished by saying, "You're the one who helped Mom back in the day, right? So she got into college and everything."

Charlie looked at me, unsure how much or what he should say.

"How have you been?" I asked. "Are you a lawyer here?"

"Yes, I..." His cell phone went off. "I'm due in court. What's your number?" He called me to capture it and promised to call me later.

The girls stood staring at me as Charlie trotted up the steps.

Maggie got her voice first. "Wow, Mom."

"What?" I couldn't quite stop grinning.

Lizzie tilted her head. "Mom, don't blow this."

"Yeah. I've never seen you like this." Maggie crossed her arms and looked at me sternly. "Not even when that douche Richard had you fooled."

Lizzie agreed. "And it's obvious Charlie feels the same way. If that scene had been in a movie, the two of you would have like floated away together or something."

"Why didn't you hunt him down when we got you to start dating?" demanded Maggie. "We could have totally skipped the Richard drama."

My joy at seeing Charlie, feeling his hug, deflated. "He's probably married. I shouldn't keep his number." I stared at my cell phone.

Lizzie took it out of my hand. "Don't be silly. He'll still call you. I'm going to put his name on it."

Maggie grinned and took my elbow to lead me down the steps. "I didn't see a ring. I bet he's going to ask you out to dinner tonight. Let's go home and decide what you should wear."

I laughed. "Dress up for Charlie? Maybe jeans and a nice shirt."

I turned to tell Lizzie to catch up.

She closed the phone and practically skipped to join us. "He's not married." She smirked. "And I told him you aren't, either."

"You called him?" I wasn't sure whether to be mad or hug her.

"He wasn't in court yet. And he *was* wearing a suit, Mom."

Maybe they were right. Maybe I should dress up for Charlie. After all, it would be our first date.

Chapter 22: Sunshine in My Future

When Charlie called later that afternoon and suggested meeting at Joe's restaurant for dinner, I decided not to overdo dressing up. He was going there straight from the courthouse, though, so I did wear an A-line skirt that flattered my figure and my favorite blouse.

Fussing over what to wear made me several minutes late. When I arrived, I scanned the restaurant.

Charlie wasn't there. My heart sank.

Joe was seating people. "You look very nice tonight, Peg."

"I was supposed to meet someone, an old friend, but I don't see him." I tried to look like it didn't matter.

"You're the one Charlie's waiting for?" Joe sounded overjoyed.

"He's here?" I looked around again and still didn't see him.

"I have him over in the café side, where you can have privacy. Charlie said you have a lot to talk about."

"You know him?" They were from different points in my life.

"Of course. Most of the lawyers eat here, but Charlie's one of my best customers, and he's helped out some people I sent to him. I had no idea you knew each other. I would have said something."

Joe let me through to the café side, which was not open during the dinner hour. "I'll give you two a few minutes, then come in to take your order."

Charlie stood as soon as he saw me and crossed the room. Our hug felt like coming home. I leaned my head against his chest and he kissed the top of my head, like he always did. We held hands as we walked to the candlelit table.

I told Charlie how the girls and I had come to live nearby and asked if he was practicing law with his father.

"No! I'm with a group that takes primarily civil rights cases involving minorities and women." His voice was full of enthusiasm as he went on with more details about his work – the Charlie I knew so long ago but more besides.

When he paused, I smiled and paraphrased what he'd said when he decided to leave. "You're making change happen instead of talking about it with a bunch of stoners."

He nodded with a big grin on his face. "You got my life back on track, you know. You made me realize it was time to grow up. You thanked me for helping you, Sunshine, but it worked both ways. Thank you."

There were long, comfortable silences as we ate.

"Did you ever remarry?" I eventually asked.

"No."

"Cheryl said you wouldn't ever settle down with one woman."

"We were married too young, and it was the seventies." He shrugged. "I did live with someone for a few years, but it didn't work out."

We talked about how much and how little we've shared with people about our past.

"I have friends who think they've known me my whole life, but there's this gap," he said. "And there are parts I can't share, especially since I'm a lawyer."

"Have you kept in touch with anyone from those days?"

"Just Lynn. John passed away a few years ago. Lynn's the one person I've been able to talk to openly. Our families spent a lot of time together when I was young, then they moved to California. They knew how I was living out there, but never told my parents, so when you needed help, I went to them."

"I never thanked them properly."

"Lynn would love to hear from you." He gave me his phone to copy the number. "She'll be glad to know you're okay."

"I'll call her tomorrow." I noticed the time on my phone. The restaurant had to be closing soon.

"Do you still beat yourself up all the time?" Charlie asked.

I smiled and shook my head. "I finally like myself."

November 8, 2000

It's almost morning and I just got home. After the restaurant, I went to Charlie's apartment and we talked all night. We shared our lives apart, before and after our time together.

He listened attentively to my whole story, every last bit of it. I'd never told anyone about the abortion. Charlie reached for my hand and I cried about it for the first time in years. He hugged me and kissed the top of my head.

There's still no judgment in him.

Then it was his turn.

"I meant to come back sooner," he said. "You were so young. I wanted you to have time to find your own way, get an education, even to have normal relationships with guys closer to your age. But I thought we'd see each other once or twice a year to stay connected. I thought you'd be ready for me by the time I finished law school."

Charlie was set to come out that first Christmas, then I wrote him about my date with Al and Lynn told him Al seemed like a nice boy. Charlie canceled his flight because he didn't want to get in the way. That's why he didn't come for my eighteenth birthday, either. Then his mother's health issues demanded his presence.

After I went to Sonoma State, Lynn couldn't tell him how I was doing anymore, and I wasn't writing very much, and he was working three jobs and going to school, and he was afraid it might be too late. So he wrote that graduation card I kept.

He said "Love, Charlie" on purpose.

When my long thank you letter arrived, he thought I'd written it in response to his card, to let him down gently. That's why he wrote so little the next few years. But he couldn't quite let go. When he finished law school, he took the bar exam at the end of July, then came out to see me, to find out if there really was the connection that he'd always felt we had.

"The girl at your apartment said you'd left a few days earlier to sail around the world with your fiancé. I was worried." He sounded distressed even with me sitting next to him, safe and sound. "So were Lynn and John. They looked back through your cards and found the place you got your first job. I went there and the woman you'd worked with said the last they'd heard, you got off in L.A."

He tried to find me in Los Angeles and later he looked for me in Fredonia, but I never lived there. It was just a sweatshirt. Finally he gave up and settled into his life as a lawyer. He hasn't been a monk, of course. He even lived with one woman for three years, but there was something missing and they drifted apart.

As the girls recognized, Charlie and I connected that moment on the courthouse steps as if we'd never been apart. Still, we took a few weeks to date and get to know each other as we are now.

November 30, 2000

Charlie works long hours while he's preparing a case, but he remembers to take time to have fun. He still likes going to rock concerts, but he enjoys the symphony as well. He took us all to the Nutcracker. The girls think he's great and want him to move in with us full time.

I've shared my fiction and the features I've written with him and he's given me good feedback. He believes in me.

Walking by the Susquehanna, we talked about our futures.

"I've been feeling restless. I love the work I'm doing, but it's getting repetitive. I'm ready for a new challenge." Charlie stopped to pull me into a hug. "With work, that is."

"It's not your restless vagabond foot?"

"No, though I would like to travel again – not hitchhiking around the country, but seeing more of the world."

We went back to holding hands and walking as I told him my plan for investigative travel once the girls were in college.

He squeezed my hand. "I have a confession to make. When you ran the girls to their dance last night, I looked through some of the research you've been doing on trafficking. Well, actually, I think I skimmed all of it, and it's important. So are the environmental issues. Sunshine, if you have an opportunity to travel while the girls are still in school, I'll be here for them. And once they're both in college, we can go together. There has to be some way I could help things from a legal perspective."

My alarm bells went off – promises too good to be true. I let go of his hand and pulled back to face him directly.

"You decided you were restless with the work you're doing *after* you looked through my research."

"No. I've been thinking of making a change for the last year or more. Scout's honor."

"Were you ever a Scout?"

"Yes, I was. But you can also bring it up when we have dinner with my father next week. I made the mistake of mentioning it to him last Christmas and he's been campaigning for me to join his firm. Not the kind of change I had in mind. Working on trafficking is a natural progression from the work I've been doing."

I let him take my hand. We continued our walk with the warmth of common purpose enveloping us.

Christmas, 2000

Charlie proposed last night.

We were standing by the creek, hand in hand, looking at the stars, just the two of us, when he said, "I always loved you." I told him he saved me twice, when we first met and again by getting me set up to go to college. He said I saved him twice, too. I kept him going after the crash and then made him reassess his life.

We haven't been together all these years, but each of us is where we are because of the other - and we are who we are partially because of the detours we each took.

Neither of us needs saving anymore. We're each okay on our own, but that doesn't mean we have to be alone.

I said yes.

Resources

The best centralized center for resources I've found is at the Rape, Abuse & Incest National Network (RAINN) website. There are resources for children, women, and men. The links for trafficking are also good for those being exploited for non-sexual purposes.

RAINN

rainn.org

RAINN **24/7 Hotline:**

800-656-HOPE (800-656-4673)

Other good resources include:

National Center for Missing & Exploited Children

www.missingkids.org

24-hour call center: 800-843-5678

National Runaway Safeline

www.nationalrunawaysafeline.org/

800-RUNAWAY (800-786-2929)

National Runaway Chat and Info

www.1800runaway.org/

800-RUNAWAY (800-786-2929)

Thank you.

Thank you for reading this book.

Please take a few moments right now, while the story is still resonating, to help others find it.

Amazon's algorithms control book sales – the more reviews and ratings a book gets, the more often it pops up for people to see. The more attention it gets there, the more attention it gets elsewhere and the more likely it will find its way to libraries, too.

So please, review this book on Amazon. You don't have to purchase it there to post a review and/or rate a book. You can copy and paste the same review at Goodreads or other places.   A review can be short and simple – "Interesting story." is enough for the review to be counted. Don't forget to give it a star rating.

Review links:

www.amazon.com/dp/1942069022/

www.goodreads.com/book/show/56630292

If you want to do more, you can:

- Talk it up – encourage your friends and your   local library or book club to get the book.

- If you do social media, post your picture with the book.

If you want to know more, you can check out my website. If you have questions, there's a contact form and I do answer messages.

Thanks. Sheri

www.sherimcguinn.com/books

sherimcguinn.substack.com/

Acknowledgments

Thank you to Harrison (not Ford) Gruman and Julie Bradley for their help with my research. Julie and her husband actually did sail around the world. Errors are all mine, of course.

Thank you to the dozens of people who offered critique through the many versions of this novel. There's no way I'm going to list each of you without missing many. However, special thanks go to Sarita Sarvate, who spent about a year reading an earlier version chapter by chapter and asking questions that eventually made me realize I needed to restructure the entire novel, and to Bob Jenkins, whose critique pushed me to make the final refinements.

Thank you to my readers – without you, what's the point?

Sheri McGuinn

www.sherimcguinn.com

September 11, 2020

Behind the Story

In *Running Away* I placed Peg in Harrisburg during Hurricane Agnes, June 1972, because I'd been there with my fiancé and it gave me a familiar locale for that novel. When I started writing Peg's story, I decided to include some other notable events of that time, fictionalizing them for backdrop to her story. Some samples are:

- The first Gathering of the tribes of the Rainbow Family was held the Fourth of July weekend that year, near Granby, Colorado. Harrison "Not Ford" Gruman loaned me his original copy of *The Rainbow Oracle*. Per the Rainbow Family website, it is one of 5000 distributed to leaders and people on the street to invite them to that first Gathering. The story timeline required moving it to Labor Day.

- The meteor Peg sees as they drive to California was inspired by an article in Wikipedia about an unusually large meteor: 1972 Great Daylight Fireball. I moved it from August to September as they drive west from Granby, as a possible sign for Peg.

- When I was researching September 1972 in Sacramento, I ran across a Sacramento Bee article describing how bereft the city was after a plane crashed into Farrell's Ice Cream Parlor near the Executive Airport on September 24th that year and realized Charlie was going to lose Cheryl and Amy.

- On October 28, 2000, Bill Clinton signed the Victims of Trafficking and Violence Protection Act. I had to have Peg mention it when I realized the timing of the story's end. That act has been updated several times since and there are international laws as well.

Sometimes a character takes over the writing. Peg did so when she got to the bus station in Erie. I was shocked and stopped writing until I saw a PBS special interviewing women who had been trafficked and realized that was her story and it needed to be told. When coercion or abuse are involved or when it's a minor, it is not prostitution, it is trafficking – a form of slavery.

Language does make a difference.

Also by Sheri McGuinn

Running Away: Maggie's Story

Maggie is already in another state when they realize she's gone. Her mother's missing journal is their only clue. While Peg races to find her daughter before she's hurt or disappears forever, Maggie finds herself in dangerous company. Told in both voices, this is a stand-alone story, yet companion to *Peg's Story: Detours*.

All for One: Love, War, & Ghosts

Youthful decisions changed the course of their lives and estranged lifelong friends. Decades later they think they've put 'Nam and PTSD behind them, until the past shoves its way into the present, bringing fear and uncertainty. By the end of the deadly month, their lives again change forever.

Tough Times

Their mother left a note: "Stay together." Michael knows the system will split them up, so he starts across country to take his young siblings to the white grandparents they've never known – because *his* father was black. While Michael deals with responsibility, grief, prejudice, fear, his first romantic relationship, and hormones, the police find his mother and label it murder. They think Michael did it, but the killer is stalking the kids.

2023 KINDLE BEST OF INDIE BOOK AWARDS FINALIST YOUNG ADULT

Alice

Thirteen-year-old Nina narrates the story of her mother, Alice, who has always been responsible, proper, and totally uptight. The school eliminates Alice's teaching position, then her hippie father drops into their lives, and then the bank sends a letter threatening their home – and Nina suddenly sees another side to her mother.

Discussion Questions

1. Peg knows virtually nothing about sex when the story begins. Today, it seems like it would be difficult for teens to be that ignorant – but are they getting the information they need? Do they talk with their parents?

2. Peg blames herself for everything that happened at the frat house. Was it her fault?

3. Peg doesn't believe she can tell her parents about what happened at the frat house and later decides she can't go home. What do you think would have happened if she had talked to her parents in the first place? What if she did go home? If she told her parents what had happened in Harrisburg?

4. What do you think of Charlie at the beginning? When you find out he's married? When they go north? When he realizes the age difference?

5. Peg loses touch with people who have helped her. What keeps her drifting?

6. She's experienced a series of traumatic events along the way. Does she have undiagnosed PTSD? How common do you think that may be in women? What are the symptoms?

7. What resources do you have locally that deal with trafficking and other abuses?

My website has:

Supplemental Materials

Puchasing Links

A Contact Form (ask questions or set up an author visit)

Media Resources

www.sherimcguinn.com

My newsletter caters to readers and writers:

sherimcguinn.substack.com

Review links for *Peg's Story: Detours*

www.amazon.com/dp/1942069022/

www.goodreads.com/book/show/56630292

Thanks for reading!

Every review helps – thank you.

Thanks for reading!

www.ingramcontent.com/pod-product-compliance
Lightning Source LLC
Chambersburg PA
CBHW020951180626
46814CB00003B/1038